MAYDAY

A KAIJU THRILLER

CHEEKY MINION

OTHER BOOKS BY CHRIS STRANGE

Don't Be a Hero: A Superhero Novel

The Man Who Crossed Worlds (Miles Franco #1)

The Man Who Walked in Darkness (Miles Franco #2)

www.chris-strange.com

CHEEKY
MINION

Originally published by Cheeky Minion 2014

First Edition

ISBN: 1497427002
ISBN-13: 978-1497427006

Mayday, Mayday, Mayday. Oh, Jesus. This is the cargo ship Maria Garuda, Maria Garuda, Maria Garuda. Position is...[static]...repeat, vessel is under attack. Some kind of... [unintelligible]...sheared us in half. We are sinking, I repeat, we are sinking. Can anyone hear me? Mayday. In need of immediate assistance. We are abandoning ship. [screaming] Shit, it's coming back around. Oh my God. I think it's seen me. It's looking right at...[unidentified screeching]

—Final transmission of the Maria Garuda

1

I don't care how many times you've seen Maydays fighting on TV, you've never really experienced a Mayday until you're right next to one. It's the smell, you see. The faint scent of earth and sweat and shit always hung over the island, but here, not a hundred metres from the creature's massive body, the stench was so thick I could barely breathe. I'd been working on the island for nine months, but I'd never got as close as this. It takes a special occasion to get me down to the Mayday pits. I figured a dead Mayday qualified.

Mud squelched in my shoes as I trudged towards the colossal creature. The rain had been coming down like hellfire for two days straight, turning the whole island into a quagmire. My broad-brimmed hat formed gutters that kept the rain off my face but sent it pouring down the back of my trench coat. Most of the other Volkov personnel were more appropriately attired. The Bio teams swarmed around the Mayday like ants, dressed in clear plastic ponchos and gumboots. A group of five of them scaled the dead creature's underbelly, using the mud-stained fur as handholds. Each hair was as thick as a mooring line.

Overhead, three Volkov helicopters buzzed like flies.

I pulled my handkerchief out of my pocket—it was soaked from the rain—and held it across my nose and mouth as I approached. The Mayday's colossal mouth hung open like a cave, a thick purple tongue rolled out into the mud like a Persian rug. One of her two black eyes stared at the heavens, rainwater pooling in the eyelids. Yllia's official data sheet said this Mayday was 72 metres high, or 136 metres from head to tail, with a 158 metre wingspan. Yllia was the smallest of the five Maydays and the last to awaken, but she was still one of the largest creatures any man had ever seen. White fur coated her from her bulbous head to the tips of her forked tail. Her four arms—each ending in three delicate scythed claws—were folded beneath her, sinking into the mud. Even lying down she towered over me like a tsunami about to break. One thin, butterfly-like wing lay open across her body; the other was folded up, out of sight. I'd watched her in a hundred fights, hovering above her opponents, swooping down with a speed that belied her size. And before that, over a decade ago, when she'd terrorised Western Europe, throwing psychic waves ahead of her that drove the citizens of dozens of cities to mass suicide. No matter whether it was sleeping or fighting, a Mayday was always moving—an antenna twitching, muscles the length of a train flexing and relaxing. It was unnerving to see one so still, so dead.

Through the crowd of scientists gathered around Yllia's left rear paw, I spotted a familiar giant in a navy blue raincoat gesturing furiously at one of the scientists. It was always good to see the staff getting stuck in. I rolled up the bottoms of my trousers to keep them out of the mud and went over to see what kind of trouble Healy was getting himself into.

Dominic Healy stopped in mid-sentence—hand still raised in defiance—as he saw me approaching. Healy was a black English kid about fifteen years younger than me, barely twenty-six, but he was easily over six and a half feet tall and as heavy as a fridge. He'd been the assistant to the last Head Investigator, and when I took over the job I figured I'd at least give him a try before sending him packing and getting someone new. Within an hour I'd decided to keep him. The kid was smart and feisty and he worked like a dog.

I gave up on the handkerchief and offered Healy a grin as I moved between Healy and the scientist. Healy returned my smile with the same look of frustration he'd been aiming at the scientist.

"Look at this shit, Boss. They're walking all over everything. The whole pit's been turned into a swamp. We could've found footprints, or fibres, or—" He turned his attention to a scientist driving a sampling drill into the thick flesh of Yllia's paw. "Hey! Hey! What the hell do you think you're doing? This is a—"

I slapped Healy on the shoulder. "It's all right, leave them alone. They've got jobs to do as well."

"But this—"

"I know, I know." I stepped out of the rain, using Yllia's fur for shelter. I took my hat off and shook the rain away before putting it back on. "Did you bring the camera?"

Healy still looked mad, but he nodded and pulled the

camera bag out of the satchel slung across his shoulder. Beneath his raincoat, the kid was wearing a dingy brown jacket and jeans. One thing I'd never got into Healy's head was that he needed to dress a little more professionally. I guess he figured that his size was enough to get him respect, but it wasn't the sort of respect you really wanted to inspire in people in this job. Except when it was necessary.

Healy passed me the camera. It was a high-end DSLR model—only the best for Volkov Entertainment Incorporated. I wondered if I could convince one of the scientists to let me borrow their poncho to protect the camera. I opened my mouth to ask the scientist Healy had been arguing with. Then I finally looked at her face.

"Dr Russell," I said, tipping my hat. "I didn't recognise you with the raincoat on. You're looking lovely, as usual."

She glowered at me. "Escobar. I'm surprised to see you out braving the rain. It's a little unnecessary. As I was explaining to your young assistant, we have this under control."

"Of course you do," I said, trying my smile on her. "You'll have to forgive me a little curiosity. Nature of the job. I love a good mystery. And this…" I patted one of the thick hairs emerging from Yllia's leg. "…this is a hell of a mystery. How many nukes did we throw at these things? Then one just drops dead? That's exciting, don't you think?"

She made a noncommittal noise, her gaze sliding past me. Maybe I was boring her. Dr Catherine Russell was a Canadian national. I'd run all her background checks when she'd joined the company to head up the Biology Division six months back, although it'd just been a formality. Dr Russell used to work under Volkov during the Mayday Wars, and he was happy to have her back. I had to admit she was a good-looking lady, retaining a slim-but-not-too-slim figure well into her mid-forties, topped with a head of wavy blond hair that I was 90% sure was all natural. Not that I was interested in her or anything. I'd learned long ago what came of mixing business and pleasure.

"Any ideas on what killed our giant friend here?" I asked her.

She shook her head. "It's far too soon to speculate. Probably natural causes. But we'll find out."

"I don't doubt you will. Now, if I may borrow my assistant for a moment?"

I took Healy by the shoulder and steered him away from Dr Russell. Once we were out of earshot, I stopped a young scientist hurrying past with a jar of Yllia's flesh and flashed her my investigator ID with the Volkov logo stamped in the corner.

"Excuse me, miss. I need to borrow that poncho."

She frowned and looked down at her raincoat. "But—"

"I know it's an inconvenience, but under Section 14 of the company guidelines, under extreme circumstances an investigator may requisition any item or equipment from a Volkov staff member. I think a dead Mayday is pretty extreme, don't you?"

"Well, I—"

"Good girl. Quickly, now."

The girl hesitated a few more seconds, bit her lip, then made a face and pulled the poncho off.

"Thank you very much, miss," I said as I took the poncho and wrapped it around the camera. "Off you go."

The girl hurried away to seek a more sheltered location. When she was gone, I nodded for Healy to keep following me.

"Pretty girl," I said. "Not very smart, though." I pointed to the helicopters circling overhead. "Are they filming?"

"I think so," Healy said.

I rubbed my chin, enjoying the scratch of my beard against my skin. I'd been trying out a Van Dyke beard the last few weeks, but I wasn't sure if I suited it. "I need you to find whoever's in charge of them at Media Division and make sure those tapes stay under lock and key."

"I think they're digital, not tapes," Healy said.

"Whatever. I'd rather they were destroyed so they don't leak, but I've never met a TV man who's willing to destroy footage. Are there any reporters on the island at the moment?"

"I think one landed a week ago, doing a piece on the lead-up to the anniversary."

"When you get a chance, find out who it is and where they're staying. We need to keep this as quiet as possible. I'm going to have a look around the pits and see what I can see. I need you to have a walk around Yllia and see if you can save any evidence from these vultures. Don't bother trying to argue with them. Tell a scientist he's an idiot and he'll demand citation. Just get what you can. Then I need you to find out the name and job of every person who had access to the pit. Trainers, scientists, security, keepers, the whole lot. All right?"

While I was talking, Healy had taken out a notebook and started scribbling in it, using his body to shield it from the rain. "Sure, Boss. You going to talk to Volkov about this?"

"Soon. When I've got something. If anyone comes looking for me, you don't know where I am, okay?"

I gave him a pat on the back, then stepped out of the shelter of Yllia's body and back into the full force of the rain. I pointed my hat into the wind as I walked. I made a mental note to get Healy to send a new suit to the office. It wasn't even seven in the morning yet, but I doubted I'd have a chance to get back to my apartment anytime soon. Today was shaping up to be a busy day. I grinned to myself at the thought.

The Mayday pits were spread out across the island. Volkov Entertainment actually owned two islands here in the South China Sea. The larger of the two, the East Island, was mostly dense forest. The East Island held the Mayday pits and all the related buildings and equipment needed to keep the monsters housed in the manner to which they were accustomed. The West Island, connected to the East by a road bridge, held Maytown, the company town where the Volkov staff lived and where all the administration happened. Both my office and my apartment were over there, as well as the headquarters for all of Volkov Entertainment.

But it was here on the East Island that Volkov's real business happened. Yllia's pit was in the south-western quadrant of the island, at the base of a set of craggy hills covered by thick jungle. A ten-foot-high concrete wall topped with razor wire circled the entire pit. Not to keep the Mayday in—no wall in existence could manage that—but to keep personnel interacting with the Maydays to a minimum. At the far end of the pit I could just make out the man-made lake Yllia would've drunk from and the automated cargo gates where the keepers brought in slaughtered cattle and sheep by the truckload. There were already scientists digging through it all, taking samples. As if a Mayday could be poisoned.

A watchtower was perched above the wall on the northern edge. I squelched through the mud and flashed my ID at the green-uniformed security guards at the tower's ground entrance. They stood aside. I swiped my card against the sensor next to the door, but it didn't beep.

"It's broken, sir," one of the guards said. "The door's unlocked."

"How about that." I switched on the camera, aimed it at the sensor, and snapped a picture. I shrugged at the confused looking guard. "So maintenance know what they're looking for."

I pushed open the door and stepped out of the rain. The interior of the tower was nothing special, just bare concrete and a spiral staircase going up to the viewing platform. I groaned a little at the sight of it. They really could've done with an elevator in this thing.

I was panting a little bit by the time I got to the top. I patted down my pockets until I found my e-cigarette. I'd given up smoking a couple of years ago at the request of my ex-wife when the ex hadn't yet been added. Marrying her hadn't proved to be a good decision, but quitting the cigarettes was, so I'd stuck with it. The hardest thing was finding something to do with my hands while I was working. You can't be a good private eye without a smoke dangling from your lips. It's a law of nature.

I took a puff of the fake cigarette and stepped out onto the viewing platform. This was more like it. Down there in the mud I couldn't see shit. But up here, even through the rain, I could see the entire pit. Yllia lay near the east wall like some sort of mutant cat/butterfly cross, the scientists crawling across her body like ants. Rainwater pooled in pockets formed by her wing. Over to the south, next to her lake, her shelter stood, twice as wide as a military air hanger and three times as tall. Strips of grass still clung to life near the walls of the pit, but the entire middle had been turned to mud by the years Yllia had spent here. The pit's supply building was on the other side of the south wall. And far beyond that, nearer the coast, I could see another Mayday.

Tempest. Due to the rise of the land, he was the only Mayday visible. The first Mayday humans had encountered. The terror of Africa. Even though I could only make out his grey silhouette through the mist, I could tell he was awake and watching what was happening in Yllia's pit. He stood on twelve colossal legs, each jointed in four places. The bulk of his body was dark and bulbous like a spider, but what I guess you'd call his thorax bent up in a swooping arc, ending in a head that was barely distinguishable from his shoulders. Two hands of serrated claws slowly flexed open and closed. His tail flicked back and forth.

"Enjoying the show?" I said quietly. I took a long drag

on the fake cigarette, blew a smoke ring in Tempest's general direction, then pocketed the cigarette and turned back to look at Yllia. As I did so, something crunched under my foot. I lifted my shoe, but there was nothing on the metal platform. I steadied myself against the railing and twisted my leg to get a look at the sole of my shoe. Stuck into the rubber, surrounded by mud, was a small fragment of glass. I prised it out and had a closer look. The surface was slightly curved, like it'd come from a drinking glass. Nothing else about it was noteworthy, but I tucked it into my coat pocket anyway, then I turned the camera back on.

I spent a couple of minutes snapping pictures of Yllia's body, the pit, the walls. I liked pictures. They made it easier to focus, easier to figure out what was important. They froze the world in a single moment where everything was clear.

I stepped back into the shelter of the tower to get out of the wind and scrolled through the photos on the camera's display. Was there an expression on Yllia's face? Was she afraid when she died? Her eyes were smaller than you'd expect for a creature so huge. Her long, pointed antennae had retained their stiffness even in death. Had she been in pain? Did Maydays even understand pain? This whole enterprise, Volkov's entire media empire, was built on the premise that they could be hurt. If not physically, then mentally. Humiliation for the 1.1 billion people they'd killed over the course of their nine year war against us. But the biologists had never been able to tell us if they really could hurt. I'd doubted it. Then again, I'd assumed they were immortal. Look how that had turned out.

Goddamn it, this was going to be a hell of a case. If I could make it one.

Then I saw it. I felt the grin split my face. I ran back to the railing and stared down at the pit again. Yes. *Yes.* I had a case.

I nearly tripped twice sprinting back down the stairs. I'd gotten fatter since arriving on the island, too much time spent behind a desk running employee background checks and keeping reporters from sneaking onto the East Island. The days were starting to blend into each other. Detective work always had an element of grunt work to it, but back on the mainland there'd been those short jolts of excitement to make it all worth it. Getting a key detail from some distant family member you thought you were wasting your time talking to, a detail that lead you straight to the guy who was skipping out on his child support payments. Catching the cheating wife going into the house with not one but three men on her arm. Occasionally, ducking a punch thrown by someone who didn't appreciate being served legal papers.

Since taking the job with Volkov there hadn't been any of that. The island and the level of security meant there hadn't been a serious case of industrial espionage in four years. I'd started to think that this was it; this was the life of a company man, nothing but boredom and flicking paperclips into the rubbish bin to pass the hours. But now I had something real. I felt as giddy as a teenage boy copping his first feel of a tit at a booze-fuelled house party.

I didn't even mind the rain hammering my face as I stepped back into the mud of the pits. After a few minutes of searching, I found Healy again, interrogating some help-less security guard. I grabbed his arm and led him away.

"I've got it," I said.

"Got what?"

I just grinned at him. "Where's Dr Russell?"

"She left."

"What? Where'd she go?"

Healy shrugged. "To fill Volkov in, I guess."

The giddiness drained slowly from me. "Shit. Shit. When'd she leave?"

"I don't know. Maybe ten minutes ago."

"Goddamn it. Volkov and Russell have history. If she talks to him first, he'll give her control of the investiga-tion." *Think.* I snapped my fingers. "Who've we got that has a day off today? Someone living near the centre of town."

Healy scratched his head with his pen. "I think Lindsey lives in town."

"Lindsey Fischer? All right. What kind of car does Dr Russell drive?"

"Most of the head Bio guys have company Falcons. She'll be the same."

"Okay, good. I have to go."

"Boss?"

"I'll be in touch," I said over my shoulder. "Thanks, Healy."

I ran for the pit exit—or at least I trudged as fast as I could in the mud. As I went out the exit and back onto the blessed concrete of the car park, I pulled my cell phone out of my pocket and found Lindsey Fischer's number. It rang four times, five times.

"Come on, come on," I muttered to myself as I found my keys and pressed the fob. The lights on my company Honda Civic lit up and I pulled open the door.

A click came from the other end of the phone line. "Yeah?"

"Lindsey, it's Jay," I said. "Are you busy?"

She made a slight groaning sound, like she'd just woken up. "To be honest, Boss, I was just about to jerk off."

"Jerk off later. I need you to do something for me."

"Jesus, I just looked at the clock. Do you need me to tell you what the time is? Because you clearly don't know if you're calling me at this hour."

I started the car and shifted into reverse. The car park was overflowing; it was going to be hell getting out of here. "Get dressed and get to your car. Right now. No time for breakfast. Dr Russell is heading from Yllia's pit to Volkov Tower in a Ford Falcon. I need you to intercept her."

"Intercept her? How?"

"You're a detective, figure it out. Try not to kill her or anything, but you have to stall her. Just for a few minutes. Okay?"

"All right, I guess so." She sounded more awake now. "Do I get a bonus?"

I dodged a pair of haphazardly parked Range Rovers and pulled out onto the road. "We'll talk."

I hung up and put my foot down. I wished I had a siren. I'd have to bring that up with someone. The forests cleared and turned to grassy plains as I headed downhill along the narrow road. The roads around the pits weren't made for the kind of traffic they'd seen this morning or the speed I was going now, but I somehow managed not to kill myself or anyone else. Cars were still heading towards the pit in small convoys, not just biologists now but other rubberneckers that'd caught wind that a Mayday was dead. I hoped security managed to keep them out. It was going to be hard enough keeping this thing under control as it was. Thank God for putting Dominic Healy on this earth and giving him the smarts to call me as soon as he heard what'd happened.

The roads had finally widened up to a whopping two lanes each way, with a handful of branching streets heading off to other parts of the East Island. It was still strange to me, living somewhere this isolated. Within a year of our victory over the Maydays, I'd packed up my meagre home in Refugee Town 2108 and headed for the newly rebuilt Sydney. I'd lived and worked there ever since, until Volkov came calling.

I reached the bridge in record time. The other side of the road was backed up, but there was hardly anyone heading back to Maytown this early in the morning. Maytown wasn't big, but it was dense, packed with the hundred and ten thousand people needed to keep the company running and the staff supported. I passed dozens of apartment buildings on my way into the centre of town. My own apartment was on the outskirts of the town, in a more luxurious building than what most of my team were given. Perks of the job. If I had to sell my soul and become a company man, it damn well better be worth it.

Traffic slowed up ahead. The line of cars crept forward until I saw what was holding everyone up. Two cars were pulled over to the side of the road, the rear of the red Ford Falcon dented from a minor fender bender. Dr Russell was out of the car, arguing with a solidly built woman with hair still mussed from sleep. Lindsey was giving as good as she got. As I drove past the accident, Lindsey caught my eye from the side of the road and winked. I grinned at her and drove on. All right, I guessed she deserved that raise. I'd pay it out of my own pocket if I had to.

Volkov's head office was an unassuming tower in the centre of Maytown, not quite as high as the nearby Media Division office building. The only thing that gave it away was the stylised, swooping "V" perched on the roof, lit by a pair of red-tinted spotlights. The building looked like it was made entirely of glass, but any perceived fragility was a lie; it'd been designed to survive the kind of earthquakes that can only be generated by stampeding Maydays. I pulled into the parking lot and showed the security guard my ID. The old guy obligingly raised the barrier arm and let me through. The car park was full of cars but devoid of people. I parked, grabbed the camera, and got into the elevator.

The doors slid open for me on the fourth floor. The building was actually twenty-five storeys tall, but Volkov had a reputation as a paranoid man. I guess when you spend a decade of your career fighting Maydays, you learn that a top floor office puts you at just the right height to be torn in half by a carelessly swung claw.

I shook the rain off my jacket as best I could and took off my hat as I stepped into the lobby. The furniture was all brushed metal and glass, the kind of stuff you have to clean three times a day just to keep the fingerprints under control. I showed my best smile to the middle-aged woman manning the reception desk.

"Hi, Carol. Hell of a morning, huh? Is the professor in?"

As I was speaking, I casually made my way past her towards the doors that led to Volkov's office. She wasn't buying it. "You can't go in there, Mr Escobar. The professor is—"

"Busy, yeah, I know." I didn't stop moving towards the doors. "He's going to want to see me."

The receptionist stood up. "Mr Escobar—"

"Thanks, Carol."

I shoved open the doors and stepped into the office. Rain hammered the wall-sized window at the far end of the office. Volkov's desk was set up in the corner, a pair of computer monitors facing away from me and a bookshelf running along the adjacent wall. Two black, rectangular couches that looked about as comfortable as concrete slabs faced each other in the centre of the room, a coffee table between them. I dropped my hat and the camera on one couch, pushed back the lapels of my damp coat, and put my hands in my pockets.

"Professor," I said loudly. "I think you wanted to talk to me."

Professor Nikolai Volkov was standing behind his desk with a phone to his ear and a long cigarette between his fingers. The guy was all eyebrows—I think they'd scared all the hair off his head. He had the kind of skull that didn't suit being bald. He didn't look like a professor. He didn't look like a businessman either. From the size of him, you'd pick him for a railroad worker or a club bouncer. Not fat, not a musclehead, just big all over.

I strolled over to his desk and offered him my hand. He still had the phone to his ear. He pointed his eyebrows at me and frowned.

The clatter of the receptionist's heels came from behind me, followed by a slightly breathless, "Mr Escobar, please."

I didn't turn to her. I held Volkov's gaze and kept my hand extended. A few seconds ticked past, marked by the silver clock above the bookshelves.

Volkov sighed. He switched the phone to his left hand and gave me his right. The guy had a handshake like a grizzly bear. "Call me back," he said into the phone. Then he laid it in its cradle and released my hand.

"Thank you, Carol," he said over my shoulder. His English was good, but his voice hadn't lost its native Russian accent. "It is all right. You may leave us. Make sure we're not disturbed."

"Dr Russell is due any minute," she said.

"I'm sure she won't mind waiting," I said. "Don't worry, I won't be long."

Carol hesitated, then clattered back into the lobby and closed the door. Volkov brought the cigarette to his lips and took a long drag. That was one thing I always admired about Volkov: the man smoked like he did it professionally. He tapped some ash into a glass ashtray on his desk and pointed me to the couches. I dropped into one, enjoying the scent of secondhand smoke that billowed towards me as he sat down opposite.

"How much are you going to lose on this?" I asked.

Volkov sat back on the couch and crossed his legs. "Short term, perhaps three hundred million. Yllia was to fight Grotesque in the anniversary melee. Now we'll have to replace her on short notice. Perhaps we will have to turn it into a team match."

Grotesque was set up as a heel, a Mayday the audiences at home could love to hate. He needed a face to fight, someone for the audience to root for. With Yllia gone, Nasir was the only one who could fill that role. "Sounds rough. How about the long term?"

Volkov raised his hands in a gesture of surrender. "Who knows? The ramifications are too much to deal with at this moment."

"Tell me about it. Once word gets out that someone murdered a Mayday, I wonder if the Alliance will be so keen to allow you to continue keeping them."

He grew still, the only movement coming from his lips and the smoke trailing from his cigarette. "Who said anything about murder?"

"Oh, that was me." I gave him a grin. "You mind if I help myself to a drink?"

Volkov's eyebrows twitched. "There is a selection of spirits in the cabinet."

"Water's fine. I'm not a big drinker." I poured myself a glass from the pitcher on the table. Volkov still hadn't moved.

"When Dr Russell called me, she didn't mention anything about murder," he said. "It sounded as if she expected Yllia's death to be the result of disease."

"I'm sure she did. She's a fine scientist. But this time,

she's way off." I took a long drink, stretching out the moment. "Someone found a way to kill Maydays. They gained access to Yllia's pit. And they killed her stone cold dead without anyone noticing."

"This is quite an allegation."

"You know how I like to shake the bird cage. I believe that's why you hired me." I reached over and retrieved the camera. "Have you seen pictures of the pit this morning?"

He nodded. "I've reviewed some of the footage."

I brought up the widest shot of the scene that I had on the camera's display and showed it to him. "The rain hasn't eased up for a second in two days. When was the last time you saw Yllia out in the rain outside of a fight? I seem to recall that was the only thing that saved London from her. So what's she doing all the way out here, so far from her shelter?"

Without waiting for him to answer, I flipped to another picture.

"Here's the ground outside her shelter. It's pretty torn up here, but you can see where the freshest footprints are." I pointed at the picture. "Look. Six of them in a row." The mud was so churned around it was hard to make it out, but I could tell Volkov saw it too. "She came right up to the watchtower."

"It is not possible," Volkov said. "The impulse control shouldn't have allowed her that close to the wall."

"Then the impulse control was broken. I remember other times Maydays broke impulse control. I think you do too. Like when the Alliance tried to force Serraton to bury himself underground. He shook off your mind control and flattened what was left of Bangkok. He could break impulse control because he was threatened. That's what happened here." I tapped the picture on the camera. "I took these from the watchtower on the north wall of the pit. Look at the way Yllia's footprints change direction, heading toward the tower. The lock on the watchtower door was broken. This was where the killer was. Right there, in the tower. Yllia knew there was someone up there. She was coming to investigate. Then she turned away, went back this way. And look at these last two steps. They're deeper. Then no more prints until we get to this groove in the ground, right by her body. You know what that looks like to me? It looks like she tried to fly, Professor. All on her own. All without impulse control."

Volkov studied me for a few moments as his cigarette burned down. His intercom crackled, and Carol's voice came through. "Professor, Dr Russell has arrived."

Volkov made no move to answer her. He rested his cigarette in the corner of the ashtray and leaned forward. "This evidence, it isn't much."

"Fuck all, I think the expression is," I said.

"Dr Russell will be expecting to be responsible for any investigation."

"And she'd be perfect for the job if this really was natural causes. Dr Russell is a fantastic scientist. I'm sure I'll need her help on this. But she is absolutely the wrong person to head up this investigation."

"And you are the right person?" Volkov asked.

"The word 'investigator' is right there in my job title."

A small smile touched Volkov's lips. I don't think it was

used to being there, so it didn't stick around. I decided to press the advantage.

"You know I'm right, Professor," I said. "You didn't hire me just to snoop on your employees. The police don't exist in Maytown. You knew one day, something would happen that would require a real detective. Today's that day. Put me on the job. I'll find whoever did this."

The intercom crackled again. "Professor?" Carol said. "Dr Russell is waiting."

Volkov picked up his cigarette again, took one more drag, then stubbed it out. He stood up and pressed the intercom button on his desk. "Apologise to her for me. I regret that I may be a little longer. I will send someone for her shortly." He released the button and turned back to me. "Do you have any idea who might have done this?"

I shrugged. "Mayday Protection fanatics? Competitors wanting to cripple you before the anniversary? Hell if I know."

"If it was a staff member, then it should have been your job to weed them out before they began work."

"Unless they started working under my predecessor's watch. In any case, we won't find out until I catch them." I downed the rest of my water and stood up so I was back on equal footing with Volkov.

He rubbed the bridge of his nose. "Very well. The job is yours. But you will work with Dr Russell where it is necessary."

"You're doing the right thing."

He didn't look so sure. He turned to the window and stared past the rain running down the glass in rivers.

Beyond, the East Island was shrouded in mist.

"Here's what I need," I said to his back as I returned the camera to its bag. "I need you to send out a memo. Make sure everyone knows that they have to cooperate with the investigation. Both Volkov staff and anyone else I feel like talking to. If you want this sorted out fast, I can't afford to screw around with red tape and corporate pissing contests."

"Very well. But you must understand that this company holds a great many secrets that allow us to maintain our monopoly. Some divisions may be reluctant to have you around."

"They can be as reluctant as they like, as long as they don't get in the way of the investigation. And don't worry. The company secrets are safe with me. The next thing I need is going to be a little trickier. You have to put the island under lockdown."

He turned slowly towards me. "What do you mean?"

"No one enters or leaves from the port or the airstrip. No flights or boats have left the island since yesterday afternoon. The killer is still here. We need to make sure it stays that way."

Volkov nodded. "I will arrange it."

"Great, but that's not all. This whole place has to go dark. Right now we have to control what information reaches the outside world. By now the whole damn island knows that Yllia's dead. I'm sure some of them have called people back home. But you have to stop it before it gets out of hand. Cut off all landlines. Internet, too. Shut down the cell towers. Some communications are still going to get out, that's unavoidable. We can't really do anything about radio. But we can confuse the issue. For every true bit of information getting out, we need ten false rumours leaking as well."

Volkov looked at me like I was speaking in Greek. He threw a hand in the air. "You are talking madness. There are more than just my staff here. There are Alliance inspectors, reporters—"

"Exactly. That's exactly my point." I crossed the distance between us. "The Alliance recognises that you're a great man, Professor. Without your impulse control technology, we'd still be fighting Maydays. We'd still be losing. But you know damn well they only let you keep them here because they had no better options. They couldn't kill them, so they might as well control them, might as well use them to entertain the world and make a profit. What was the alternative? Let one country or another take sole possession of the greatest weapons we'd ever encountered?" I shook my head and gestured out the window. "That out there, all of this, it's a compromise. But this morning we just experienced the biggest paradigm shift since you captured the Maydays in the first place. If Yllia's dead, then maybe all Maydays are now killable. Will the Alliance let you keep running Mayday fights when they finally have a way to end them once and for all?"

"You were the one who suggested that it was more than natural causes that killed Yllia."

I nodded. "Isn't it better to know for sure? Then you can prepare. You can do something about it." I held his gaze for a few seconds, then I returned to the couch and put my hat on. "Twenty-four hours. Keep the truth from leaving the island for twenty-four hours. Blame it on the weather or something, I don't care."

"The Alliance may interpret our sudden silence as a threat," he said. "The compromise, as you put it, is delicate."

"Contact the board and the joint leaders. Now, before you cut comms. Tell them something, just to stall them and stop them trying to pull off an armed takeover. You've been their darling for ten years. They'll give you the benefit of the doubt for twenty-four hours."

"And you'll have found the killer by then?"

"You'd better hope so. Or this company, Professor, is fucked." I started for the door.

"One more thing before you go," Volkov said, his voice quiet as he took his time lighting another cigarette. "I am putting a great deal of faith in you here. Know that if you betray that faith, your career will be over. Not just with this company. If I have to, I will bury you."

I grinned and tipped my hat to him. "I'll see myself out."

I shoved the doors open and walked back into the lobby. Dr Russell was perched on the edge of a couch. Her face went through a series of interesting contortions as I emerged from Volkov's office. I hit the elevator call button and smiled at her.

"I'll be seeing you soon, Doctor."

She was going to get wrinkles if she scowled so much. I waved goodbye and stepped into the elevator. As the doors slid closed, I pulled out my cell phone and dialled Healy.

"We got it," I said.

"Got what?" Healy said.

"The case, we got the case."

"You sound like my cousin when his parents got him a dirt bike for Christmas."

I grinned into the phone. "Get everyone to the office. Everyone. They'll kick themselves if they miss out on this. This is a career case."

"Right, Boss. Want me to order some breakfast burritos for everyone?"

"Healy, my son, I have a feeling this is going to be a damn good day."

2

The Investigative Division's offices were a big step up from anything I ever had back in the real world. I'd been operating out of a corrugated iron shack in Refugee Town 2108, and my upstairs office in Sydney wasn't much better. I'd always figured that all I needed to do my job was a phone line, a filing cabinet, and an Internet connection that was relatively stable. Now that I'd experienced what it was like to be treated as a true professional, I didn't think I could go back.

The office was an open plan outfit, with glass dividers between the various investigators' desks. As head investigator I had a corner office to myself, though I rarely closed the door except when I wanted to catch an afternoon nap on the brown suede couch along the wall. We shared the building with the Security Division, or maybe I should say that we borrowed a little space from them. But despite that, it never seemed like we were tacked on. Head Office had approved every equipment request I'd made without haggling over costs. As a result, all of our investigators had recently upgraded their computers, and more portable equipment was available for them to use. My computer tablet was still unopened in my desk drawer—I preferred a good notepad when I went into the field. Still, I guess Volkov could afford to be generous when televised and streaming Mayday fights still drew massive worldwide audiences. Even this many years down the line, the public showed no sign of growing bored of watching Maydays kick the shit out of each other in the ruins of the old cities. I suppose it was kind of cathartic.

The one thing our office didn't have was a conference room. It'd never been an issue before, but today was something special. Once I'd got changed into a dry suit in the privacy of my office, I went out to the front of the main office. Healy passed around the box of breakfast burritos he'd picked up from the place around the corner. When everyone had something to eat and I'd been warmed up a bit by some coffee, I called for everyone's attention. A dozen pairs of eyes looked up from their computers and breakfasts. We were a pretty small crew, given the size of the company. The team was so diverse we could've formed our own miniature United Nations. I played the part of the stodgy old white guy. Lindsey Fischer was a white woman from South Africa, while most of the rest of the team were Asian or Hispanic. Healy was the youngest, while the oldest was Su-jin Ho, a tough Korean woman who used to be a cop and could get a Mayday talking if she was left in an interrogation room with it.

"All right, quiet down, everyone," I said. "You've all heard what's going on, but let's make sure we're all on the same page. Professor Volkov, our glorious and all-powerful leader, has graciously given us a chance to bathe in wealth and fame. Yllia, the youngest of the Maydays, was brutally murdered sometime during the night."

Lindsey Fischer put up her hand. She was sitting in the far corner, but her voice had a natural boom that carried easily across the office. "It's been a while since I've looked at a law textbook, but I seem to remember that the term 'murder' only applies to humans."

"How can you think like that?" I said. "Where's the compassion? Sure, these Maydays might have wiped out entire cities. But monsters are people too." I leaned on a desk. "Anyway, thanks to Lindsey's quick thinking and terrible driving, Volkov has handed control of the investigation over to us instead of the Biology Division. Your job right now is to make sure he doesn't regret that decision and send me swimming back to the real world. This is, without a doubt, the biggest case any of you sorry bunch will ever encounter. If we solve this, we've got it made. I know a dozen private dicks who would kill each and every one of us to have a crack at this case. Luckily, I've convinced Volkov to put the island under lockdown for the next twenty-four hours. No one gets in or out. No contact with the outside world."

A low groan went through the room. "Jesus, Boss, my girlfriend's back in Chicago. It's her birthday today. If I don't call her, she's going to have my balls."

"Sounds like she already does," Lindsey chipped in.

I put up my hands to quieten everyone. "All right, all right. If we solve this case, you'll all be famous enough to get new girlfriends. Better. Stronger. Faster."

"Bigger tits," Lindsey added.

"Shut up, Fischer," I said. "Your cell phones will be useless within an hour. Healy, give everyone one of the walkie-talkies from the emergency supplies. The range should be long enough to allow communication from pretty much anywhere on the island, but keep case details to a minimum when you're using them. The walkies have privacy encoding, but that doesn't mean they're secured. We can't be sure who else is listening to our frequency. Bear in mind that all the information we're dealing with here is highly sensitive and may include company secrets. You all signed non-disclosure agreements when you started working here. If I find anyone has leaked information, intentionally or accidentally, I'm going to personally make sure Legal sues the pants off you."

Healy handed the box of radios around, and everyone started fiddling with them. I gave them a couple of minutes while I drank my coffee, then I started talking again.

"We've got a lot of ground to cover and not enough time. I want a couple of people trawling the old Mayday war files, including anything you can get your hands on that wasn't made public. Someone found a weakness in Yllia that wasn't supposed to exist. Maybe there's a hint in the old reports. And don't just look at Yllia, either. It's possible all the Maydays are vulnerable to the same thing."

"That's going to take forever," someone said. I recognised Chiaki Okawa's voice and found her behind her desk.

"Great, thanks for volunteering, Chiaki," I said. "Get Luis to help you out. Healy, did you find out who that reporter is?"

Healy nodded and flipped through his notebook.

"Guy's name is William Cunningham. He's done some war correspondence, supposed to be a tough bastard. He's visited the island a few times before to do stories."

"You think you can send some security people to sit on him? We can't have him leaking stories off the island."

"Sure, but we may want to talk to him. He's that reporter who attached himself to the Mayday Protection Front for six months to make a documentary about the group. If the MPF was involved in this, Cunningham might know something."

I nodded. "That's a good thought. Su-jin? You want to see what you can wring out of him?"

The Korean woman nodded.

"Good," I said. I turned to Lindsey Fischer, who was still fiddling with her walkie-talkie. "Lindsey, if you want to put your smart-arse tendencies to good use, you can head over to the pits and get in Dr Russell's face. Bio is going to want to dissect Yllia and see what they can learn. Make sure they know that the investigation takes priority. Don't let them cut up anything important. And contact me to let me know if they find anything out."

"No problem, Boss."

"The rest of you can get started interviewing everyone who had access to Yllia's pit. Healy should have a list." I turned to Healy and pulled the small glass fragment out of my pocket. "I found this on top of the watchtower at the pit. Is there someone on the island who can tell me where it came from?"

Healy took the fragment and turned it over in his hand. "I suppose I can take it to Chemistry and see if they can do anything."

I nodded. The Chemistry Division was much smaller than Bio, but they still had some of the best chemists Volkov could headhunt from around the world.

"What are you going to do while we're all working our arses off, Boss?" Lindsey asked. "Take an early lunch?"

"You think I'd miss a chance to show up the rest of you bastards? I've got the most important job. I'm going to talk to Yllia's trainer. Miss...." I clicked my fingers at Healy, and he found the name in his notebook.

"Priya Dasari, Yllia's primary handler for the last four years."

"That's the one," I said. "All right, any questions?" No one said anything. "Fine. Well, stop dicking around, you bunch of layabouts. We have work to do."

The hubbub of quiet talk once again filled the office. I put my hat on and took a step towards the door, but Healy's heavy hand came to rest on my arm. "Boss, can I talk to you for a second?"

"Sure. My office?"

He nodded and followed me into my corner office. I sat down heavily in my chair, took my hat off again, and tossed it at the hat stand in the corner. It bounced off the wooden stand and flopped to the floor. One of these days I was going to make that shot.

Healy perched himself on the edge of the chair opposite and dry-washed his face with his hands.

"You look like hell," I said. "What's eating you, kid?"

He looked at me over the tips of his fingers. "I'm not sure about this, Boss."

"Not sure about what?"

"This. This case. We should be getting the Alliance inspectors involved. High level guidance. This is big stuff. Really big stuff. This office has never worked on something like this before. Not even close. Do you really think we can do this?"

"Well, maybe not the rest of you. But luckily you've got me here to pick up the slack. Don't worry, I won't tell Volkov I did all the work."

His face remained as tight as a Mayday's arsehole. "Boss...."

I put up my hands in surrender. "I get it, Healy, I get it. You're worried this is going to backfire. You're worried this is all going to go to hell and you'll find yourself out of a job and that pretty girl you're shacked up with will leave you for someone with a fatter wallet and a pair of Italian loafers. But you're worrying over nothing, son. If we started inviting the Alliance in here, you know what would happen? They'd shut us down like that." I snapped my fingers. "I already explained this to Volkov. You and me and the people in this office are this company's best chance of managing the situation. We're the ones in the driver's seat. These islands aren't that big. The killer is still here. We'll find them. And once we find them, we'll figure out how they did it." I leaned back in my chair and put my feet up on my desk. "And that'll be that. Volkov will be able to contain the situation. And we'll be richly rewarded. Trust me. It'll be a piece of cake."

He stared at me for a few seconds after I finished talking. It was hard keeping up my smile when he was giving me that look.

"I'm not worried about my job," he said. "Jesus Christ, Boss, they killed a Mayday. A Mayday. If this is the MPF, they've upped their game a whole lot from Internet campaigns and bombing Volkov's mainland offices. I want to know if we're safe."

I chewed on my thumbnail while I thought about it. I had to admit, that hadn't occurred to me. But I shook my head anyway. "The MPF are crazy, but they're not that crazy. They know if they start hurting people they're not going to make themselves any friends. I reckon a little Mayday euthanasia would fit with their ethos, but I can't see them coming after us."

"What if it's someone else? Someone less concerned about who they hurt."

I shook my head again. "Whoever it is didn't touch anyone human. They got in, killed Yllia, and got out. I don't know what they want, but they're happy just killing Maydays. So we have to stop them before they kill any more. We do that, and Volkov won't be able to thank us enough."

Healy didn't look convinced, but he shrugged and stood up. "Okay, Boss. If you're sure."

"Trust me." I stood, picked my hat up off the floor and followed Healy out of my office. I stopped him before he could walk away and spoke quietly to him. "One more thing before you go. You've been here longer than me. I haven't had a chance to go through all the old staff records since I took the job. But every company detective I've ever talked to keeps a file of problem staff hidden away somewhere. The usual suspects. Did the last Head Investigator have something like that lying around?"

Healy nodded. "Want me to go through it and see if I can find anything?"

"You're the best, Healy. And stop looking so glum, you sad sack. Career case, son. How many times do I have to say it? Career fucking case." I put on my hat and grinned widely. "Let's go have some fun."

3

It was raining sideways by the time I parked outside Psi Division. It was the tail end of the monsoon season, but it looked like we hadn't seen the last of the bad weather yet. I braced myself, then opened the door and climbed out of the car. The wind tried to take my hat almost immediately. I pushed it down hard on my head and jogged across the empty car park to the glass double doors that were the only entry into the compound.

Psi Division was the beating heart that made Volkov Entertainment the only organisation in the world capable of controlling the Maydays. Unlike the rest of Volkov's staff, the Psi folks didn't hold apartments on the West Island. They lived, worked, and played all within the confines of the Psi Division compound near the centre of the East Island, not far from Yllia's pit. Most of the time they never travelled further than the Mayday pits. Food, entertainment, everything they needed was brought to them. But there was one freedom they had over the rest of us. When the Maydays were shipped out to do battle in a ruined city somewhere in China or Vietnam or India, the handlers went with them and observed the battle first-hand. No, not observed it. Controlled it.

I'd only been to a single melee since I took on the job—I'd wrangled it out of Volkov as a condition of my joining the staff. One of the aerial film crews had taken me up in their chopper, and I'd watched as the huge, lumbering Nasir fended off attack after attack from Yllia and Grotesque on the outskirts of Jakarta. Even from so high up, the helicopter had shuddered with every thundering crack of Nasir's fist. Braver Volkov film crews had been in the city, filming the battle from the stumps of skyscrapers that'd had their tops ripped off a decade before. And most insane of all were the Maydays' handlers, following the battle through the streets in Humvees armoured to resist RPG blasts. The Psi crews may be a weird bunch, but they had balls, I'd give them that.

The doors to the Psi Division compound were locked, as usual. I ducked under the shelter of the entrance building's overhang and held my thumb on the buzzer for a few moments. I let go, and when the intercom didn't come to life immediately, I jammed the button down for another ten seconds. There's only one way to get anything as an investigator, and that's to be as annoying as possible until they can't ignore you anymore.

The intercom crackled. "Yes, all right, what is it?"

I showed my teeth to the black-shielded camera perched above the intercom. "Jay Escobar." I pointed my ID at the lens. "Head Investigator. Open the door, will you? I only just put on dry socks."

The door stayed shut. "What do you want?"

"I want to come in, wasn't that obvious? I need to talk

to Priya Dasari."

"Miss Dasari is indisposed. Please come back later."
The intercom went silent.

I checked my watch. It wasn't even ten in the morning
yet. Much too early to deal with this sort of bullshit. It was
a good thing I was in such a jovial mood. I leaned against
the buzzer again. After two minutes, the voice came back.

"Mr Escobar—"

"Ah, there you are," I said, releasing the button. "I was
beginning to think I was going to have to drive my car
through these doors. I'm sure you've received Professor
Volkov's memo asking you to cooperate with my investigation into the death of the Mayday Yllia. So I'm a little
confused about why I don't hear this door opening."

"Mr Escobar, please. The Psi Division is isolated for a
reason. Our handlers are all highly sensitive individuals,
and right now several of them are suffering from some
kind of psychic backlash as a result of the Mayday's death.
I'm sure what you have come about is very important, but
I must insist that you return another time. I suspect that
by tomorrow, Miss Dasari will be more inclined to speak
to you."

I nodded slowly and scratched my beard. "I'm going to
get my gun."

"What?"

I released the intercom button and jogged back to my
car. I opened the glove compartment and pulled out the
small lock box inside. After a few seconds of fiddling with
my keyring, I found the right key and lifted the lid. My
Smith & Wesson Model 15 revolver still looked as new as

the day I'd got it from a black market dealer in the refugee town. Which really wasn't all that new, since the thing had been plenty battered and bruised before I got my hands on it. But since I'd never fired it outside a firing range the whole time I'd owned it, it wasn't in bad nick. I fished the box of .38 Special cartridges out of the glove box as well and started feeding them into the cylinder as I walked through the rain back to the doors.

The glass doors stayed firmly closed. The lobby inside was dark and empty, nothing but a lonely indoor palm tree to welcome me. I waved at the camera. Then I pulled back the revolver's hammer and aimed it at the doors.

The crackle of the intercom had a note of desperation to it this time. "Wait, wait, wait, don't, I'm unlocking it. Fuck."

There was a buzzing sound. I tried the doors again. This time, they swung open easily. I decocked the revolver and emptied the cartridges out of the cylinder. I shook my hat dry as I came inside. The light overhead flicked on, and a nervous face appeared from around the corner of a hallway at the back of the room.

"Damn it," I said as I slipped the revolver into my pocket. "Don't you hate that feeling when you get rain dripping down the back of your neck? I'm going to have to start carrying around dry shirts in my car. Anyway, no matter." I put my hand out. "Jay Escobar, Head Investigator. And you are?"

"Curtis Stills, sir." It was the same voice I'd been talking to over the intercom. "I manage logistics here." He hesitated and inspected my hand for any concealed weapons before emerging fully into the lobby and carefully putting his hand in mine. His palm was sweaty.

"Curtis, great. I'll be sure to note your eager cooperation in my report to Professor Volkov." I reached into my pocket. Stills flinched at the motion. I grinned quietly to myself and brought my e-cigarette to my lips. I took a puff, then waved it in front of my face. "You don't mind, do you? It's not a real cigarette."

He shook his head quickly.

"Good man. Now, where's Miss Dasari?"

He glanced at the pocket with the gun in it. "Uh, like I was saying, she's suffering some ill effects from Yllia's death."

I blew a puff of fake smoke in his face. "I need to speak with her, Curtis. It's very important. Show me to her."

The man licked his lips, then nodded. He turned and made his way down the corridor he'd come from. I followed.

"My Mayday psycho-biology's a little rough," I said. "Remind me. Miss Dasari is the only one who maintained a psychic link to Yllia?"

"Yes. She's been her handler for the last four years, since her predecessor retired. The bond between a trainer and a Mayday is a delicate thing. It can't be easily transferred. Even a day's break from the training can undo everything we've worked towards. It's similar to the way hawks are trained for falconry."

"I imagine there's a little more room for error when you're training birds." There were windows on either side of the corridor, showing a courtyard crawling with vines

and carefully cultivated moss. If the rain hadn't been bar-
relling down, it might've been a nice place for me to take
an early lunch break.

"Like all our handlers, Priya's work never ends. She
hasn't taken a weekend or a day off since she began. Psi
Division is organised into teams to support each of the
handlers. Drivers, assistants, and the like."

"Like pit crews in Formula One. I get it. I'm going to
need a list of everyone in Yllia's crew. My people will need
to interview them in the next couple of days. You can either send them to our office or my men can come to you,
I don't care."

The back of his neck went pale, like he was imagining
a whole lot more people like me stomping around his precious Psi Division. "I think I'll send them to you."

"Make sure it's fast. Some of my people aren't as patient
as me."

We were past the courtyard now and into a wide indoor
lobby. The ceiling in the middle of the room was two floors
up, with office windows looking down at us from either
side. Pool tables and couches and vending machines lit-
tered the lobby. I figured this was where the staff mingled
when it was too wet to hit the courtyard and they were too
scared to venture over to the East Island with the rest of
us. We took a right and went down another long hallway.
Curtis was power walking like he couldn't wait to get rid of
me. I was going to have to lose weight if all this excitement
kept up.

I thought he'd be taking me to the handler's quarters
or an office or something, but when we reached the end of

the hallway we came out in what looked like a GP surgery. Finally, Curtis stopped outside a door that was indistinguishable from the ones on either side of it. I looked at the painting of a bland English landscape on the wall behind him.

"Where the hell are we?" I said.

Curtis hurriedly brought his finger to his lips. In a low voice, he said, "These are our quiet rooms. The division is very careful to select only the most stable individuals to receive the LIM—the linkage implant module."

"I know what it stands for," I said. I doubted there was a person on the island who didn't. The LIM was Volkov's masterpiece, the technology that had won the war and saved us from extinction. Once a LIM was surgically implanted into a person, they could control the impulses of a Mayday, toning down all the rampaging and destruction that they were so fond of. "What's your point?"

"Despite everything we do to alleviate the burden, the handlers suffer from the mental stress of their job. Many of them experience severe migraines, among other things. These rooms can help reduce the symptoms."

Twin streams of fake cigarette smoke blew from my nostrils. "Look, Curtis. I don't have time to worry about a bunch of antisocial psychics with headaches. Is this Miss Dasari's room?"

"Yes, but—"

I shouldered him out of the way—I probably had a good thirty kilograms on him—and opened the door.

The room was dark, no windows that I could see. The only light was that from the hallway, casting the sparse furniture into shadowy shapes. It was a small space, even smaller than my old shoebox office back in Sydney. Big enough for a desk and a single bed and space to walk between them, if you were skinny.

A small figure lay on the bed, on top of the covers. She groaned and rolled away from the light, pulling the pillow down over her head.

"Priya Dasari?" I asked. When I got no response, I took a couple of steps into the room. I felt Curtis' hands on my arm, trying to pull me back, but I shrugged him off. "Miss Dasari, I'm Jay Escobar. I'm an investigator. I need to talk to you about the Mayday's death."

The woman looked like she was trying very hard not to move.

Curtis tried to pull my arm again. "Please, Mr Escobar," he whispered.

Goddamn Psi Division. I found the light switch and flipped it.

The woman jerked and shuddered as light flooded the room. She really was a tiny thing; I'd guess she wouldn't even be five foot high when standing in stilettos. A ponytail of dark hair poked out from under the pillow. She wore a set of simple blue pyjamas—probably standard issue for the Psi Division.

I clapped my hands twice. "Come on, Miss Dasari. The sooner you talk, the sooner you can get back to sleep. Curtis, get her a Panadol or something."

He didn't leave. I could feel him hovering behind me. I let him. I drew up the chair from the desk and sat down next to the bed.

Slowly, the woman pulled the pillow away from her face and rolled towards me. Her eyes opened into slits. Her forehead was all creased up. When she spoke, her voice was quiet and strained. "Why are you here?"

Her accent faintly reminded me of somewhere in London, but like a lot of young people these days she had a mongrel accent, a by-product of spending childhood being shipped from country to country as a refugee, mingling with thousands of others in similar situations.

"That's an ambiguous question, Miss Dasari. Why are any of us here? Did God or Zeus or Buddha put us on this Earth only to see what happened when he threw giant monsters at us? I always ascribed to the 'kid pulling wings off flies' view of God, myself. He doesn't have a plan, He's just been left unsupervised." I leaned back in my chair. "But as for why I'm here on this island, I guess I'm here because it sounded like a good idea at the time. I was a private detective in Sydney, you see, and I'd taken a case investigating the guy who used to be the administrator of the refugee town I'd been living in during the war. This guy, get this, had been running a black market economy in the town for years without anyone ever catching wind. How he'd do it was when people, families and the like, wanted to get into the town, he'd turn them away, saying there was no more room. Then when the family were walking away, one of his agents would come out of the shadows and offer to smuggle the family in, for a price. The agent would send the man of the family into a nearby ruined city to go looting for whatever was in demand on the black market: sugar, booze, porn, that sort of thing. If the man got killed by bandits or ran into a Mayday, the administrator's agent would strip the rest of the family of everything they owned and send them naked back into the wild. So whatever happened, the administrator was never out of pocket." I shook my head. "Sickening stuff. It wasn't until after the war was over that I got enough of the pieces together to do anything about it. I used my considerable charm to get one of the agents talking, and he ratted out the administrator. After that, it was a simple enough matter to put together a case against him. I suppose I became a bit of a D-list celebrity for a couple of weeks after that. Made my money back selling the story to the news. That was when Volkov came knocking. And here I am. I'm not the best detective in the world, but I've a knack. I knack for choosing the right jobs. Until this morning, I was starting to think my knack had run out, that I'd made a terrible mistake working for a corporation like this. But now..." I tapped my temple. "...now I know that my subconscious was right all along, telling me to take this job. So tell me, Miss Dasari, does that answer your question?"

The whole time I was talking, the woman's hand had tightened on the duvet cover. I knew both Priya and Curtis thought I was being a bastard, and in truth, I was. That's what being an investigator is all about. No one likes to give up what they know. Even if they aren't thinking about it, everyone instinctively knows that knowledge is power. Power that can be used against them. So the only way a detective gets anything is by playing it tough. And that's all it is, play. Just acting. Mostly.

Priya let out a long, slow breath. Her eyes were still

screwed up, but I could tell she was forcing her muscles to relax. I waited as she eased herself into a sitting position. A sudden dizzy spell seemed to hit her and she threw her hand to her face. Curtis rushed in to help her. He eyed me—his fear of the gun in my pocket seemed to be wearing off. But I smiled and said nothing. There was a time to be a bastard, and a time to be patient.

When she was upright, her eyes slowly opened. She wasn't a particularly pretty woman—her jaw was too square for that. But she was younger than I expected. She must've been a kid during the war. Now here she was, the puppet master of a Mayday. Did she really understand the danger she was dealing with? The sheer destructive potential she controlled?

She fixed me with a steely look like she knew what I was thinking. Hell, maybe she did—the inner workings of the LIM were some of those company secrets Volkov was so protective of. I gave her a grin and a small wave.

"All right," I said. "Sorry. Why am I here? I'm here because Volkov wants me here. I'm here because your Mayday is lying dead in three feet of mud and no one has any idea why. I'm here because I think someone killed her. When someone is killed, the cops always talk to those who knew the victim." I shrugged. "I figure no one knew Yllia like you did. Does that answer your question?"

Priya nodded slowly.

"Good. Then I think I'll handle the rest of the questions from here on out." I turned to Curtis. "Are you going to get her that Panadol or what? Can't you see she's suffering?"

Curtis looked to Priya. The woman nodded and gestured that it was okay. He chewed his lip for a second, then disappeared out the door. When he was gone, I stood up and pushed the door closed. There was a lock, but I didn't flip it. An interrogation was always a delicate balance. You wanted to wind them up, scare them a little, but not too much. Push too far and everything crumbles. That's what makes it so much fun.

I sat down again and leaned forward. Priya's dark eyes were bloodshot and ringed with dark circles. Sleep had mussed Priya's hair, revealing a thin scar behind her left ear. The LIM implant site.

"You felt something," I said.

"Yes."

"You're still feeling something."

She nodded.

"Tell me what happened," I said.

She took a moment to compose herself. Her face was drawn and pale, a thin sheen of sweat coating her forehead. She kept her head completely still, as if moving it even an inch might set off a bomb in her brain.

"You know when you stretch a rubber band," she said. "You stretch it and it gets tighter and tighter. And then, suddenly, it snaps, and one end flings back and strikes your hand, and it stings for a moment. What I feel is like that, but a thousand times worse." Her face tightened for a moment, her lips forming a line. She exhaled as the pain passed. "You can't understand, Mr...what did you say your name was?"

"Escobar. But call me Jay," I said. "You're saying you felt the moment Yllia died?"

"I can't explain it." Her eyes were far away. "What it felt like. Since I began this job she's always been there. She was always this tiny ball of someone else in the back of my head. Now that part of my brain is empty, and the rest is curling in on itself."

"I understand. Now, this is very important, Priya. What time did you feel Yllia die?"

She rubbed her hand back and forth across her forehead. "I…I don't know. I was asleep when it hit me. At least, I think I was. I woke up, and all I could feel was pain. I couldn't see, I couldn't hear, I couldn't smell. It was like waves crashing into me. I was drowning, and then it faded and I could almost see the light again, and then another wave of pain came and drove me further under. I don't know how long I was like that. It wasn't until my assistant came in to tell me what had happened that I came out of it. It was morning by then."

"You can do better than that. Think hard."

She shielded her eyes with her hand. "I'm thinking as hard as I'm capable of, Mr Escobar." She spoke with a hint of a growl. "I went to sleep around eleven. I woke up once. I think it was about one-thirty. I got up and had a drink of water and went back to bed around two. So I suppose she died after that."

"What woke you?"

She shook her head, then looked like she regretted it. "I don't know. A feeling. I felt uneasy. Or maybe it was Yllia who felt it. I don't know."

"You could feel the creature's emotions?" I said. I was sceptical that they could even feel emotions, at least the same way we did. What use did a 50,000 tonne invincible monster have for an emotion like unease? Another thought occurred to me. "Could Yllia…communicate with you?"

She hesitated. "In a way. Not really with words. It's more like images, feelings."

That was news to me. Volkov had managed to keep that little piece of information under his hat. Did the Alliance heads know? Had they tried to interrogate the Maydays, find out where they came from, why they attacked us? Had anyone tried to negotiate with them since Volkov captured them? Then again, it made sense for Volkov to keep the world from knowing. Groups like the Mayday Protection Front might not look so insane talking about Maydays as people if everyone knew we could talk to the creatures. I grinned to myself. Volkov, that cunning bastard.

"What's funny?" Priya asked.

I shook my head. "Never mind. All right, so Yllia was uneasy. Did she tell you why?"

"No."

Something in the way she said that made me curious. "What is it?"

She licked her lips. "Nothing. It's just that Yllia had been quiet the last few days. Quieter than usual. The other trainers have said that their Maydays are more…talkative, I suppose. Some of them enjoy putting images of broken cities in their trainers' heads. I've heard that Grotesque in particular likes to throw insults at his trainer, tell her about what he plans to do to the human race. But I never experienced that with Yllia."

"Sounds like you were pretty chummy with her," I said.

Priya's eyes darkened. "She was a monster, Mr Escobar. A quiet killer. She may not have levelled cities like Nasir or Tempest, but she killed more than her share. Nine hundred and sixty thousand estimated civilians dead from her plasma attacks. The destruction of the Allied European Fleet—four hundred thousand souls. Another hundred and forty-two million driven to suicide by the force of her psychic waves. She was not my friend. She was my war prisoner."

I grinned. Feisty, this one. "So your war prisoner had absolutely nothing to say on the topic of who killed her."

"I think she knew something was coming. I didn't realise it at the time, but I think she knew. She's been marked for death for days, maybe weeks."

"Are you aware she broke impulse control before she died?"

Her face went tight. "That's—"

"Impossible. I know, I've already heard it from Volkov. But it's still true. Yllia broke free of your impulse control. She tried to fly. You feel anything like that?"

I could see the gears in her head turning. "Maybe… maybe it wasn't her dying I felt. Maybe it was her breaking free. I've read the reports of handlers who have lost impulse control. I suppose what I experienced could match that."

"I'll assume for now that you're good enough at your job to not lose impulse control from negligence. What could have caused her to break it?"

"There are only a few things we know of. Fear of being trapped. Starvation. Nasir once broke free when the

Alliance tried to bury him at the bottom of the sea."

"I remember," I said. "My pet theory is that Yllia was trying to get away from her killer."

"That fits, I guess."

"You're not convinced?"

"I don't know, detective. I'm tired and I can barely think."

I stroked my beard. I was getting the feeling in my gut that this whole interview was a bust. Not surprising, there were always more dead ends than true leads in any serious investigation. Still, I had to admit I was disappointed. I'd expected a psychic to be more…well…knowledgeable.

Something beeped in my pocket, and a crackly voice came out. "Boss, you there?"

I fished the walkie-talkie out of my pocket and looked at Priya. "Excuse me." I stood up and depressed the radio button. "I'm here. Who's this? You sound like you're talking through a kazoo."

"It's Lindsey. I'm at the pit with the Bio nerds and they're not happy about it. They're trying to keep me out of the autopsy."

"They're scientists. They're all weak from lack of sunlight. Just push them over and force your way in."

"There's a lot of them, Boss. And your lady friend Dr Russell is throwing a hissy fit. She seems to think that our little car accident this morning was engineered by you to get control of the investigation."

"How could she think I was capable of such a thing? All right, I'm pretty much done here anyway. I'll be there as soon as I can."

"Roger," Lindsey said. There was another beep, and she was gone.

When I turned back to Priya, she was sitting with her legs dangling over the edge of the bed. Maybe it was my imagination, but her pain seemed to have faded. Maybe she didn't need that Panadol after all.

"They're going to dissect Yllia?" she asked.

"If they can. I don't know how deep they'll get through that invincible hide of hers, though." I pocketed the radio. "I better get out of here before your mother comes back."

"My mother? Oh, right. Curtis just worries about us, that's all."

"I can see that. I hope you feel better soon, Miss Dasari. I may be back to talk to you again. If you think of anything else, send a message to my office." I took out a business card and put it on her desk. "The address is on there."

She nodded, but said nothing. Her face was set, like she was thinking. I waited a few seconds, expecting her to talk, but she never did. I said, "Thanks for your help," and then I left the room.

Curtis was hovering outside in the hallway. I tipped my hat to him and smiled. "The exit's this way, right? I'll figure it out. Don't forget to send those people to my office to be interviewed. It'd be a hassle if I had to come back."

He nodded quickly, his lips pressed together. I gave him a wink and strolled back down the hallway towards the exit. The handler hadn't been able to give me as much as I'd hoped, but at least I'd got a time frame to work with. Yllia died sometime between two and six, when her body was discovered by the keepers. Security was limited at the pits themselves—guards were posted mainly around the coast and at the bridge to stop nosy people sneaking onto the East Island. There had never been any concern about the Maydays' safety before. But now that I had a time frame, maybe something one of my other investigators picked up would click.

I stopped back in the lobby and stared out at my car across the car park. I didn't think it was possible, but the rain had got even worse. I decided to give it a few seconds in the hope that it would die down. I pulled out my radio and adjusted the frequency to the one Healy was using.

"Healy, how's it going?"

There were a few seconds, then his voice came through the static. "Busy."

"Good. I just wanted to let you know that Yllia died sometime after two a.m. Her handler had a breakdown overnight. Let the others know when you get a chance. I'm heading back to the pit to save Lindsey from some ravenous biologists."

"Right."

"Having fun yet?" I asked.

"Ask me again when I'm not neck-deep in old paperwork."

The crackle disappeared and I returned the walkie to my pocket. If anything, the rain was heavier. To hell with it. I shoved open the glass doors and jogged for the car.

When I climbed in my car and slammed the door, I returned my Smith & Wesson to the lock box and leaned over to put it in the glove box. It'd be a comfort to have a gun when dealing with Dr Russell, but I figured it might end up more trouble than it was worth. I sat up, started the car, and flicked the headlights on. Only then did I see the figure walking through the rain towards the car.

I sat in surprise for a second, watching her approach. Then I leaned over and opened the passenger door. Priya Dasari climbed in and hugged herself, rubbing her arms. She'd gotten changed into jeans and a white shirt with a cardigan, but she was still completely under-dressed for the weather. I cranked up the heater and brought my e-cigarette to my lips. We sat in silence for a moment while I took a couple of drags. Then, finally, she spoke.

"I want to come with you."

"Nope."

"Why not?" she demanded.

"Why should I let you?"

"Because you're investigating the death of a Mayday when you don't know anything about Maydays."

I shrugged. "I've been around a little longer than you, Miss Dasari. Those were some nice statistics you rattled off back there. But those were just numbers. I was in Sydney when Grotesque tore it to the ground. The war wasn't history for me. I lived it."

She scoffed and put her hands up to the heater vent. "When I was a kid, my parents were always talking about taking me to Mumbai to meet my mum's family. I'd never been outside London. So when I was eight, they took me to India. I'd been in Mumbai two days before Serraton came out of the sea and attacked."

"Bad?" I asked.

"There was so much confusion. No one knew what was

happening. He seemed to be everywhere at once. We'd see him silhouetted against the sky. He'd swipe his tail and three buildings would disappear. There were bodies hanging from his teeth. Then he'd dive behind a line of buildings and all you could hear was the rumbling as he ran through the streets. You could feel his footsteps, feel them vibrating through your bones. And then he'd rise up out of nowhere, snarling like he was laughing, and then…." She shook her head. "My mother and I made it to a shelter, but we were separated from my father. When Serraton passed, we went looking for him, but it was hopeless. There were too many bodies. We never found him."

The story was familiar enough. Everyone on the planet had a similar one or knew someone who did. "Tragic. But you're still not coming with me. Go home."

She swivelled in her seat to face me. "And do what? What am I supposed to do now? I began training for this when I was fourteen. From the beginning I was always intended to be Yllia's handler. This was my life. Now someone's killed her, and by doing that they put me out of the only job I was ever trained for."

"That happens to lots of people. You're still young. Go back to the real world, go to university. Hell, you could write a book and become a millionaire that way. *My Pet, the Mayday*. There, how's that for a title? Needs a bit of work, but—"

"I'm not leaving this island without knowing who did this to me."

I tucked my e-cigarette away. "I'll send you an email when I figure it out."

"You won't figure it out. Not without someone who knows about Maydays."

"I've got the Bio Division at my beck and call," I said. "Don't worry about me, sweetheart."

She smirked and stared out the windshield as the rain peppered it. "The Bio Division. What makes you think they know anything? What was the last major paper they published, do you know? I do. *Mayday sleep patterns unaffected by combat fatigue.* Behavioural science is the only thing they've managed to do in a decade. A live Mayday is impossible to study in any detail. We have no tools capable of taking tissue or bodily fluid samples. Every gastrointestinal probe they've tried to use has been destroyed by the acid in the creatures' systems. Even when they shed skin cells or hair, all the intracellular material degrades instantly, turning it into sludge. The Bio Division doesn't know a damn thing about how Maydays work. What makes you think they'll be able to tell you how they die?"

I tapped the steering wheel with my thumbs. I was getting the feeling she wouldn't get out of the car voluntarily. Too bad I'd already put my gun away. I considered hauling her out bodily, but my detective sense was tingling. She wasn't telling me everything. That made me curious.

"All right, kid," I said. "Tell you what. You come with me to the pit and we'll have a look at your dead Mayday. If you know so much, maybe you can help me deal with the scientists. Afterwards I get one of my people to drop you home. Deal?"

"Deal," she said.

I started the car and pulled out of the parking lot. "You

get that Panadol in the end?"

"It's a psychic backlash, not period pain. Shut up and drive."

I did what the lady said.

4

Yllia's pit had been transformed in the last few hours. A huge, white tent had been set up over Yllia's body, the plastic straining against the ropes that held it down in the wind. I strolled through the mud and the rain, Priya behind me. She was close enough that I could hear her breath catch when a flap of the tent billowed open and Yllia's massive face came into view. Maybe it was my imagination, but the Mayday looked thinner than she had this morning, like she was rotting from the inside out. I glanced back at Priya, but her face betrayed nothing. She couldn't fool me. War prisoner or not, she'd lived in this Mayday's head for four years. There was something between them—not a friendship, maybe, but a connection. I filed that away for later consideration. I'd have to bring it up with Volkov. It could be dangerous if the people who controlled the Maydays were sympathetic towards them.

I flashed my ID at the security guards at the entrance to the tent. They let me past and I pushed open the tent flaps. The smell hit me first, harder than it had this morning. The earthy, meaty scent nearly made me gag. I found a rack of odour respirators by the entrance. Before I keeled over, I slipped one on and handed another to Priya. I had to wipe the tears from my eyes before I could see properly.

Yllia's body stretched out in both directions, looking even more colossal in the confined space. The complement of scientists had thinned out, only thirty or so remaining. Most of them were gathered near the head, dressed up in thick plastic coats with long surgical gloves stretching to their elbows.

I turned to Priya, who hadn't taken her eyes off the Mayday. "What do you reckon, burial or cremation?" I was nearly yelling to be heard through the mask and over the sound of the rain on the plastic tent. "I once had an aunt who demanded to be buried when she died. She weighed about two hundred kilograms. I was one of the pall bearers. I had to get physiotherapy afterwards." I pointed at Yllia. "Could be worse, though, right?"

Priya said nothing. I was going to get a reaction out of her one way or another. I turned back to the group of scientists gathered around the head. Just off to the side, I spotted a large blond woman, the only person around not dressed like they worked in an abattoir. Lindsey seemed to be lacking her trademark good humour today. I squelched through the mud to her.

Her eyes met mine over her odour mask as I approached.

"Thank Christ you're here," she said. "I was about to start screaming. Goddamn scientists have been blocking me all morning. Won't even tell me what they've found. Who's that?" She nodded at Priya, who was wandering towards Yllia's flank.

"The Mayday's handler. She followed me home."

Lindsey looked confused but she shrugged. "You've got to help me out here, Boss. Dr Russell's got a bee up her arse about you, and—"

"Escobar!"

I turned around at the sound of my name and found Dr Russell storming towards me, her boots kicking up mud around her. I winked at Lindsey, spread my arms, and met Dr Russell halfway.

"Doctor, I love the new decor."

She stopped a foot inside my comfort zone and got in my face. A hairnet covered most of her blond hair, except for a couple of strands that'd fought free. She tugged her odour mask down and snarled.

"What do you think you're doing, sending your lackeys to interfere with my autopsy?"

I put my hands in my pockets and rocked back on my heels, which wasn't easy in the mud. "Is that what this is? An autopsy? I figured you'd just been setting up a circus tent. You know, 'Come one, come all, see the Great Dead Mayday.' Makes sense that you'd be preparing for a new career seeing as how you and everyone else in this company will be out of a job if you keep stopping my investigators doing what they need to do."

"You're the one who's going to ruin this company. You have no expertise in a matter like this. I don't know how you convinced Volkov to put you in charge of the investigation, but I'm not going to stand idly by and let you send your people to interfere with a scientific investigation."

"Catherine—"

"Do you understand the implications of what has happened here? Since this Mayday has died, her tissue has become vulnerable to our instruments. For the first time in the history of megabiology, we are able to obtain tissue samples from a Mayday. Our first chance to truly understand them. And every second I waste arguing with you or one of your people is a second more of degradation that the remains are subjected to. This chance may never come again. We will find out what killed this Mayday, Escobar. And we will do it without your interference."

She sure was precious. "Aw, hell, Doc, I didn't realise this investigation meant so much to you. I never meant to freeze you out. I just wanted to offer Volkov my help in the matter. I guess it just panned out that I got the chance to talk to him first. But I have no doubt that if he'd heard the passion in your voice like I did just now, he wouldn't have hesitated to let you take control of the investigation." I spread my hands. "Oh, well. *Que sera, sera.*"

Her eyes looked like they were about to burst out of her skull. I was enjoying this much more than I should have been.

"Listen to me, you smarmy son of a bitch," she said, her voice dropping so low that only I could hear it over the pounding of the rain overhead. "I'm not an idiot. I know you had your dog over there crash into my car to delay me."

"Your car? I always thought you drove a company car."

"I could have been killed."

I raised an eyebrow. "From a fender bender?"

"Volkov is a smart man. He'll soon realise he made a mistake putting you in charge. Until then, I will not abide the presence of a gorilla like you. Leave."

I shook my head. I'd let her blow off a little steam, but now she was pushing the bounds of good taste. I was getting sick of everyone on this damn island thinking they knew better than me. I stretched up to my full height and loomed. She'd put herself only inches away from me, so now her options were to look up at me or take a step back. She went for the former, but she didn't look happy about it.

"Catherine, this isn't optional. This isn't your specimen. This is my crime scene. You are here at my liberty. If you get in my way—and I'm starting to feel like you are—I will get some big heavy guys from Security down here to haul your arse all the way back to your apartment where I will hold you until this case is finished or I feel like you're no longer a danger to it. You and Volkov may be old buddies, but I've got his ear on this. I am his best chance to save this company. He knows that. And if I say you need to go, you're gone. Now, are we going to have a problem?"

We had gathered a small audience of scientists who were pointedly not looking at us. They had all decided—apparently in unison—that they needed to edge slowly towards us to better analyse their samples. So none of them noticed when Priya Dasari slipped behind them and sneaked towards Yllia's monstrous head.

Clever girl. I met Lindsey's eye and saw that she'd noticed the handler's sneaking as well. She raised her eyebrows a fraction of a centimetre at me. I gave her a wink and a shake of my head. I didn't know what Priya was up to, but I wanted to find out.

Dr Russell had gone quiet, like the part of her brain

that controlled speech had melted. If I squinted, I thought I could spot a little bit of it leaking out her ears. I decided to press my advantage and keep her distracted at the same time.

"All right, now that we're on the same page, let's get down to business. I know you've found something, or you wouldn't be so determined to keep my investigators away. So why don't you just tell me what that is?"

She gave me a look that shortened my lifespan by two, maybe three years. I shook it off and said, "If you don't tell me, I'll get it out of your scientists. After they've watched me drag you away."

She was chewing the inside of her mouth like it was my face. Her eyes burned, her lips twisted. But she broke. They always do.

She stretched up, put her hand delicately on the small of my back, and brought her lips next to my ear like a lover about to promise me the world. "I will see that Volkov ruins you."

I grinned and tugged my mask down. "Sweetheart, I can't wait to see you try," I whispered in her ear. "One last warning to make it all official. If you ever, ever call one of my investigators a dog again, I will come for you. It will not be a measured or reasonable response. I will worm my way into your life, find out all your secrets, and destroy you piece by piece. And if you don't have enough secrets, I'll invent them. I'll destroy your career. I'll turn your friends and family against you. I'll make it so you can't set foot in any country more civilised than Somalia without the police knocking on your door. This won't be on company time. It'll be personal. No one—no one—insults my investigators."

She stepped back and met my smile with one of her own. I'd like to think there were more daggers in mine.

"Very well, Mr Escobar," she said in a voice made of false silk. "Our initial investigations revealed no physical trauma to the Mayday. She has not participated in a melee in two months, and the only recent attack landed against her was Serraton's acid, which delivered no more than surface damage. Therefore, we can conclude that it was not a physical attack that killed her."

I twirled my hand in the air, telling her to get on with it.

"It's too early to be sure," she continued, "but no unusual chemical compounds have been identified in Yllia's food or water supply. If we expect an unknown poison to have a dose-response relationship that is even remotely comparable to most identified poisons, any concentration that is enough to kill something as large as a Mayday should be measurable in the source. But none has been identified. Radiation poisoning has also been ruled out."

"Which leaves us with?"

"A biological cause of death."

I pushed back my hat and rubbed my forehead with the back of my hand. Did no one listen around here? "Yllia didn't catch a cold. Someone killed her."

"I didn't say she wasn't murdered."

"So, what, you're talking about a biological weapon? Like anthrax?"

Her mouth formed a tight line. "In principal, yes. But

so far we have been unable to find it."

I glanced behind her at the Mayday's body. If Dr Russell was right, was this thing contagious? And where the hell had Priya got to?

"Excuse me for a moment," I said. I stepped away from Dr Russell and jerked my head at Lindsey. She followed me towards the massive expanse of Yllia's unfurled wing, out of earshot of the scientists.

"You see where the girl went?" I whispered.

Lindsey pointed with her chin. "Round by the Mayday's ear. Why the hell is she here, Boss?"

"Never mind that. Go get these lazy scientists back to work. I'll be back in a second."

I pulled my mask back onto my face and fought my way through the mud. Dr Russell tried to get my attention as I went past, but I played dumb and kept walking. Plastic crates full of equipment sat on white sheets designed to protect them from the mud. I went past them and made for Yllia's head. Her fur was drooping now. Deep holes peppered her skin, each about the size of a coin. Inside, the flesh glistened like dried resin.

Yllia's eyes stared blankly as I strode past her head. Still no sign of Priya. Mud leaked into my shoes and made each step a minor misery. I started the journey round to the other side of the Mayday's head.

I saw her shoes first, then the legs of her jeans. Priya was pressing her cheek against Yllia's temple, arms out-stretched like she was trying to give the creature a hug. As I approached, I saw her eyes were closed. What the hell was she doing?

"Miss Dasari?" I said. "You might not want to do that. The geeks reckon it was a biological weapon that killed—"

A loud *crack* split the air. A moment later, pain roared in my skull.

My first thought was that I'd been struck by lightning. What rotten luck. Finally get the case of a lifetime and then I get hit by lightning. God really was a funny guy. Guess he had to get his kicks somehow.

A second blinding pain thudded through my head.

Lightning? Twice? What a stupid idea. I was under cover, wasn't I? It was getting hard to remember. A part of my body a few miles distant—my knees, maybe—felt cold and damp. Come to think of it, my face did too. I was lying in something. Lying down on the job, disgraceful.

The third thud in my skull barely hurt more than an electric drill to the eye. Or a bullet to the head. Was that it? Had I been shot? I must have a hell of a skull if I could still wonder about it. Something was screaming, roaring, a long way away. I tried to turn my head towards it, but I didn't seem to have a neck anymore. I didn't seem to have a body at all. I floated a few moments, weightless. I had no eyes, but the fog that'd been clouding my sight began to clear.

Images flashed before me like a bad film reel.

I was looking at the world from a thousand feet in the air, a wasteland sprawled out below me. Colossal shadows stalked across the horizon, hundreds of them, one slithering across the desert on a dozen twisting tentacles, another taking slow, lumbering steps on legs the size of skyscrapers.

Wings stretched out to either side of me, carrying

me across the landscape. Alien sensations assaulted me, tastes and smells forming cloud trails all around. A dozen strains of musical humming, far outside the normal range of hearing, echoed across the earth as the massive creatures called to each other.

Another bomb went off in my head. The vision changed.

I was flying again, but instead of desert, a coastline spread out below me. Where huge creatures had once roamed, tiny bipedal mammals now scurried through landscapes made of concrete and metal. Their screams didn't reach this high, but I could taste their fear as I swooped towards them.

Jets and helicopters buzzed around me like gnats, spitting harmless balls of fire at me. I wasn't excited as I moved in to destroy the city. I barely felt much of anything. I had woken up from a long sleep and found my home infested with vermin. So I did what you do with vermin.

Another blow struck my brain and sent me reeling through time once more. Distantly, I thought I could hear myself screaming—me the real, human me. But then it was drowned out by another feeling—alien and yet familiar. Horror.

I recognised where I was this time. Rain came down relentlessly, turning my fur cold and damp in the night air. I lumbered through the mud, my wings tucked tightly away to protect them from the moisture. Neither the darkness nor the tiny human fence around the edge of the pit obscured my view of the island. I could feel eyes on me—not human eyes, but the eyes of a creature with real intelligence, real cunning. I met Tempest's eyes across the distance. The massive creature stared at me, standing tall on his spider-like legs.

My strength was failing. It was time. I was already dead. I could sense Tempest's rage. But I wouldn't give him the satisfaction of watching me die.

I turned from the watchtower and bounded. The earth groaned in protest as I launched myself into the air. My wings unravelled, caught the air.

And then I fell. And when I hit the ground, I experienced something I'd never experienced before.

Pain.

5

A little part of me wanted to stay asleep, but on the whole, drowning face-down in a mud pit seemed like a more embarrassing death than I could abide. So I dragged myself out of unconsciousness and out of the mud.

I was going through suits faster than a teenage boy goes through tissues and Internet porn. I found my handkerchief and wiped the mud out of my eyes. It didn't help much. My eyes still burned. So did the rest of me. There was a panel beater in my brain trying to knock all the kinks out. What the hell had all that been? Had I had a seizure? And why hadn't anyone come to help me?

I sat on my arse in the mud for a second, trying to get the world to stay still. When it refused, I said, "To hell with you, then," and stood up. I went down again straight away. Goddamn mud was like trying to get up on roller skates. I grabbed a couple of Yllia's hair fibres and used them like ropes as I pulled myself to my feet. My head wasn't too appreciative of the action. My gut tightened and I doubled over, pulling the mask down around my neck. For a second I thought I was going to throw up. No such luck. I stood with my head between my knees for a second or two, blinking back tears. Then I looked up and saw a small body lying face-down in the mud in the shadow of Yllia's head.

"Priya!" My voice sounded foreign to me. I slipped and plodded over to her. Hell, was she breathing? I couldn't tell. I sank to one knee at her side—my suit was a write-off anyway—and rolled her onto her back.

I used my sleeve to wipe the mud out of her mouth and nose. Her face was grey underneath. I gave her a couple of slaps to the cheek—it always worked in the movies—and lowered my head so my ear was just above her lip. A light breeze tickled my ear. She was breathing. The knot in my stomach loosened a little.

I felt the roar before I heard it. A high pitched scream that I hadn't heard since the day I got to watch a live melee. It vibrated up my legs and shook my heart. It shook the rest of me as well. Grotesque. He was angry.

The second scream came a moment later, and then another one after that. Serraton. Tempest. The roars echoed through my skull. I pressed my hands to my ears to try to block them out, but it was hopeless.

My pocket crackled. "Boss," Lindsey's voice came through the radio. "Boss, you hear that?"

"Of course I bloody hear it," I yelled back into the walkie. I found my hat lying in the mud and picked it up. "Forget about it. Are the geeks alive?"

"Yeah, they're fine. A bit muddy. We all blacked out. Did you see—?"

"Later. We're around the other side of Yllia's head. The handler's still out. I'm going to get her out of this mud."

"All right, hold on, I'll come to you."

"No," I said, a little rougher than I intended. My brain wouldn't stop pounding. "I need you to keep the geeks contained, all right?"

"Contained?"

"Don't let them talk to anyone else. Not until I've figured out what's going on. Don't tell them you're doing it if you can help it. But keep them working and under control."

There was a pause on the other end of the line that the roaring Maydays were more than happy to fill. Whatever Priya had done, she'd sure riled them up. I scooped the mud off my hat as best I could and put it back on.

"Boss," Lindsey said. "Don't you think that's a little extreme? Everyone just passed out. Maybe we should get a doctor down here to check everyone out."

Priya was light enough that I could lift her out of the mud and carry her with one arm. I thought she groaned as I put her over my shoulder, but it was difficult to tell, what with all the angry monsters screaming.

I depressed the walkie button. "If Dr Russell and her people saw what I just saw, they are now in possession of extremely sensitive information that could be crucial to this case and the well-being of this company. I can't have them talking to anyone, and I need them figuring out what killed Yllia. If you can't do that, I'll get Healy down here to do it for you."

I took the few moments of silence to adjust Priya's weight and begin trudging through the mud. If I could, I wanted to get out of the pit without talking to Dr Russell again. It was the first day and this investigation was already going tits up. What the hell had Priya done?

When Lindsey finally replied, her voice was tight, completely empty of her normal good humour. "Roger, Boss." The radio crackled and went dead. Now all I could hear was the rain and the echoing cries of the Maydays. My ears rang.

I peered around the side of Yllia's head. The scientists weren't interested in me; half of them were still sitting in the mud with their heads between their knees. The other half glanced nervously towards the Mayday screams.

I took my chance and trudged towards a loose tent wall to my right, Priya hanging limply from my shoulder.

The white plastic of the tent wall flapped up in the wind as I approached. I glanced back once more. Lindsey was watching me from where she stood apart from the biologists, her frame tiny against the huge beast behind her. I nodded at her and ducked under the tent wall.

I was hoping the rain would wash off some of the mud. It didn't. I tugged off the odour mask, tossed it on the ground, and made my way out of the pit and back to the car park. As light as Priya was, she got heavier the farther I had to carry her.

I glanced across the island as I walked. Through the rain, I saw Tempest standing tall, muscles flexing with agitation. His roar had turned to a low growl that echoed across the island.

By the time I got to my car the Maydays had quietened down enough that I could hear Priya starting to stir. I had to hurry this along. I balanced her awkwardly with my left hand while I fished through my pockets with my right. When I finally found my keys, I unlocked the passenger door and lowered her into the seat. Her eyes flickered and she moaned lightly.

I opened the glove box and found my handcuffs. I hadn't found a chance to use them since taking the job. Not even recreationally. Figured it was about time to christen them. I snapped one cuff around Priya's wrist and the other to the grab handle above the door.

It was time to get some goddamn answers.

\\\

Priya jerked her hand back and forth, testing the strength of the handcuff chain. I hoped she was suitably impressed. They were my own cuffs, police standard. Illegal for civilian use in most places. Good thing we weren't in most places.

"Give me a break," she said. "What is this?"

I grinned at the road from the driver's seat, one hand on the wheel and another laying casually on my lap in case she did anything stupid. The road I was taking her down wound around the banks of a river swollen with rainwater. The road was little more than a service way, a back road that connected Yllia's pit to Serraton's near the coast. I wanted her out of the way of the city proper in case she did anything else weird and psychic.

"This, sweetheart, is me being a generally untrusting sort of guy."

"Where are you taking me?"

I looked around and found a dirt nook underneath an overhanging bank. "Here will do."

I pulled over, switched off the ignition, and pulled the handbrake. Rain pattered on the windscreen. The Maydays were all quiet again, thank Christ. I'd spoken to Healy over the radio and determined that everyone on the West Island was freaked out by the roaring, but they hadn't blacked out or had any visions. It seemed like the incident was localised to those of us who'd been near Yllia's body at the time. If Lindsey could keep the scientists from blabbing, we stood a chance at containing the visions.

"How's the head?" I asked.

"It feels like I've been kicked by a horse," Priya said. "Let me go."

"Soon, maybe. First I want to ask you some things. Until I know what the hell's going on, I want you where you can't do any more damage."

"Damage? What are you talking about?"

"That really hurt, you know. My head's still throbbing. I don't appreciate having the experiences of a dead Mayday stuck in my head."

Priya's eyes widened. "You…you felt that?"

"I did more than feel it, honey. I had it burned on my retinas. So did one of my investigators, along with every geek in Yllia's pit. So I'm going to ask you once, and I'm going to ask you real nice. What the fuck did you do?"

"I was helping."

I dug deep and gave her my best sneer. "Real helpful."

"This morning, when I could move again, when the pain had faded enough for me to form thoughts, I felt something. There was a hole in my mind where my connection to Yllia had been. But there was a fragment remaining, a tiny thread. I thought maybe if I could get close to her I could fix the connection. I thought maybe I could see what'd happened."

"Well, if you saw what I saw, you got a whole bunch of bullshit. Do you have a killer for me?"

"No, but—"

"Then you're not much use to me, are you? I'm taking you back to the city. You're going to sit nice and quiet in a cell until all this is over. You've made me nervous, and I don't want you getting up to any more mischief until I've figured this out."

She jerked her hand in the cuff. "You can't do that. What about my family?"

"What about them?" I started the car.

"They won't know where I am."

I doubted she even had a family on the island. Handlers didn't make good spouses. "Don't care."

She let out a frustrated growl and tugged at her wrist again as I pulled back onto the road and headed west.

"That ain't gonna help, sweetheart."

"You need my help. You're going to screw this whole thing up."

I grinned. "Have a little faith. I've been doing this a while."

"You don't have a clue how to find the little one."

The hell was she talking about? I shot her a sideways glance. She stared at me, raising her eyebrows. I shrugged.

"You didn't see the little one?" she said. "I thought you said you saw what I saw."

"Jesus, maybe I'm not as much of an expert psychic as you," I snapped. "Just tell me what the hell you're babbling about."

"It was during one of the visions. Yllia was somewhere

else, when she was still free. There were other Maydays there. Not together, not in the same place. But I could see them in my mind's eye. I got the feeling the Maydays were communicating somehow. I couldn't understand it. But then Yllia did something. One of her powers, something I hadn't seen before. And then the others—I couldn't really see very well—but it almost looked like they were… sweating."

"Sweating?" I raised an eyebrow.

"Not really. I couldn't understand it. And then the vision was gone. But there was something else there as well, something small, tiny to a Mayday. Smaller than a person. It looked like some kind of slug. Didn't you see any of this?"

"I guess I don't get that channel."

I chewed the inside of my lip as I thought. I tried to replay the vision in my mind, but it was murky, dreamlike. I was pretty sure Priya was just screwing with me, trying to get herself off the hook. Then again, what if she was telling the truth? What did it mean? How the hell was I supposed to derive meaning from a half-seen vision broadcast from a dead Mayday brain?

"Well, whatever you saw, it's all Greek to me. You have any idea how it's connected?"

She shook her head. "I think the little thing, the slug, was important in some way to the Maydays, or maybe just to Yllia. But other than that…." She shrugged.

"Great." My stomach let out an angry growl. "And to top it off, I'm starving." I glanced at Priya. "All right, I'll make you a deal. I unlock the handcuffs, buy you lunch, and you go through these visions of yours again until you manage to get me something useful. And if you can't, maybe we'll talk about that cell again. How's that sound?"

She gave me one of her looks. I'd like to think I was getting pretty good at interpreting them by now. I'm a fast learner.

"Come on, you can't still be angry about the cuffs," I said. "You nearly blew my brain out. I had to be sure I could trust you."

"Do you trust me?"

"Not at all. How do you feel about Chinese food?"

6

I learned long ago that when you're trying to untangle yourself from a whole bunch of confusing bullshit in the middle of a case, the best course of action is to head to the nearest Chinese restaurant and get eating. Thai food works in a pinch, but for a really tough puzzle, it has to be Chinese. Don't ask me why. It's not for the fortune cookies—you can toss those right out. But you can't argue with the results.

Priya wasn't taking to the idea with as much gusto as me. There were a few Chinese places on the island, but my favourite was this yum cha style restaurant where they didn't give you a knife and fork just because you were white. The waitresses weren't bad company either. I took a couple of dishes off the cart each time they came around, but Priya was still on her first.

"Come on," I said, pointing at her with my chopsticks, "you've got to eat something."

"I still don't feel well."

I shrugged. "Suit yourself. But if you're not going to use your mouth to eat, you might as well talk. There's still things you're not telling me."

Priya pushed the food around on her plate with her chopsticks. "Some things are hard to articulate."

"Try."

She rubbed her head. "I feel like there's a pressure in my mind. Something that shouldn't be there. I didn't really notice it before. I was in too much pain from the break with Yllia to sense it. But there's something in my head, something foreign. Something that's been there since she died."

"Okay," I said. "I have no idea what you're trying to tell me."

"Neither do I," she said, her hand curling into a fist to knead her forehead. "It has to be some remnant of my connection with Yllia. But it's locked up. I can't get to it. I've never experienced anything like this before."

"As soon as we're done here we'll find a hypnotist in the phone book. Maybe they'll get to the heart of your suppressed trauma."

She narrowed her eyes at me like she wasn't sure if I was kidding. I was. She figured it out and scowled.

"Don't be like that, sweetheart," I said. "I was just pulling your leg. Are you going to eat that?" I reached over and picked up a dumpling from one of the dishes in front of her.

"There's something else as well," she said as I stuffed my face. "That vision. I can't stop thinking about it."

"The one with the slug?"

She nodded. "In the earlier visions, there were hundreds of creatures everywhere. But in that one, I could only see a few. The ones who attacked us during the war. Why only those ones? What happened to the others? Maybe these Maydays were the few remaining. The survivors of something."

I'd been thinking about that as well. If our Maydays were survivors, that implied the others had died. Maybe whatever had killed the other Maydays was the same thing that'd killed Yllia.

"The little one," she said. "The small creature. I think it's a Mayday as well. And I think it's still alive. If the others I saw are survivors, why not that one? Maybe we just didn't notice it because it wasn't crushing cities."

"You think it's important somehow."

She nodded. "I can't explain why. It's just a feeling."

"Like this pressure of yours."

"Exactly. But I know we need to find it."

"All right," I said. "Where do we start looking?"

"I have no idea."

I grinned. I knew it. Just another distraction. "Well, in that case, I'm taking a bathroom break." I folded my napkin and stood up. "If I come back and find you've run off, I'll track you down and you really will be seeing the inside of that cell. Got it?"

"Sounds better than having to put up with you."

I batted my eyelashes at her and left her to continue playing with her food. The bathrooms were down a short hall at the back of the restaurant, the walls painted a sickly maroon. I went into the Men's and checked all the cubicles. I had the place to myself. I flipped the lock on the door and pulled my walkie-talkie out of my pocket.

"Healy, it's Jay. You there?"

There was a short pause before the radio beeped and his voice cut through the crackle. "Hold on, Boss, there's a call coming through on the emergency line."

"I thought we were blocking all calls."

"All except the emergency number. Hang on."

"Just let the Security boys take it," I said. "That's their job. I want to know what you guys dug up on the handler, Priya Dasari."

There was a long burst of static. He really was answering the call. It'd be nothing. There was no crime on the island. Not until this morning. We'd got emergency calls a grand total of twice since I started working here.

After waiting a minute, I depressed the radio button again. "Healy, come on. What've you got on Dasari?"

The walkie crackled. "Boss, I've got a kid on the line. He says a few guys broke into his house and now they're roughing up his grandmother. He's locked himself in the master bedroom."

"Jesus. Well don't tell me, get Security to haul arse down there. Where is it?"

"Four nineteen Ifukube Avenue. Boss, the kid's name is Oliver Dasari."

I stared at the walkie. "Wait, Dasari? Is that what you said?"

"Confirmed. He's the handler's son."

I rubbed the back of my head and tapped the radio against my forehead. What the hell was going on here?

"Boss?"

I depressed the button. "All right. All right. Gimme that address again."

"Four nineteen Ifukube."

"Okay. Send Security. But I'm closer. Is the kid safe?"

"For now."

"That's not reassuring, Healy." I unlocked the bathroom and jerked open the door. "I'm on my way. And send someone to that Chinese place on the corner of Darrow and Thirteenth. The handler will be here. Get her somewhere safe. She won't like it, but don't give her a choice. And don't tell her what's happening. Understand?"

"Sure thing."

I pocketed the radio and crossed the restaurant as fast as I could without running. Priya frowned as I came rushing up.

"What's wrong?" she said.

"Something's come up. I'm going out. You're staying here. I'm sending someone to pick you up."

She stood. "Wait, what's happening? Is it about Yllia?"

I put both hands on her shoulders and shoved her back down into her seat. "Stay put or I'll get the handcuffs out again." I turned and shouted to a pair of waitresses. "Hey, you. You know who I am?"

The two women glanced at each other and gave short nods. I was drawing stares from the restaurant's other patrons.

"Good," I said. I pointed at Priya. "You don't let her leave until one of my investigators comes. If she moves, you'll both be fed to the Maydays."

"What do you think you're doing?" Priya said.

I didn't answer. I pulled on my hat and ran for the door.

7

419 Ifukube was only a five minute drive from the res-taurant. I cut it to three with a reckless disregard for the safety of both myself and other road users. For a moment, the rain considered letting up, but then it changed its mind and poured down even harder.

The house was in one of the few suburban areas of the island. Since all the houses around here were prefabs installed by the company, 419 was the exact same box-shaped architectural bore as all the other homes on the street. The only way you could tell them apart was by the car in the driveway and how well-kept the small garden sections were. In 419's case, the garden was threatening to go wild but hadn't quite managed it yet. No car outside. No signs of anything amiss. The rain was keeping everyone off the streets. I parked the car a few houses down and fished the gun case out of the glove compartment. My hands trembled when I tried to get the key in the lock. I tried again. Missed.

I closed my eyes and took a breath. My stomach was twisting. What the hell was wrong with me? *Come on, Escobar. Get it together. Something fucking weird is going on and the handler is at the centre of it. Now get your gun, get out of the car, and do your damn job.*

I opened my eyes and unlocked the gun case. Funny, all these years and I'd never actually had cause to use the revolver in anger. I was so proud of myself when I first got it. I didn't feel so excited now. I just felt sick.

I loaded the revolver, got out of the car, and jogged towards 419, keeping an eye on the windows. I thought I saw something move, then it was gone.

I slowed as I approached the house, but my heart didn't. I held the gun close against my chest as I crept down the driveway and cut through the garden towards the front-facing windows. The curtains had been hastily pulled, but there was a gap in the centre where they didn't quite meet. I peeked inside.

The lights were off, but there was enough ambient light to see by. Two men dressed in jeans and black sweatshirts were doing their best to fill up the small lounge. Both wore balaclavas, and both were as heavy as me and a bit taller. At their feet lay a heavyset Indian woman. She was moving, but not much. One of the men jabbed her in the ribs with the end of a baseball bat. He was talking, but I couldn't make out the words.

The other man turned towards the window. I ducked out of sight, clutching the gun in both hands. My palms were beginning to ache. *All right. Think it through.* Security wouldn't be far away. Maybe. You never knew with those goddamn grunts. The woman—Priya's mother?—wasn't looking so good. And there was a kid in there somewhere. Jesus Christ, she never told me she had a son.

There was a thud and a cry from inside. *Fuck*. I couldn't wait. There were only two of them. I had surprise and a gun. It'd be enough. I crept back to the door and wiped the rain out of my eyes. It felt like I was wearing baseball mitts on both my hands. I tried the doorknob. Locked. Muffled shouting leaked out of the house before being swallowed by the rain. I eyed up the door. Cheap prefab piece of shit, just like the rest of the house. I stood as tall as I could make myself, took two deep breaths, and aimed the gun just below the lock.

Jay Escobar, big fucking hero.

I turned my head aside and squeezed the trigger. The gun barked in my hands. I was used to the kick, but I normally wore ear protection on the odd occasions I actually practiced with the damn thing. My ears rang. I checked my aim and fired again. Another round splintered the wood. Then I stepped back and slammed my foot into the door where the lock met the door jamb.

The whole thing had taken about two seconds. In that time one of the thugs had taken three steps out of the lounge and into the narrow foyer. He took one look at me, his eyes wide behind his balaclava eyeholes, and turned to shout to his friend.

I brought the butt of the revolver down over his right eye. He was halfway down when I hit him again, harder this time. I was moving faster than I could think. I came around the corner, stepped into the lounge, and pointed the gun at the thug with the baseball bat.

"Throw it over there," I said. The words echoed strangely, like I was hearing myself on the radio. "Throw it now, you piece of shit."

He tossed it on the carpet. The two of us were separated by a two-seater couch and the woman lying on the floor. I spared a glance for her. She was breathing, bleeding a little from a cut under her eye, and moaning softly. Her eyes flickered. I didn't think she was fully appreciating the current situation. I hoped the Security boys brought a paramedic with them. But first things first.

I jerked the gun at the thug. "Go over there, slowly. Over by your buddy."

The nauseous feeling was slowly fading. I didn't know what I'd been so worried about. The whole thing was over in fifteen seconds. I didn't even stub my toe. I stepped backwards and sideways to keep the couch between me and the thug as he moved over to his groaning, barely conscious friend. The thug who was still standing breathed heavily through his teeth, but he didn't say anything. Probably wise. He didn't want to give me any excuse to teach him manners like I did his friend.

"There," I said, moving closer to the hallway that branched off the lounge. The kid was around here somewhere. But I couldn't afford to take my eyes off these guys until backup came. "That's real nice. Now lie down on the floor with your hands on your head. Then we'll have a couple of minutes to chat before my friends show up. How does that sound?"

He slowly lowered himself to the ground.

"You're a natural at this," I said. "So tell me, what possessed you to take out your frustrations on this poor old—"

The floor creaked in the hallway behind me. There was

a smell, a man's sweat.

Another guy. Shit.

I turned. But not very far. Something hard and sharp and weighing about as much as your average rubbish truck connected with the top of my head.

It hurt like hell, I don't mind telling you that.

My legs went out from under me. The third man took pity on me and held me upright. By my neck. Thick, sweaty fingers crushed my windpipe. I tried to scream. No dice.

The man doing his best to murder me was yelling something, but I was too distracted to pay much attention. My vision cleared just enough to see the other thug rising from the carpet and coming to his friend's aid, fists raised.

There was something cold and metallic in my right hand. My gun. Somehow I'd kept hold of it. While my left hand struggled vainly at the fingers closed around my throat, I forced my right arm up. My finger found the trigger. The thug who was rushing me hesitated. I squeezed the trigger.

The force of the shot kicked the gun right out of my weakening hand. The other guy came off worse. He toppled onto the injured Mrs Dasari, trying to keep his left cheekbone from falling out of his head.

That just left me with the one thug to deal with. Trouble was, he had me in a bit of a tight spot. My legs kicked wildly, out of my control. But he had me off balance, no chance of getting a good knee into his balls or even a boot to his shins. My gun was somewhere around me, but both my hands were too busy trying to get the thug's fingers off my throat for me to spend time searching for it. I clawed at his hand, but it was hopeless. The guy must've eaten steroids with his Coco Pops every morning. My lungs burned and spasmed and screamed.

The rubbish truck hit me over the head again. My vision narrowed even further. You know that tunnel of light they always talk about? For me it was a tunnel of black. God didn't want anything to do with me, that son of a bitch. I was powerless, more powerless than I'd ever been in my life. The terror's grip was even tighter than the thug's. I silently begged to any and every deity I'd ever heard of. Just a few seconds more life. That's all I wanted.

To think I'd wasted all that time smoking a goddamn electronic cigarette like some sort of sandal-wearing yuppie who'd let his wife carry his balls in her handbag along with her Chihuahua. What a fucking chump.

More shouting. I couldn't see a damn thing. Then a thud. The fingers came free of my throat.

Air rushed into my lungs. Too fast. It was cold and sharp, like breathing ice. I doubled over and went into a coughing fit. Tears streamed down my face. I realised I wasn't being held up any longer when I collapsed to the carpet, curled up and sucking in air between coughs.

My vision came back like pinpricks in a blindfold. I flinched as a hand came to rest on my shoulder.

"Boss." Healy's voice. "Boss, are you all right?"

Did I fucking look all right? I tried to suppress the urge to cough. Where was my hat? "The hell took you so long?" I choked out. My throat burned with every word.

"We got here ASAP."

"Well it wasn't fucking fast enough, now, was it?"

Another wave of coughing wracked my body. I became aware that there were other people in the room—half a dozen guys in Security blues. One was putting cuffs on the thug I'd pistol-whipped, while another two had rolled the guy I'd shot off Mrs Dasari.

Healy turned and spoke to one of them. "How far away are the medics?"

"Thirty seconds," the Security guy said. He checked the woman. "She's alive but she's pretty beat up."

I was getting a splitting headache in addition to everything else. "Help me up," I rasped at Healy. "Where's the one with the fingers?"

I tried to get up, but Healy's big hands stayed on my shoulders, keeping me down. "How about you sit still until the medics arrive?"

"How about you work for me and I'm telling you to help me up." I knew I was being a son of a bitch, but I didn't much care. My heart wouldn't stop pounding. I rubbed my hand across my face and realised I was slick with sweat. I could still feel the fingers on my neck, clawing, choking, breaking....

Enough. My hat and my gun were lying a couple of feet away. I pocketed the gun, put my hat on, and jerked an irritated hand at Healy. Reluctantly, he took it and helped me up. I tried to pretend I didn't need his other arm around my shoulders to keep me upright. The thug with the strangling fetish was lying slumped in the hallway. I couldn't tell if he was alive or not, but I guessed he must've been since a couple of Security boys were taking care to cuff him good and tight. The thug wasn't that tall, but he was wide enough to nearly fill the hallway. Someone had tugged his balaclava off, revealing a pair of ears that stuck out so far he looked like Mickey Mouse. His fingers were still curled into claws as Security secured him.

I realised I was rubbing my neck. I forced my hands into my pockets. "Who took out Dumbo the elephant?" I asked Healy. "Was that you?"

Healy nodded and helped me around the back of the couch, towards the foyer. We met the paramedics—a skinny guy and a chubby woman—coming the other way. They hurried past us to attend to Mrs Dasari. The Indian woman was coming around, but she wasn't happy about it. With bruises like that, I wouldn't be either.

"Did you send someone to take care of Priya Dasari?" I asked.

"Of course. Luis and Chiaki will be picking her up now. They'll have her back at the office in fifteen."

"No," I said. I caught myself touching my neck again. It was going to bruise. "Radio them and tell them to keep her at the restaurant. I'll pick her up and take her myself."

Healy's hands tightened on my arm as he stopped me. "Boss, I really think you should get the paramedics to check you out before you head back out there."

"I'm fine." I doubled over in another coughing fit to prove it.

"Boss—"

"Jesus, Healy, drop it," I said when I could speak again. "Get these masked arseholes into a cell and find out who the hell they are and what they were doing here. And make sure when the old woman and the kid go the hospital they get false records. You personally. Don't tell anyone except me where they are." I stopped. "Wait, the kid. Where is he?"

"Still in the room. Security's keeping him there until we can clear out the mess." Healy pointed his chin at the dead thug bleeding his brainstem into the carpet.

I nodded. "Is he all right?"

Healy went and called down the hallway. "How's the boy?"

"Scared," came the voice of one of the Security guys. "But he didn't get hurt as far as I can tell."

Healy nodded and turned back to me. "There'll be another ambulance here in a second to take a look at him. When the bastards came in they stuck him in his room and locked him in to keep him out of the way. So the first thing he did was get on the emergency line. I don't think they even knew he had a phone in there."

"Smart kid," I said. "See what you can get out of him. And find out who the hell these guys are. If they work on the island or are related to someone who does, I want to know what company or Division they came from. And if they don't work here, I want to know how they got on the island in the first place. Volkov's going to give us hell about this."

I made for the door. Healy grabbed my arm again. "Seriously, Boss, take a second. You nearly got killed. Who knows what he did to your throat. You need to—"

"Healy, if the next words out of your mouth are: 'Get checked out by the paramedics,' you're fired. Understand?"

Healy's mouth formed a line. He glanced around

and took me out to the relative privacy of the house's entranceway.

"What were you doing in there, Boss? Why didn't you wait?"

"Why didn't you tell me there were three guys?" I countered.

His voice went quiet and his eyes went hard. "I don't agree with the way you're handling this investigation," he said. "You're treating it like a game. There's a man in there with half his head caved in."

Something inside me snapped. I tore Healy's hand from my shoulder and jabbed him in the centre of his considerable chest with my finger. "You're not paid to agree with me, you're paid to do what I fucking say. Now get back inside and help me figure out what's going on here."

Healy said nothing as I turned and walked back to the car.

8

I took a moment after I parked outside the Chinese restaurant to check my throat in the mirror. Blotchy purple bruises were already spreading across the front of my neck. Breathing hurt, and the frequent coughing was worse. The rain had washed the sweat off my face, but it couldn't stop the heavy, slithering feeling in the pit of my stomach.

Shake it off, Escobar. It's over, you're alive. Deal with it.

I scowled at the mirror, threw open the car door, and stomped through the rain to the restaurant. Luis's car was parked askew on the footpath outside. I shouldered through the restaurant doors and beheld the argument going on inside. Luis' and Chiaki's backs blocked Priya from my view, but it wasn't hard to hear her chewing them out. The restaurant had become considerably emptier of patrons since I'd left. The two waitresses were huddled together in the corner, like if they didn't move no one would notice them there.

"You can't keep me here," Priya was saying. "And I don't care what your boss said. Tell me what's going on, or get the fuck out of my way."

"Language, Miss Dasari," I said as I crossed the room.

Luis and Chiaki both turned to me, looks of relief plain on their faces. Priya took the opportunity to slip between them and head for the door.

I grabbed her arm as she tried to rush past me. "I don't think so. We need to talk."

She gave a roar of frustration. I ignored her struggling in my grip as I turned to my investigators. "Good work. Head back to the office. I want that report on the war as soon as you can get it to me. And I want you looking at Volkov's role as well. And anything you can find me on the handlers." I paused. "Well, what are you waiting for?"

"Your neck," Chiaki said. "What happened to you?"

I waved my hand. "Get to work." I turned my back on them and dragged Priya out to the car.

The handler struggled as I shoved her into the passenger seat.

"Do I have to get my cuffs out again?" I asked.

She sneered but grew still. "What right do you have to keep me—"

I slammed the door in her face and went around to the driver's side. She was still shouting as I got in and buckled my seatbelt. I turned to her and snarled.

"Sweetheart, shut the fuck up. We're taking a drive to my office. On the way, we're going to have a talk. And you're going to tell me everything you've been keeping from me."

"What are you talking about?"

I started the engine and skidded away from the curb. "You see this?" I jabbed at my neck. "Some rhino just tried to punch my ticket. All because I interrupted him and his pals beating the shit out of your mother."

She stared. "My...my mother?" Her eyes widened. A hand shot out and snatched hold of my coat. "What happened to my mother?"

I tore her fingers from my coat and threw her hand back at her. "A bunch of thugs just hit your mother's house. Now, either you're the unluckiest woman in the world, or they were trying to get to you. Why would they do that?"

Priya stared straight ahead for a moment. Then her gaze snapped back to me. "Oliver. Is my son all right?"

"They're fine. He hid and called for help. Your mother's hurt but she'll be fine." I didn't know that for sure, but I didn't want her getting distracted. "They're both at the hospital."

"I have to go to them."

"Not now. We're talking."

"I have to see my family! What if someone comes for them again?" The anger left her voice. I glanced over to see her giving me puppy-dog eyes. "Please, Mr Escobar. Let me go to them."

I shook my head and gave a mirthless smirk. "Nice try. You're good at that. 'Please, Mr Escobar.' "

"Fuck you."

I grinned, showing her my teeth. "That's more like it. Look, Security's with them. They'll be safe. You, on the other hand, are not safe. You can glare at me all you want. It's not my fault your poor mother had a goon stomping on her face. That's down to you. They wanted to get to you. If you want to protect your family, you better start talking."

"Talking about what? What do you think I know?"

"I don't know," I said. "That's why I'm asking. That's

my job."

"Well, you're doing a fantastic job so far."

Fire roared inside my head. I slammed on the brakes and brought the car to a screaming halt. I jabbed a finger at her. "I nearly got killed protecting your goddamn family. Who were the thugs attacking them?"

"I don't know."

"What did they want from you?"

"I don't know."

My grip tightened on the steering wheel. Someone behind me honked their horn. I shoved open the door and stuck my head out. "Shut the fuck up!" I yelled. I slammed the door and turned my attention back to Priya. "Are you affiliated with any anti-Volkov organisations?"

"I work here. Of course not."

"Did you kill Yllia?"

She narrowed her eyes. "No."

"I don't believe you."

"I don't care what you believe," she said.

I ran my tongue along the tips of my teeth.

"Can I go now?" she asked.

I barked a laugh. "Sweetheart, you ain't going nowhere."

I walked into the office, dragging Priya with me. And got hit by a roar of applause.

My investigators stood up from behind their desks. Several of the Security boys that had been at the Dasari house were lounging around as well, adding their own applause. I stood in stunned silence at the attention.

"There he is." Lindsey Fischer appeared from behind

me, carrying a box full of wrapped sandwiches from the bakery down the road. She dropped the box on a table and slapped me on the shoulder. "Dirty Harry himself." She spread her arms, addressing the office. "So there he was, minding his own business, when he heard the scream of a damsel in distress. He kicks in the door and goes in with all three guns loaded." She held up her fists. "Fuckin' A, Fuckin' B…" She grabbed her crotch. "…and this one right here."

The office laughed. I tried to grin along, but the churning in my stomach was starting up again. I pulled at my collar; it was too tight.

"In he goes," Lindsey continued. "Alone against three bad guys. I bet he wasn't even afraid, were you, Boss?"

I licked my lips. "I thought I told you to stay on the geeks, Fischer."

"They're under control. I left Gordon and a couple of Security guys there to cover for me for half an hour." She seemed to notice Priya for the first time. "You two sure are spending a lot of time together, huh, Boss?" She grinned.

I tugged Priya over and put her in Lindsey's hands. "Take her to an interview room. Get her a drink if she wants, but she's not to leave without my say so."

Lindsey's grin faded a little, but she nodded. "Sure. I brought sandwiches. Do you want—?"

"I'm fine," I said. I glanced at the rest of the office. "Shouldn't you all be working?"

The smiles slipped off everyone's faces and their eyes turned back to their desks.

"Are you okay, Boss?" Lindsey asked. "I didn't mean to

embarrass you."

"I'm not embarrassed." I looked around the room. "Is Healy back yet?"

"I think he's down in the tank with one of the bad guys."

"One of them?"

She nodded. "One's being taken to hospital and the other…." She slit her throat with her thumb.

I tugged on my collar again. "All right. I'll be back to talk to Miss Dasari." I headed for the doors, then turned back when I thought of something. "Did Su-jin find that reporter? What's his name? Cunningham."

"Interview Room Two," Lindsey said.

I waved my thanks and headed downstairs to the interview rooms. The door to room 2 was open. I knocked and entered.

Su-jin was a short woman, but she was no smaller than the man opposite her. William Cunningham had streaks of silver in his dark hair and a nose that looked like someone had bitten a chunk out of it. He was well-dressed in a thin tie and a shirt with the sleeves rolled up. Next to a small pile of folders, a mug of coffee and a vending machine cookie sat on the table in front of him, untouched.

I nodded to Su-jin, then put on my best face and rounded the interview table. "Bill," I said, shaking his hand. "I'm Jay Escobar, Head Investigator here on the island. Thanks for agreeing to talk to us."

The smile he gave was guarded. "I'm not sure I've agreed to anything yet. You're the man investigating Yllia's death?"

"Whose death?" I asked. "I don't know what you're talking about."

An eyebrow rose. "You may have cut communications, but people still talk, Mr Escobar."

I waved like it didn't matter. "Jay, please. I'm terribly sorry about the communications. I heard it was a solar flare. Knocked everything right out, if you can believe it." I put my hand on Su-jin's shoulder. "Thanks, Su-jin. Go upstairs and grab yourself a sandwich. I'll take a look at what you've got for me in a moment."

Su-jin didn't buy my bullshit, but she didn't argue. "Very well," she said as she stood up and excused herself. I waited until she was gone, then pushed the door shut behind her and sat down in her seat.

"I'm not at liberty to discuss any possible investigations that may be underway," I said to Cunningham. "Certainly not with such a dogged reporter as yourself." I shrugged. "Then again, maybe if you give us a hand with something, maybe I can share a few tidbits with you when we get the phones and Internet fixed."

"Such as who's been strangling you?"

I smiled a smile I didn't feel. "You know, I think you and I are on the same wavelength. You were attached to a cell of the Mayday Protection Front for a time, weren't you?"

"That's correct."

"We've got someone in custody here. I'm about to go discuss some things with him. I wonder if maybe you'd like to watch the interview and let me know what you think."

"What I think?"

I nodded. "Whether or not he could be a member of the MPF or a similar organisation. Any other insights you could offer."

"You suspect the MPF of killing Yllia? Their mission is to free Maydays, not kill them."

"Some might say death is a kind of freedom. Not me. I enjoy life too damn much."

"There are also ethical considerations," he said. "The MPF let me interview them with the understanding that I wouldn't identify them to the police."

"I'm not the police. But I understand. You have your journalistic integrity to consider. Then again, if there really was a dead Mayday on the island, I would think getting an exclusive story on it might be enough to brush aside any ethical concerns. So what do you say, Bill? Care to help us out?"

He considered the offer, but I could tell he'd already made up his mind. Cunningham and I were cut from the same cloth. He could recognise a once-in-a-lifetime opportunity as well as I could.

"It would be a pleasure," he said.

"Fantastic." I stood. "Let me introduce you to our guest."

The tanks were our holding cells in the basement of the building we shared with the Security Division. They were larger and cleaner than most police holding cells I'd seen back on the mainland, mostly because they were so rarely used. Occasionally a Christmas party would get out of hand and Security would put a drunk or two in the tanks until they sobered up. A few months ago one of the administrators' husbands got thrown in here prior to deportation. The neighbours had reported that he was fond of using his fists to convey the love he had for his family. But this was the first time we'd had an honest-to-God attempted murderer locked up.

I stared at him on the security monitor. The place was wired for sound, but the Security guys told me he hadn't said a word since they'd locked the door on him. The thug with the ears—the one who'd given me this lovely purple necklace—was in there, perched on the edge of the bunk. His hands were still cuffed behind him. My throat went dry looking at him.

"Are you all right?" Cunningham asked.

I ignored the question, steeling myself. "Do you recognise him?"

"No. But I only saw a handful of MPF members without masks in the time I was with the cell. That leaves another thousand or so more around the world."

I figured that would be the case, but it was worth a shot. Enough procrastinating. It was time for me to show this big-eared thug who was boss.

"Buzz me in," I said to the Security guys as I headed for the tank.

"Do you want anyone else in there with you?"

The thought was tempting, but I shook it away. "No. I'll be fine. Just have someone outside in case it gets ugly and we need to rearrange this guy's face for him."

The Security guy nodded and pressed a button on his

console. There was a loud buzz. I swallowed, pulled the tank door open, and stepped inside.

The thug kept his eyes firmly straight ahead. I shut the door behind me and planted myself in front of him.

"Remember me?" I asked.

The thug said nothing.

"I have to admit, you nearly had me there," I said. "But you're on my turf now. And I don't take kindly to people trying to strangle me."

The thug looked away, making a show of looking bored.

I curled my hand into a fist and gave him one across the mouth. It was like hitting a brick wall. The force of the blow sent shockwaves up my hand, all the way to my elbow. The thug dropped from the bunk and hit the ground.

"Didn't your mum ever tell you to respect authority?" I asked as I massaged my knuckles.

"Go fuck yourself."

I stomped on his face. Blood spurted from his nose. I wiped my shoe clean on his shirt.

"Here's the thing," I said as I kicked him in the gut. "I'm not a nice guy. You've got no rights here. You want to call a lawyer? You want Amnesty International to come along and stop me from hurting you? Tough. I'm a company man. You got my attention. That means you got the attention of Volkov Entertainment Incorporated. It's something you'll regret." I put my hand in my pocket and touched my e-cigarette, but I didn't draw it. "What's your name, friend?"

He groaned and spluttered at the blood streaming down his face. I bent down and grabbed his broken nose between my thumb and forefinger, wiggling it back and forth.

"Wakey wakey." I raised my voice so he'd hear me over his moaning. "Name."

"Fuck. Craig Hall."

I released his nose. "Well, Craig, I've got a few questions for you. The faster you answer them, the sooner I'll be out of here. How's that sound?"

He spat a glob of chunky blood onto the floor and glared at me.

"Great," I said. "Tell me, why were you and your buddies beating up that poor woman. Did she call you names?"

"It wasn't about her."

"I already guessed that. You were after Priya Dasari. Why?"

He scowled. "She's a slaver. What other reason do we need?"

"Nice try. I suppose it was a coincidence that you attacked her family on the day of Yllia's death?"

He shrugged, or tried as best he could while handcuffed and lying on the floor.

"Not a talkative one, are you?" I said.

I lined up my shot and booted him right in the solar plexus. He pulled himself into a fetal position, eyes bugging out. As he gasped for breath that wouldn't come, I bent back down and grabbed him by the chin. His skin was sticky with sweat and blood.

"That's what it feels like to not be able to breathe, you piece of shit. You thought you could kill me. Me?" I snarled at him. "No. You're mine now. You hear me? You're mine.

If you cooperate, maybe I'll go easy on you. Maybe we can come to an arrangement. If not, well…." I slugged him in the face again. "So are you going to tell me what I want to know?"

"All right!" he gasped. "Stop. Jesus. If I tell you, will you let me go?"

"Maybe. When this is over."

He looked unsure. But he didn't have many options. "All right," he said. "He told us Dasari was the key to freedom for the Maydays."

Now we were getting somewhere. "You're MPF?" I asked.

"Yes. Well, not anymore. Ex. There was a split."

"How sad. Now, Craig, this is very important. Who told you to go after Dasari?"

"I don't know his name. He wasn't that stupid."

"He can't have been that smart if he hired you," I said. "Why should I believe you?"

"It's the truth. And he didn't hire us. He runs our faction. But he's careful. We're kept separated."

"Sleeper cells," I said.

He nodded,. "Exactly."

I exhaled loudly. "So what can you tell me?"

He hesitated. I raised my fist again.

"Wait," he said. "I think he's on the island."

"What makes you say that?"

"Things he said. Things you couldn't know unless you were here. Staff activities, specific details about the weather, things like that."

Well, it was a start. "How does he contact you?"

"Email. The last message we got before the Internet went down was to destroy anything incriminating and find Dasari."

"And do what with her?"

"Keep her under wraps until we were contacted."

I growled. "I'll find out if you're lying, Craig."

"I'm not lying."

"What's so special about Dasari?"

"I don't know. He never said."

I watched his eyes. "There's something you're not telling me."

"I...I don't know. But I think Dasari wasn't really the important one."

"Then who was?"

"Yllia."

I sat back on my heels. Were they trying to get their hands on Priya to get Yllia out of Volkov's control? Maybe they thought if they threatened Priya's family, they could make her their own personal puppet master. But that didn't make any sense. Why wait until Yllia was dead?

Nevertheless, it made me nervous. As soon as we were done here I'd get security boosted at Psi Division and find out what other handlers had family on the island. If there were more thugs on the island, they might try the same thing again with someone else. Imagine if they managed to get their hands on Tempest's handler. It could be devastating.

I stood and stared at Hall. I could feel my collar scraping against the bruises on my neck. I wanted to keep going. I wanted to make him hurt some more for what he tried to do to me. But I had a job to do.

"Thanks, Craig," I said. "You've been a big help. Enjoy your stay."

It took all my strength to turn away. I opened the door and left him lying on the floor in a pool of his own blood.

9

Cunningham raised his eyebrow at me as I returned to the security station.

"Interesting interrogation techniques."

"I hope I can trust you to keep what you saw to yourself if you want to stay involved," I said. I brushed past him and a Security guy.

"Where are you going?" Cunningham asked.

"Go upstairs and wait in my office. Someone will tell you where it is. I'll meet you there in a few minutes."

I headed for the bathroom and locked the door behind me. My head was still swimming. I turned on the tap and splashed some water on my face. It didn't do a damn bit of good. I couldn't meet my own eyes in the mirror. Why wouldn't my heart stop pounding? There was nothing to be scared of.

I pulled my collar up so it covered the bruises as much as possible, then got some toilet paper from the cubicle and wiped the thug's blood off my shoes and the cuffs of my trousers. With a bit of luck it'd be mistaken for mud. I tossed the blood-stained paper into the toilet bowl.

A wave of nausea rolled through me. I slammed my

hand against the wall of the cubicle to steady myself. My stomach threatened to rebel. I screwed my eyes up tight. My bruised throat throbbed. Slowly, the urge to vomit subsided. I grabbed some more toilet paper and wiped the sweat off my face. *Get it together.* This was no way for the head investigator of Volkov Entertainment to act.

I took a few deep breaths. All right. It was all right. Just nerves and adrenaline. I flushed the bloody toilet paper and headed back upstairs.

Healy still hadn't returned to the office, which was fine by me. But most of the other investigators had come back for a break and to compare notes. I put my game face on and called for attention.

"All right, everyone, shut up for a minute. Time for us to regroup. Let's hear what you've got. Who wants to go first? Roberto?"

Roberto shuffled through his notes. "We're just finishing up the last of the interviews with all the Security guys and keepers that had access to Yllia's pit."

"And?"

"Nothing. No witnesses. There's only a handful of patrols for the whole Eastern island. None of them saw a thing. Security at the bridge reports no one crossed after about eight in the evening."

"Does everyone who had access to the pit have an alibi?"

He shook his head. "We're still chasing that up. But several of them live alone and claim to have been at home all night. We're not going to be able to verify everyone."

That was to be expected. "All right. Start investigating

anyone who can't alibi out. And triple check the alibis you do have."

"No problem," Roberto said.

"What about the glass shard I found at the pit? Any word back from Chemistry yet?"

Lindsey spoke up. "One of the Chemistry admins just dropped off the report to Healy." She went to his desk and searched through the papers. "Here we go. Apparently it was borosilicate glass."

"All right," I said. "And what the hell does that mean?"

She scanned through the report. "It's a type of glass that's resistant to heat and chemicals. Used in cookware, lab glassware, medicine ampoules, things like that."

"They can't narrow it down any further than that?"

"It says they'll keep trying, but that's all they've got for now."

I nodded. "Make sure Healy chases them. See if it came from somewhere on the island."

"Righto, Boss."

"How's Bio getting on?"

Lindsey shook her head. "When I left them they were still taking samples. It's a big corpse."

"I noticed."

"They'll be there a while. You ask me, they don't know what the hell they're doing. They're just poking it and hoping for the best."

Another dead end. I made a mental note to go bother Dr Russell again when I got the chance. If she needed the scare put in her to get her working, so be it. Maydays weren't subtle creatures. I doubted whatever killed Yllia was subtle either.

"Chiaki? Luis?" I said. "Tell me you two have done better than the rest of these losers."

"We've been looking through the war reports all day," Chiaki said. "And we've barely scratched the surface. Many countries and organisations had developed weapons they hoped would be able to kill a Mayday. None were successful. We have identified some teams that were still developing weapons when the war came to an end. Perhaps they continued development. But the Alliance cut off all funding to these research teams."

"Except for Volkov's team, you mean," I said.

"Correct," Chiaki said. "It is interesting, though. Before the end of the war, it seems Professor Volkov's team were considered poor prospects. They received only minimal funding from the Alliance until the LIM was developed."

I scratched my beard. "Okay. So what?"

"Three months before the end of the war, after the attack on Anchorage, Yllia crossed the Bering Strait and attacked Irkutsk, where Professor Volkov's laboratory was located. Reports state that tens of thousands of the city's civilians committed suicide while they sheltered. The public was unaware of the location of Volkov's lab, but Luis found the Alliance's reports."

Luis took over. "Yllia blew the shit out of Volkov's lab. The Alliance analysts speculated that Volkov's lab might have been the target of Yllia's attack. It made sense when Volkov unveiled the LIM. Perhaps Yllia knew what was being developed and tried to destroy it pre-emptively."

"Sounds fishy to me," I said. "What kind of defences

did Irkutsk have? If Yllia wanted to kill Volkov, I don't think he'd be sitting with his feet up in his office right now, giving himself lung cancer one cigarette at a time."

"That's the weird part," Luis said. "Irktusk was barely defended. Yllia had a history of maintaining her attack on a city for up to twelve hours. In that time she could wipe out the population of most large cities. But this time, her attack lasted two hours and eleven minutes. Then she turned around and headed north-east. The Alliance lost track of her somewhere over Siberia. She didn't appear again until she was the last Mayday still at large. She was captured with little resistance."

I leaned against a desk and folded my arms across my chest. "So your theory is that there's something linking Volkov to Yllia?"

Chiaki and Luis nodded. "There may be a reason that Yllia specifically was killed," Chiaki said.

Interesting. I'd been thinking that Yllia had been selected to be killed almost at random. Perhaps to sabotage the upcoming melee, or just because she was the most convenient Mayday to kill for some reason. But maybe I'd been thinking about it all wrong. The Maydays weren't interchangeable animals. They had personalities, like us. And when a person is murdered, it's rarely at random, rarely because they were in the wrong place at the wrong time. There's usually a reason someone killed them. Often a stupid, simple reason, one that makes sense only to the killer, but a reason nonetheless. If there was some link between Yllia and Volkov, maybe that link had something to do with her murder. I had to go have another chat with

Volkov.

"Nice job, guys," I said to Chiaki and Luis. "Gold star for both of you. As for the rest of you, I wouldn't worry about trying to beat the five o'clock rush. You'll all be working late tonight. Keep digging. I want someone figuring out who that thug downstairs is. He calls himself Craig Hall, but who knows if that's his real name. Ask Healy if he matches anyone in the problem employee file. And see what you can dig up on the other two as well. I want to know if they worked here, who their friends are, how long they've been on the island, everything. All right? Get to it."

I scanned the room and found Su-jin sitting at her desk. I crooked my finger at her as the others went back to work. She nodded and came over.

"What did you get out of the reporter?" I asked, jerking my chin towards my office, where I could see Cunningham waiting.

"He claims he is here to report on the preparations for the anniversary melee as part of his channel's retrospective on the war. He has been on the island one week, permission granted by the Media Division. It seems he has been asking to be granted an audience with the professor. So far, he has been unsuccessful. Security stopped him getting access to Yllia's pit this morning after her death. He claims willingness to cooperate with us."

"But?"

Su-jin's mouth formed a line. "I do not trust him."

"Of course not. He's a reporter. That's why we're keeping him on a leash."

"It is not that. I suspect he is a sympathiser of the MPF."

I glanced through my office door at him. Interesting. I hadn't picked up on that. But I knew better than to doubt Su-jin's intuition. "Does he have an alibi for last night?"

"He claims he was at his hotel. We will see."

I nodded. "Keep at it."

"Sir, your neck…."

"Jesus, not you too." I pulled my collar back up. "It's a bruise, nothing more."

She studied me, her face a mask. "Very well. I will keep you updated."

"You do that."

She returned to her desk. She didn't look at me again. I processed what she'd told me about Cunningham for a moment. Then I walked to my office and stepped inside.

"Sorry about that," I said to Cunningham. He'd taken a seat in the corner. I walked around my desk and looked out the window. Rivers of rain ran down the glass. I caught myself rubbing my neck, so I forced my hands into my pockets and turned to face the reporter. "What are your impressions of our friend in the tank?"

Cunningham looked thoughtful. "I'm inclined to believe him. Although it's difficult to determine whether someone is telling you the truth when you use more…extreme interrogation techniques."

I ignored the last part. "You know anything about this split in the MPF he's talking about?"

"I've heard rumours. I doubt it's a real split, more of a splinter group breaking away. There are more opinions on how to run the MPF than there are members. Factions split off every now and then, reorganise, merge together. If he's telling the truth, though, this particular group seems well-organised. Most of the splinter groups get too zealous, bomb a few places, then get caught and broken up. This one seems more sophisticated."

"Any clues who the boss man is?" I watched his face as I said it, but he betrayed nothing.

"Unfortunately, no."

"The thug says he's someone on the island."

Cunninham shrugged. "It's possible."

"They're brazen if they're targeting handlers. We're rushed off our feet here. You want to give us a hand? You know these people better than us. Why don't you go talk to him? Be the good cop to my bad."

He appeared to consider it. "Would I be authorised to use any information I get from him in any story I write?"

"I don't see why not, as long as it doesn't interfere with the investigation. Nothing published until the case is closed and I've run it past Head Office, though. You won't be allowed to write anything that seriously damages Volkov."

"I'm not your company's mouthpiece, Mr Escobar."

I showed him my smile. "Of course not." I rounded the desk and clapped him on the shoulder. "This is just professional courtesy. We can negotiate further once you've got something written. Head on down there and tell them I said it was okay. I'll have someone clear you. Sound good?" I put out my hand.

He rose and grasped my hand. "Thank you very much."

"No, thank you." I steered him out of the office towards the elevator. "Good luck."

Cunningham smiled and got into the elevator. I waited

until the door closed, then I went back in and found Su-jin.

I bent down to speak in her ear. "Head down to the tanks and keep a discreet eye on Cunningham. I've got him interviewing the MPF thug. See what you can find out."

She nodded and slipped out of the office.

One last person to see, and I wasn't looking forward to it. I passed through the hubbub of the office and went downstairs to the interview rooms. Lindsey had left Priya in Interview Room 1. I opened the door and was greeted by a look so cold it'd make Serraton himself shiver.

I countered her look with the biggest grin I could muster. "Before you start, here's the deal. It's non-optional. I take you to visit your family at the hospital. You get thirty minutes with them. After that, you come with me again. It's not safe for you to go back to Psi Division. You may be being targeted by an MPF splinter group. I don't want to let you out of my sight. So you stay with me. And you tell me everything you know about Yllia. Either that, or I take you straight to the tanks where you'll wait for as long as I damn well feel like. Do we have a deal?"

Priya stood. We stared at each other for ten long seconds.

"All right," she said. "Are we going or what?"

I grinned, opened the door for her, and bowed. "After you."

10

I got nothing but frosty silence out of Priya as I drove her to the hospital. That gave me time to sort through the investigation in my head. I had a lot of little pieces, lots of maybes and conjecture, but nothing substantial. This MPF splinter group had to be linked in somewhere, but how? Had they orchestrated Yllia's death themselves? Or were they just reacting now that she was dead? We needed to find out how long the three thugs had been here and if there were any others. I didn't know much about sleeper cells. Maybe Cunningham could put it together. Assuming he wasn't working with them. If he was, Su-jin would find out.

The question then was what interest the MPF had in Priya and Yllia. And what did Volkov know that he wasn't sharing?

I turned the problem this way and that in my head, but it didn't make any sense. I needed something real. A witness, a fingerprint, anything. Someone had to have seen something. The Mayday pits weren't well guarded, but someone must've noticed something odd. I'd have to growl at them myself to get an answer.

I pulled into a car park outside Maytown Hospital. It was a squat building, clean and white and glistening from the rain. I opened my door and started to step out.

"Don't you have an umbrella?" Priya said, the first words she'd spoken since we left the office.

"Afraid of a little rain?" I asked. I got out. After a moment, she did as well. We dodged puddles as we jogged to the hospital entrance. An unused ambulance was parked in a bay near the entrance. The hospital doors slid open for us and we went inside.

"I'm not talking to my family with you in the room," she said as I led her to the emergency department.

"Don't sweat it, sweetheart. I'll be in the waiting room. There'll be security outside the door."

I flashed my ID at the triage desk and asked for the Dasaris by the fake name Healy had set up for them. I got the directions and the boys from Security—well, one was a girl—met us at the door to their room.

I jerked my thumb at Priya. "She's with me." I turned to her and tapped my watch. "Thirty minutes, remember."

Priya nodded curtly and entered the room. I caught a glimpse of Mrs Dasari propped up in her bed, purple blotches across her face. Her eyes were glassy. The door closed in my face.

My hand moved halfway to my own bruises before I caught myself. Forget it. I had half an hour to kill. First stop, the store in the lobby. This afternoon had taught me something about the importance of living. I couldn't believe I'd ever let my ex-wife convince me to give up smoking. I tossed my e-cigarette in the rubbish on the way and bought a lighter and a pack of Winfields. The girl behind the counter gave me the eye as she handed them over. I guess buying cigarettes in a hospital wasn't very classy. But to hell with her.

I left the store and went back to the lobby. My stomach was still churning, but I decided I should take the chance to get some food in me since I hadn't finished my lunch at the Chinese restaurant. I returned to the hospital's entrance. There was a cafe, but I couldn't face the queue so I found a vending machine instead. Nothing looked particularly appetising. I finally settled on a chocolate bar and fed my coins into the machine. The spiral holding the chocolate bar in place turned and stopped, threatening to steal my money without giving me anything in return. I put my boot into it to change its mind. The chocolate bar dropped down in surrender. I grabbed it and returned to the waiting room.

I wasn't a big fan of hospitals—it was the smell, mainly. That and the ugly people. If you want to see some truly hideous specimens of humanity, head to a hospital. But I was going to be here for a while, so I decided I might as well get comfortable. I sat down in the corner, forced down a couple of squares of chocolate, and closed my eyes.

I never noticed myself slipping into sleep.

Choking. I was choking. My lungs strained, but the air wouldn't come. My arms were pinned to my sides. Colossal beasts walked the lands, footsteps pounding in my head. The pressure tightened on my throat. I struggled. My head spun. The world collapsed around me. A creature turned his massive bulk towards me. I recognised him. Tempest. His arms flexed, claws pointed towards me. His eyes burned with fire. He watched me die, impassive. His mouth hung open like a cavern of darkness.

He roared.

My eyes snapped open and I jerked awake, grasping at my throat. Air rushed into my lungs. The glow of the fluorescent light overhead burned my eyes. A figure appeared in front of me. I held up my hands to ward him off.

"Boss, easy." Healy's voice came to me through the dream fog. My vision cleared and his face resolved. "You all right?"

I looked around. The rest of the waiting room was staring at me. I must've only been out a couple of minutes. I could feel sweat trickling down the back of my neck.

"Come on," Healy said. He took me under the arm and silently urged me to stand. I followed his lead as he guided me to the bathroom.

He pushed the door closed behind me and left me by the sink while he checked the cubicles were empty. I grabbed a couple of paper towels and wiped my face.

Healy leaned against the sinks and eyed me. "What was that about?"

"Just a bad dream. My mum always told me chocolate before bed was a bad idea." I glanced at him to see if he was buying it. He wasn't. I changed the subject. "What are you doing here?"

"The thug you coldcocked came around, so I spent a few minutes leaning on him. You look like hell."

"Ah, piss off," I said. The nausea was back with a vengeance. I swallowed to keep my stomach inside me.

"Boss, tell me what's going on with you."

"Give me a break, kid. I nearly got killed today. Is a man not allowed to be affected by that?"

He shrugged.

I whirled on him. "What the fuck's that supposed to mean?"

"This is more than just nerves, Boss. You're not coping."

"Tell me how well you cope next time someone strangles you."

"I'm just having trouble understanding," he said. "You've faced death before. You were in Sydney when Grotesque hit. This was bad, but it can't have been as bad as that."

I curled my lip. "I wasn't in Sydney."

"What?"

"I was out of town on a case for a defence team." I shook my head. "That's a lie. I'd finished conducting the interviews three days before. I stayed away because I'd brought the junior assistant I was screwing with me. We turned it into a long weekend. You know, a hotel room and room service, that kind of weekend. We were heading back on the Monday when news of the attack came over the radio. We were less than an hour out. My wife—my second wife—was still in the city, right in the centre of town. She didn't drive, I had our only car." I closed my eyes. "Radio said Grotesque was tearing the place up. So I turned the car around and followed the traffic fleeing the city. I never saw Grotesque, only what they showed on TV. I looked up the aerial pictures of the city after the attack. Our apartment building was gone. Not flattened, just dust."

Healy was quiet for a moment, pursing his lips. "Did you ever hear from your wife?"

I shook my head.

The bathroom door opened and a man walked over to the urinal. I tossed the paper towels in the bin and headed for the door.

"Boss," Healy said.

"Forget it."

He followed me back into the hospital corridor. "Go home," he said. "Get some sleep. Or better yet, stay here and get your neck looked at. You need to rest."

"I don't need to rest," I said. "I need all this shit to start making sense. If we don't get some answers, Volkov's going to have our heads." I turned away and stared out the window at the rain hammering down outside. "This day. This fucking day." I sighed. "Did you get anything out of the other thug?"

"Nothing substantial. Not yet. I need more time."

I exhaled and leaned against the wall. A nurse walked past carrying a cup of coffee. I could go for one myself.

"I wonder," Healy said. "That roar before. All those Maydays, roaring at once. Do you think they mourn their dead?"

"I don't think they have any concept of death."

"Maybe. Even animals mourn sometimes."

"That's the thing, though. They're not animals. They're not like us either. Maybe they see that Yllia's dead, but I don't think they...." I trailed off. Something clicked in my head.

"Boss? What's up?"

I licked my lips. That was it. That was the answer. I grabbed Healy's sleeve. He looked taken aback. Maybe it was the wild grin I could feel creeping across my face.

"Where's Dasari? Has she come out yet? She was visiting her family." I checked my watch. Her half hour was just about up.

Healy stared at me. "Uh, I can check."

"Do that. Bring her to my car." I shook my head. "No, wait. I'll get her. You head back to the office, find the reporter, Cunningham. He'll want to see this. Get Cunningham and meet me at Tempest's pit."

"Tempest? Boss, what's going on?"

I grinned. "He's our witness. Tempest. He's our witness."

11

It was still an hour from sunset, but the rain and the heavy clouds darkened the road in front of us as I drove across the bridge towards Psi Division. Priya had one hand on the dashboard and the other on the door grip.

"Do you have to go so fast?" she asked.

"The sooner this is over, the sooner you can get the hell away from me. I thought you'd like that idea."

"What do you expect me to do?"

"I just thought you'd be able to introduce me to Tempest's handler. What was his name again?"

"Miguel Garcia," she said.

"He good?"

"He has to be to control Tempest."

I nodded, easing off the accelerator just a bit to take a wide turn. The roads were empty over this side of the bridge. "Good point. I forgot to ask, how are your family doing?"

"Terribly, thanks for asking."

I grinned. "No need to be snarky. Where's the boy's father? I take it he's not in the picture?"

"How about you focus on the road and stop asking me

about my personal life?"

"That's no fun. You know me, I'm just nosy, that's all."

She shook her head and stared out the passenger window. Well, she could suit herself. The car's headlights slashed through the rain and lit up Psi Division's compound as I parked on a set of yellow lines right outside the front doors.

I got out, hurried to the doors, and leaned on the buzzer. Priya was slower getting out of the car. That was all right. She didn't need to be excited. I had enough excitement for both of us. The nausea and clamminess had been replaced by a sense of exhilaration. This was what I needed. A break in the case.

The buzzer cut off and a voice came through the intercom. "Yes? Oh, Mr Escobar."

"Curtis, I've got another favour to ask. I need to borrow Miguel Garcia."

Crackly silence was the only response.

"This is not optional," I said. "Tell him, Priya."

She sighed and spoke into the intercom. "Just get him, Curtis. Indulge this son of a bitch."

"What do you need Miguel for?" Curtis said.

"He's going to help us with a crucial part of the investigation," I said. "Get him ready to go. Now. Does he have a car?"

"Y…yes."

"Good. I want him at Tempest's pit in fifteen minutes. If he's not, I'll be cranky."

I jerked my head at the car and we got back in. I peeled away from Psi Division, heading back to the road.

"You really expect this to work, don't you?" Priya asked.

"Why wouldn't it? Tempest's pit looks directly over Yllia's. He saw something. He must have."

"And your plan is to, what, interrogate him?"

"Precisely."

She shook her head. "You're insane."

"You yourself said you could communicate with Yllia. Well, it's time to see what Tempest knows."

We rounded a bend and Tempest appeared. The mist clung to him like a cloak. His massive bulk towered above us, so high I couldn't see his head without leaning forward to peer upwards through the windscreen. His chest puffed in and out with long breaths, each one taking more than half a minute. Steam poured from the nostrils in the centre of his flattened snout.

The ground shuddered slightly as his twelve legs moved, each one rising and falling in slow motion as he twisted round to face us. His claws flexed at the ends of his arms, rain streaming from the points. Thick grey scales, each the size of your average four-door sedan, coated his body, the layers folding at his joints. His tail swung lazily behind him. Far above us, glossy black eyes watched us approach.

"I think he knows we're coming," I said. "Don't you, big guy?"

He stared at us in silence. I grinned and kept driving.

The road turned to gravel as I pulled into the parking area outside Tempest's pit. Healy and Cunningham were waiting for us in Healy's Civic. I parked next to them and wound down the window.

"You're in for something special tonight," I said.

Cunningham frowned. "I'm not entirely sure what you're planning, Mr Escobar."

"You'll see. Care to accompany me to the watchtower?"

Healy had an umbrella ready for Cunningham as he got out of the car. Priya shot me a look. "How come he gets an umbrella?"

"Sorry, sweetheart," I said. "You're going to have to get wet again."

We got out of the car and crossed the parking lot to the pit's entrance. Tempest's smell clung to the damp air; a scent like vinegar and dirt and something else, something alien. There was a creaking, grinding noise as he shifted his weight. I smiled up at him, ignoring the rain pouring off my hat and down my coat.

Two guards were huddled under an overhang at the entrance, both wrapped up in thick coats. Healy and I showed them our ID.

"Nice night, huh?" I said. "We're meeting Tempest's handler here. Send him up when he arrives, will you?"

"Yes, sir. Can I ask what this is about?"

"You boys are in for a treat. We're about to conduct the greatest interrogation the world has ever seen."

I clapped the guards on the shoulders and walked between them. The others followed in silence as I led them through the gate and into the pit. The mud tried to suck me down as soon as I set foot in it. I could hear Tempest breathing over the sound of the rain, like huge bellows used to fuel a furnace. His nearest leg was fifty metres away, a tower against the darkness. I could feel his eyes on us.

I led our small group along the fence until we reached the nearest watchtower. I examined the electronic lock on the watchtower door. Unlike at Yllia's pit, this one was intact. I swiped my pass and was greeted with a green light and a click as the lock snapped open. I shoved open the door and led the group up the winding stairs.

I was nervous, but the feeling was mixed with excitement. I was going to make the King of the Maydays talk. And the monster's testimony would help me solve the case. He saw what happened. He must have. Tempest was no animal. You couldn't look into his eyes and tell yourself there wasn't a sly, primal intelligence behind them. He knew, and I was going to make him squeal.

We emerged onto the viewing platform. We weren't even at knee-height with Tempest. The sky was darkening rapidly, but Priya flipped a switch on the watchtower wall and floodlights lit up the pit. Tempest's scales glistened with rainwater. He grunted and huffed at the light. His wide mouth opened, scaled lips peeling back to reveal jagged, irregular teeth.

"I think he's trying to intimidate us," I said.

Priya shook her head. "He doesn't care enough about us to try to intimidate us. He finds us amusing."

"We'll see how amusing he finds us in a few minutes." I turned to Cunningham. "Got your camera? Feel free to take some photos. It's the least I can do. What did our MPF friend have to say?"

Cunningham fished a compact digital camera out of his bag and aimed it in Tempest's direction. "He's not repenting his sins yet. He seems to believe they're on the brink of revolution."

"I guess killing a Mayday is pretty revolutionary. Unless we can squelch it."

"He claims not to have been involved with Yllia's death. He seems…saddened by it."

"Well, we'll soon find out." I turned back towards the car park and spotted a pair of headlights pulling in. "This must be Garcia. It's almost show time. You excited, Healy?"

Healy licked his lips but didn't answer. His eyes were focussed on Tempest. Fine, he could be that way. He always was a sourpuss.

The headlights flicked off and I saw a figure crossing the car park. A couple of minutes later, footsteps clanged softly on the metal stairs of the watchtower. The door opened and a young man stepped into the light.

He was Hispanic and not particularly handsome, his thick hair badly maintained and his nose two sizes smaller than the rest of him. His glasses made his left eye look bigger than his right. His face was strained like he was in pain.

"Mr Garcia." I held out my hand and he took it gingerly. "I'm Jay Escobar. Thanks for coming."

His eyes shifted from me to the others to Tempest and back again. "What is this about?"

"Tempest here is a witness to Yllia's death. I want to ask him some questions. You're going to tell me what he says."

Garcia's eyes widened. "I…I'm not sure I can—"

"Sure you can. Miss Dasari here has told me all about it, haven't you?"

Priya looked the other way. Garcia gave her a look like she'd personally throttled his puppy.

I clapped my hands. "Excellent. Time's a-wastin'. Do you need to do anything to, uh, mind-meld with Ugly over here?"

"We are always connected," Garcia said. "But I can save you some time. I know his mind. He won't talk."

"Humour me. Come stand here, next to me." I addressed the others. "How about you guys give us some space?"

Healy, Cunningham, and Priya moved along the viewing platform a short way. With a little urging, Garcia joined me at the railing overlooking the pit. I put my hand firmly in the centre of his back so his only way of escaping was through me or by jumping the forty metres into the pit.

"Ready?" I asked.

His eyes shifted around uncertainly, then he nodded in defeat. "Yes."

"Great." I looked up at Tempest. His black eyes caught the floodlights, shining wetly. "I don't think he'll be able to hear me way up there. Make him kneel."

Garcia licked his lips and glanced at me. I smiled encouragingly. My heart thudded in my chest. Behind Garcia, Cunningham raised his camera and snapped a picture of me.

Garcia looked up at Tempest. His lips moved slightly, but no sound came out.

Tempest snorted like a horse, the force of the exhalation powerful enough for me to feel it all the way down here. Then he began to kneel. His bones groaned as he lowered his massive bulk. The grinding sound made the hairs on my arms stand to attention. His scaled flesh formed huge folds that could swallow a man. Gouging holes in the ground with his claws to support his weight, he lowered himself until his abdomen came in contact with the mud. The watchtower shuddered. He was still far taller than the watchtower, but he was low enough now that I didn't have to strain my neck to look up at him. The knotted muscles of his arms rippled. When he exhaled, I could taste something acidic in the back of my throat.

"That's more like it." I grinned up at the monster. This was a rush. Tempest looked down on me. I could sense the intelligence behind his eyes as he studied me. A serpentine tongue longer than a bullet train snaked across the scales of his lips and touched the points of his teeth.

I cupped my hands around my mouth. "You need to visit the dentist, big guy," I yelled. "You've got something rotten in there. Can you hear me, huh?"

I could've just talked to Garcia and let him translate my words to Tempest. But I wanted to address him directly. I wanted him to hear me. Maybe he was once the terror of Africa, but now he was nothing more than an oversized tarantula, defanged and kept on a leash. A schoolyard bully who'd finally been dragged into the principal's office.

Garcia nodded to me and spoke in my ear. "He can hear you."

"Can you tell me what he's saying?"

Garcia licked his lips. "He's…asking how many of your friends and family he killed. He's asking if you want to know how they tasted."

I showed Tempest my own teeth. "Not you, pal. You were too busy on the other side of the world. You were never a big fan of swimming, were you?"

"He says whales don't taste as good as humans," Garcia said.

I glanced over at the others. Priya had her arms crossed, her gaze directed towards the city. Healy's back was stiff, his jaw tight. And Cunningham was scribbling away in a notebook not much different from the one I used. If my case bringing down the administrator of Refugee Town 2108 had bought me some publicity in the investigative world, this right here was going to put me on TV screens across the globe. I put my hands in my pockets as I turned back to Tempest. Steam rose from his shoulders as the rain hammered him.

"I didn't come here to trade insults with you," I yelled at him. "You're done. You're ours now. Your mind belongs to us. I don't care how much contempt you hold for me. I really don't give a damn. I'm here because a friend of yours is lying dead in the mud over there." I pointed. The rise of the land hid Yllia's pit from me, but Tempest would be able to see. "Do you understand what that means? Dead?"

A puff of steam blew from Tempest's mouth, carrying with it a scent like week-old meat. I kept my eyes on him as Garcia spoke.

"Dead. I know. Like you humans. So brittle. So many ways to be killed. I enjoy it when you squirm in my mouth as I bite down. But burning is the best. Do you know what a city of burning humans smells like?"

I gave Garcia a sideways glance. "Take it easy. I don't need to get the whole running commentary of his mind." I raised my voice so Tempest could hear. "All I want is to ask you a couple of questions. Then I'll be on my way and you can go back to your eternal captivity. Really, this is good for you. I'm trying to save your life. Someone out there just killed one of you. Me, I want to keep you alive. My job depends on it. So you might as well cooperate."

I waited a moment. Tempest's tongue snaked back and forth, his eyes fixed on me. He shifted his weight, making the watchtower rattle beneath us. But Garcia said nothing. I took the silence for acceptance.

"Excellent," I yelled. "Question one: Did you see Yllia die?"

A throaty rumble emanated from Tempest's throat. "Yes," Garcia said.

Yes. This was it. My heart pounded. I could feel my cheeks stretching into an involuntary smile.

"Question two," I said. "Did you see any humans at Yllia's pit at the time of her death?"

Tempest's tongue whipped back and forth. "Yes."

My hands tightened on the railing. "Last question, winner takes home this lovely sixteen-piece glassware set kindly provided to us by Volkov Entertainment. Can you describe the human you saw there?"

Tempest remained still, his breathing quiet now. The seconds ticked past. I chewed on my lip. Why wasn't Garcia talking? I glanced at him. "What's the problem?"

"He's…he's not answering."

"Then dive in yourself and find out. You have access to his mind, don't you?"

Beads of sweat were appearing on Garcia's forehead. The skin behind his glasses was creased, his eyes strained.

"Maybe, but—"

"No buts."

"But he's resisting."

I grabbed his sleeve. "Look at me. Hey. Look at me." I took hold of his chin and forced his eyes to meet mine. "This is non-negotiable, Miguel. I want my answer. You're going to dig it out of his brain if you have to."

His eyes darted around for a second. Then he froze, like he was listening to something I couldn't hear. His gaze focussed on me and he nodded. He closed his eyes.

"Stop it," Priya said. She stormed over, her shoes clacking on the metal grating. "You don't know what you're asking him."

"If it's not going to kill him, I don't care," I said.

She grabbed my sleeve and pulled me around. "You're asking him to dive into the memories of a monster. You remember what you felt at Yllia's pit? That was a dead Mayday and a few echoes. This…" She gestured at Tempest. "…this is torture."

I brushed her off. "Then go report me. I have a job to do, sweetheart."

"You stupid—" She spun and grabbed Garcia. "Miguel, stop. Don't do this."

Oh no, she wasn't screwing me out of my answers this time. I took hold of her collar and dragged her off Garcia. I snapped my fingers at Healy. "Get her out of here."

Healy hesitated. Behind him, Cunningham was watching the drama unfold, a hungry look in his eyes. For a moment I felt a sliver of hatred for the man, for reasons I didn't even understand. I buried the emotion and gestured to Healy again. "Now, Healy."

He sighed and stepped forward. Priya tried to brush him off, but Healy's grip was strong.

"Take her to the car," I said. "We're nearly done here."

Healy nodded doubtfully and dragged the handler to the staircase.

"You bastard," she said. "You're pushing him too far!"

"Get her out of here," I told Healy. He nodded and disappeared through the doorway. I could hear her shouting as he dragged her down the staircase, but I took no notice.

I turned back to Tempest. The monster's mouth was stretched wide in what I could almost imagine was a grin.

"How are we going, Miguel?"

The muscles on the man's neck were taut. He trembled slightly. "It was…it was a woman."

Yes. Here we go. "Great. You're doing great, Miguel. What else?"

Seconds ticked past. A groan left Miguel's throat. "A woman. No. Not a woman. *The* woman." His eyes snapped open. "The handler. Priya Dasari."

I knew it. I knew she was hiding something. I had her now.

I reached for my walkie-talkie to call Healy. Damn it, I'd left it in the car. I brushed past Garcia and headed for the staircase to call down to him.

The ground shifted beneath me. My balance went and I grabbed the wall as the grating trembled beneath me. The watchtower groaned. I glanced back to see Tempest slowly rising. His legs extended and his arms came up, claws flexing.

Garcia stood slumped, his back to me. His head rolled slowly towards me. His eyes flickered in his head.

"What the hell are you doing, Miguel?" I demanded.

His mouth opened and closed like he'd forgotten how to use it. I glanced at Cunningham. He was staring at Tempest and slowly backing up. His cool exterior had fallen away.

Tempest continued to rise. The Mayday's shoulders pulled back, his massive chest expanding. He turned to his side, towards the other Mayday pits. He tilted his head back.

And he roared.

I clapped my hands over my ears, but it did nothing to block out the screeching stabbing agony that rumbled through my bones and made my heart go still. Tempest shook his head back and forth as the roar left his throat. It felt like my head was splitting in two.

And then, as quickly as it had begun, the roar ceased. My ears rang in the silence. The old familiar slippery feeling in my stomach was back. I saw Cunningham pressed against the wall. He was crouched down, hands pressed to his ears. I tried to call to him, but my lungs were empty.

Tempest turned his eyes back towards the watchtower. He seemed to be considering us. I fought the urge to cower and run and piss myself.

Garcia jerked towards me. His eyes were on me, but there was something wrong behind them.

I found my words. "What the hell is this?" I hissed at Garcia. "What's he doing?"

Garcia's lips spread in a wide, alien smile. A single

word emerged from his throat, guttural and monstrous. "Watch."

I stared at the man for a moment. I couldn't make sense of any of this. This wasn't supposed to be happening. Tempest couldn't stand on his own, couldn't roar. But he had.

Because he'd broken impulse control.

The realisation hit me as the sky went dark. I looked up to see a massive, clawed palm descending from the heavens towards the watchtower.

12

I couldn't move. I couldn't close my eyes. I saw it in slow motion. The monstrous hand raced the rain. Behind it, Tempest bared his jagged teeth. *How is this possible?*

I waited for my death. But it never came.

A single claw slammed into Cunningham's chest. It slipped through him like butter and kept going, piercing the viewing platform's floor and the watchtower wall beneath. The building shuddered and groaned. Cunningham blinked once, staring down at the claw going through him. Then his eyes glazed over. No screams. He no longer had lungs.

Garcia looked at the impaled reporter with a detached smile on his face. He turned the smile on me. But it wasn't him behind those eyes.

"Slave no longer," he slurred, the words barely discernible. "I do not kneel for you, human."

The watchtower shook as Tempest withdrew his hand. Cunningham remained impaled on the claw, limbs flopping limply. I stood, still rooted to the spot, as the reporter was lifted into the sky. Thick redness dripped from Cunningham, falling on me.

Tempest straightened and brought the claw to his mouth. With his eyes on me, he dragged the claw along his front teeth. When he delicately withdrew the claw, Cunningham was gone. Tempest ran his tongue across his scaled lips, like a starving man savouring his first meal in days. Dimly, I was aware that this action was more precise, more human, than anything I'd ever seen him do in footage from the war. His time with us had taught him cruelty. Sadism. He'd learned to make his violence personal. I couldn't break from his black gaze as he swallowed.

Tyres screeched in the car park, snapping me out of Tempest's hypnotic trance. Garcia grinned at me with his blank eyes. I shoved him out of the way, jumped over the blood-slicked hole in the grating of the floor, and darted to the other side of the watchtower overlooking the car park. Healy's Civic squealed, kicking up rainwater, as it roared away. It cut through a patch of torn-up grass and went skidding onto the road, heading away from the pit. I could just make out Priya's panicked face in the back seat, staring past me through the window.

The ground shifted again. I gripped the railing to keep my balance. The world was slipping away from me. I squeezed my eyes closed for a moment, shutting everything out. The image of Cunningham's eviscerated body was burned into my retinas. The watchtower groaned as I sensed Tempest moving. I opened my eyes.

Tempest's front legs smashed through the wall surrounding his pit as if it were made of polystyrene. I couldn't believe how fast he could move, as big as he was. As he crashed through the wall and out into the car park, the claws of his left arm swung past the watchtower. Close enough for me to make out the pattern of red staining one of the claws. Tempest cast a look at me as he passed. He snorted.

And then he smiled at me.

Not a human smile, not quite. His mouth was too wide and misshapen, his eyes too blank. But even so, it was an unmistakably human expression.

I backed away until I hit the watchtower wall again. I wanted to crawl into a ball. *It's not real. God, it's not real.* My stomach rebelled and I heaved. There was nothing left inside me but acid. The burning tears cleared from my eyes and I stared towards the west. Healy's car was a dot now, tearing down the road towards the bridge, towards the city. And behind him, Tempest's massive form skittered across the landscape, tearing a path through the trees as he gave chase.

No. No no no no no. Healy. I had to warn him. My hands went to my pockets. The walkie.

No. It was in the car. I remembered. Jesus, I had to contact him. I ran my hands through my hair. I'd lost my hat somewhere along the way. When I brought my hands down, my palms were streaked with Cunningham's blood.

The car, you piece of shit. Get to the car.

I turned towards the staircase as Garcia slammed into me. His fists wrapped around my lapels and shoved me back against the railing. I was twenty kilograms heavier than him, but he came at me with such wild ferocity that he had me dangling over the railing in an instant, the wind screaming in my ears.

"Do you know hate, human?" Garcia yelled in my face, spittle flying. "Do you think you hate me? You have no idea. Combine the hate every one of you pathetic creatures feels for me and it will not be a single drop in the flood of hate I feel for your swarming, screeching species."

I shoved my hands in Garcia's face, trying to push him away, but an insane strength held him in place. He twisted his face away and bit down on the flesh between my thumb and forefinger. Razor-sharp pain stabbed through my palm. Garcia twisted his head, tearing a chunk of bloody flesh from my left hand. I howled into the sky.

"You try to question me?" Garcia screamed. "ME?! I will show you hate. You are my chosen subject now. The human Volkov, he will die for what he did to me, to my people, how he twisted them, after I saved them. But you. You will not die. I will hurt you until you hate me as much as I hate you. Your world will fall. You are nothing. You are not animals. You are not insects. You are fungus. You are a growth. You are dust."

I kicked out and felt my shoe connect with something solid. A knee. Garcia flinched and the strength went out of his arms. I got my balance.

My lips peeled back in a snarl as I tucked my good fist into his gut. Whether or not he was possessed by a monster, his body still reacted automatically to the blow. He doubled over. I grabbed the back of his head as I brought my knee up. The crack of his shattering nose jarred my bones. Screaming, yelling, wild, I took hold of the scrawny handler and hurled him back against the watchtower wall. He slammed into it, gasping, thick pulpy blood streaming from his nostrils.

I threw myself at him. I put my shoulder down and crashed into him, the whole of my body weight crushing him against the wall. Something else cracked, a rib. Not mine.

"Why?" I yelled as I buried my fist in his stomach. "Why is this happening? What did you do?"

Garcia cackled even as he slumped against the wall. I kicked him in the teeth. One came loose, skittering across the metal grating and out the hole left by Tempest's claw. He continued to laugh. I kicked again. My heel crushed his throat. The laughs turned to short, gasping rattles.

I stumbled back, panting, and took hold of the railing to keep the world from spinning. Garcia giggled, blood staining his clothes. His glasses were skewed on his face, one lens cracked.

I gripped the sides of my head. My inner self wouldn't stop screaming. "I don't understand," I whispered to myself. "How could he have broken impulse control? I was here the whole time. How?"

Garcia continued to giggle.

"How?" I screamed at him.

But he said nothing. Something had changed in his face. The rage, the alien snarls were gone. Now there was just the laughing of the pleasantly mad. Tempest had left him, for now at least. Why? Was he too far away? Was he distracted?

Distracted....

I turned away from Garcia and stared over the island. Tempest charged through the fog and rain. His bulk formed a huge grey silhouette against the sky, like a moving mountain. He was still on the East Island, but he was closing quickly on the bridge. No sirens called out. Someone must've spotted him by now. The East Island wasn't that deserted. Why hadn't they called ahead, raised the alarm?

The phones. I'd made Volkov cut the phone lines. Did the city know? Could they see their doom striding towards them?

Tempest seemed to pause. The rise of the land hid Tempest's feet from view, but I knew he was standing over the road heading to the bridge. The one Healy had been driving down. I could swear Tempest turned his head towards me. As if he was making sure I was watching. Then he raised his hand and stabbed his claws downwards.

I never saw what he actually struck. But I didn't need to.

"Healy!" I screamed, my words drowned out by the rain.

Tempest lifted his arm a little and made a flicking motion. Something arced through the air and disappeared from my view again.

"No," I said.

Tempest tilted his head back, held his arms out as if addressing God, and roared. My stomach tightened as the screeching, grating sound echoed across the island.

I broke from the railing and sprinted for the stairs, passing the giggling Garcia without a single glance. My shoes slipped on the stairs, nearly sending me tumbling to a broken neck. But my arm shot out and grabbed the handrail, saving me from the plummet.

It would've been a mercy, I thought as I stared down the spiralling stairs. *What the hell kind of mercy do you deserve?*

I pushed the thoughts away and ran down the stairs. I nearly slipped twice more, but both times I caught myself at the last second. I burst out of the bottom of the watchtower, into the pit.

The wall was demolished. Where the gate had been was just rubble. The guards were nowhere to be seen. Probably running scared or lying crushed in Tempest's footprints, rubble piled across their broken bodies. I didn't know. I didn't care. I clambered and climbed and shoved my way through the shattered concrete. A length of rebar sliced a hole in the upper sleeve of my coat and opened a burning cut over my bicep. But the wall had only been ten feet high and although it was topped with razorwire, it wasn't particularly thick. So I managed to scramble through the rubble and the uneven ground where one of Tempest's feet had landed and soon I was in the car park. A car belonging to a guard or a keeper had been flattened, the concrete cracked and broken all around it. But by some miracle, my car was in pristine condition.

It took me three tries to get the key in the door. My hands wouldn't stop shaking. I finally got the door open and climbed inside. I used both hands to get the key in the ignition. My wounded hand throbbed and trickled blood over the steering wheel where Garcia had bitten me. I'd survive. No time to bandage it. I turned the ignition and the engine came to life. I followed Healy's off-road path out of the car park and back onto the road.

The window wipers couldn't keep up with the pounding rain. I could barely see the road ten metres in front of me, but that didn't stop me tearing through the growing dark, following the trail of destruction left by Tempest. I gritted my teeth and tightened my grip on the steering wheel. My head pounded. I knew I was breathing too fast, but I couldn't stop. I dragged my sleeve across my forehead to wipe away the sweat, tore open the button on my collar so I could breathe in the thick, humid air. No help. *How can this be happening? Jesus Christ, how?*

A fallen tree appeared on the road in front of me, its roots uptorn and the branches scattered across the concrete. My heart stopped. I slammed on the brakes. The car slowed. Not enough. The wheel felt loose in my hands. Then the car began to slide. Everything I'd ever been taught about how to deal with an aquaplaning car ran through my head. *Ease off the accelerator. Steer into the skid until traction is regained, then straighten. If brakes are required, use them gently, pumping them.*

But I was frozen. I couldn't do anything except press down harder on the brake as I slid out of control.

The road ended abruptly. The front of the car clipped the fallen tree as I went off into the ditch. The left headlight went out and the car suddenly spun. My head slammed against the side window. And that was that.

13

I always hated the rain. Ever since I was a kid. You'd be trying to sleep, and there'd be the constant patter of raindrops on the roof, the window, everywhere, all around you. They said some people found it relaxing. Well, good for them. I guess I'd hate that Chinese water torture stuff.

That was the first thing I noticed when I woke, the rain pattering on the car. Pissed me off. The second thing was the guy swinging hammers in my head. It felt like he'd landed a glancing blow on my neck while he was at it.

My eyes drifted open. Sometimes in movies when they've been knocked out they take a few minutes to work out what happened. Not for me, though, not this time. I must've only been out a few seconds. And I remembered everything. In crystal clear motherfucking high definition.

The car was tilted over to the right, on account of the ditch I'd found myself in. I'd been caught by one of the few trees Tempest hadn't knocked down on his way through here. The whole rear passenger door behind me was caved in by the tree trunk. Rain was leaking in through the shattered window. If I'd hit the tree at a slightly different angle, I'd probably have a broken neck. Wasn't I just the luckiest son of a bitch?

I peered through the spider-webbed windshield in the direction I thought was west. The left window wiper was stuck in position halfway along the windshield; the right one had snapped off. The engine ticked and groaned. Between the cracked windshield and the forest, I couldn't see shit. I couldn't hear shit either. Nothing except the fucking rain.

My head was thick and heavy, like it was filled with unset concrete. I shook my head, trying to clear my thoughts. Bad idea. The hammer guy behind my eyes started pounding even harder. My own words to Curtis at Psi Division drifted back to me.

Are you going to get her that Panadol or what? Can't you see she's suffering?

Why the hell was I thinking about that? There was a Mayday on the loose. And Healy was out here somewhere. He couldn't be far. Tempest was near here when I'd seen him pick up the car. I had to find it. And then…

…then I didn't know. Get to the port, maybe, or the airstrip, get off the island. Pray Tempest didn't follow. At least he wasn't like Serraton or Grotesque. They loved to hunt boats.

Quit wasting time. I wiped the sticky blood from my head, unbuckled my seatbelt, and leaned over to snap open the glove box. I hesitated, then took out the handgun box. I unlocked it and weighed the revolver in my hands. It almost made me laugh, the size of it. Tempest had shrugged off bunker busters, MOABs, once even a 25 megatonne H-bomb. The footage had been broadcast on the public television when I was in the refugee town. The Alliance had dropped the bomb from a high altitude stealth bomber as Tempest strode across the Algerian desert on his course for Morocco. The aerial footage showed Tempest glance up as the bomb screamed down towards him. Then it detonated. The explosion turned the whole screen white for a long time, I couldn't tell you how long exactly. We were all standing there, watching the screen, waiting. It cleared slowly. And there was Tempest, curled up in a ball. We held our breath. And then his legs began to unfold. He stood up, stared directly at the camera. And he roared.

And here I was, feeding rounds into this tiny revolver. Well, to hell with it. Tempest wasn't the only thing I might need to use it on. The port wasn't equipped for a panicked evacuation of the whole city. This gun might be the only thing guaranteeing me a ticket out of here.

There was a flash of light against the sky. A few moments later, something boomed in the distance. My mouth went dry. It had started. I swallowed and went back to rummaging through the glove box, looking for anything that might be useful. I took a tiny first aid kit, the kind that you put in your car to make yourself feel better even though you know if you get in a real crash a couple of Band Aids and an alcohol swab aren't going to help you put your brains back inside your head. I found a small torch as well. By some miracle, the batteries weren't dead. That was everything. There wasn't even a bottle of water in the car. Screw it, I could always drink the rain.

A thought hit me. *The walkie-talkie.* Where was it? I'd left it on the centre console, I knew I had. Where the hell had it gone? I reached over to the floor of the passenger seat—nothing. Under the seat, maybe. I tried under my seat, then under the passenger seat. My fingers closed on something plastic and rectangular. *Yes.* I pulled it out from under the seat and held it to my mouth. I depressed the button. Nothing, no beep. I switched the frequency knob back and forth. It wasn't doing shit. I turned it over. The casing was completely busted. Wires hung loose and a small circuit board was cracked. The crash had killed it.

I screamed at it and slammed it on the steering wheel. The casing cracked further and the whole back fell off. I slammed it down again and again until its innards hung out like a gutted pig. Piece of shit. Goddamn it.

I took a few deep breaths. My head throbbed. I had to keep moving. I put the first aid kit and the torch in my left pocket and the gun in my right, along with the rest of the ammo.

I tried to open the driver's door, but the frame was so bent out of shape it wouldn't budge. I climbed over the centre console, cursing the weight I'd put on in the last few months, and jiggled open the passenger door. As soon as I'd opened it a crack, the wind caught it and flung it wide. Rain poured in. The tilt of the car made it a bitch to climb out. I wriggled out until my shoes sank into the mud. Needles of rain stung the cut on the side of my head. I pushed the pain aside and clambered up the slippery side of the ditch, back to the road. At least the mud covered Cunningham's blood and the slivers of flesh still clinging to the fabric of my coat.

Panting, I finally made it onto the road. The wind whistled down the road, between the trees and the devastation. Another boom sounded somewhere over the city, followed by a crashing, crunching sound. Dizziness gripped me as I began to walk down the centre of the road towards the sound. *No.* No time to stop. I had to find Healy. I clung to that thought. Find Healy.

I shone the torch's beam ahead of me as I stumbled down the road. The rain caught the light like fragments of glass. I felt like I was walking through a booze dream, like I used to have in my youth before I gave up the drink. None of this seemed possible. I didn't know why I was still walking, what I hoped to find. But my feet kept going.

I didn't even notice the cracks in the road until I stepped right on one and nearly broke my ankle. I blinked and shone the light around. The road was shattered, cracks radiating out from a central point, like a meteor had hit it. One of Tempest's feet. I stepped over the cracks and kept going. Twenty metres down the road I found a car's wing mirror. I looked around. There were three huge gouge marks in the road. Claw marks. My heart rate sped up. He'd been here. This was where Tempest picked up the car. But where had he tossed it?

I went to the edge of the road and shone the torch through the trees in the direction I thought Tempest had hurled the car. The light glinted off something metallic deeper in the forest.

"Healy!" I yelled. No answer. I scrambled off the road and slid down into the ditch. "Healy, I'm here! Can you hear me?"

I fought through the thick undergrowth towards the

car. I couldn't see anything moving inside. My foot caught a root and I tumbled into the mud. I pulled myself up and crawled for the car.

Somehow the car had landed on its wheels, but it wasn't happy about it. The frame was crumpled. It looked like the suspension was completely broken. I was approaching from the passenger's side. Through the shattered side window I could see a figure slumped against the wheel. Bits of tree branches clung to the doors and the fenders. It looked like it'd come down through the forest canopy. Healy had been lucky that the car hadn't got stuck in a tree.

My light flashed across a set of shoeprints in the mud, leading away from the car. There were only a handful before they disappeared beneath the undergrowth.

I reached the car and scrambled around to the driver's side. The driver's door was lying loose in the undergrowth next to the car. There was a hole in the roof the shape of Tempest's claw. Rain poured in the hole, dribbling onto Healy's head.

"Healy." I shone my torch in his face. His normally dark skin was grey. His eyes were closed. There was a cut on his cheek and it looked like his nose was broken. The car was filled with the iron smell of blood. "I got you, pal."

I glanced in the back. The passenger door was lying open. Priya was nowhere to be seen. Those must've been her footprints. No matter. The important thing now was to get Healy out of here.

His eyes remained closed. I reached in, tapped his cheek. His skin was cold and damp with rainwater. "Come on, we have to go. Wake up."

His eyelids drifted slowly open. I breathed a sigh of relief.

"Thank Christ you're alive," I said. "I thought...never mind. Are you hurt?"

His gaze tracked towards me. His lips moved slightly, but no words came out. One arm was tangled in the steering wheel, the other hung limply in his lap.

"Healy?"

His eyelids slipped closed again. Jesus, he wasn't doing good. He must've hit his head worse than I thought. We had to get to—where? A hospital? There were still crashes and booms coming from the city.

No. I had to take him to Psi Division. They had basic medical facilities, and they were closer. It wasn't ideal, but it'd have to do.

I reached in to unbuckle his seatbelt. That's when I realised his leg was missing.

No, not missing. It was there, severed at the hip, dangling by a few strands of muscle and tendon. Blood pooled around the pedals.

I staggered back and emptied my stomach onto the ground, clutching a tree for dear life. The heaving forced my eyes closed, and when I closed them I saw Healy's leg, which made me heave all over again.

Get it together. I exhaled, forcing my stomach back down where it belonged. I spat out the acid taste, wiped my mouth with the back of my sleeve, and turned back to the car. Healy's eyes were open again. He looked up at me, through me.

"It's okay," I rasped, more for myself than him. "We're

going to get you out of here."

I kept my gaze on Healy's face as I reached in again and unbuckled the seatbelt. Healy didn't react as I lifted his arm to get him free of the belt.

"All right, this might hurt a bit," I said. I leaned in, tucked my arms under his shoulders, and tugged him out. Christ, he was heavy. The severed leg came with him, dangling. I tried not to look at it. Panting, I pulled him out and laid him down as gently as I could on the forest floor.

Bleeding. Have to stop the bleeding. I pulled out the pathetic first aid kit, stared at it for a moment, and shoved it back in my pocket. I looked around, found a piece of twisted metal on the ground. I used it to extend the cut in the shoulder of my coat sleeve, then ripped the sleeve the rest of the way off.

Kneeling, I tore the sleeve into strips and wrapped it around the stump of Healy's leg. There was barely anything left, barely anything for the makeshift tourniquet to grip. I pulled it up as high as I could and tied it tight. It was still bleeding, but maybe it was less, I couldn't tell. Maybe he'd already lost most of his blood. I didn't know.

How far away was Psi Division? A couple of miles? I couldn't carry Healy all that way on my back. I looked around. My eyes fell on the car door that'd broken off. It wouldn't be comfortable, but it would have to do.

I dragged the door alongside Healy. Tying a few of the strips of my coat sleeve around the snapped hinges, I fashioned a simple sled out of it.

"All right, here we go," I said to Healy. I grabbed him again and dragged him onto the door. I studied his severed leg and chewed my lip. We couldn't afford the weight. Besides, it wasn't like we were going to be able to reattach it. Swallowing my nausea, I bent down and used the piece of twisted metal to cut through the remaining flesh connecting his hip to the leg.

I could feel myself sweating, but the rain washed it away as fast as it came. After a few seconds, the leg came free. I dropped the metal and quickly wiped my hands on my coat.

"You're going to have to hold on, Healy." I took his hands and closed them around the edges of the door. "Just like that. Okay, here we go."

I took the strips in either hand and pulled. My muscles ached at the strain. But after a moment the sled started to slide.

"Easy," I said. "Hold on tight." I pulled him behind me, dragging him back towards the road.

It was hard going. The forest was thick, the ground uneven and slick with mud. I kept slipping and catching the sled on roots and undergrowth. I was panting by the time we emerged from the forest, back to the ditch on the side of the road. I went along the ditch a few metres until I found the place where the slope was shallowest, then dragged him up onto the road. I felt him start to slip, so I turned and grabbed him by the collar with one hand as I pulled the sled with the other.

Finally, I managed to drag him up onto the road. I sat there breathing heavily for a moment. I'd kill for a smoke. But there wasn't time to stop. I stood, took hold of the sled, and kept dragging.

The scraping of the door on the road was loud in the early evening. Almost loud enough to shut out the distant sounds of destruction and roaring.

"Hey," I said over my shoulder. "You want to know something stupid? About a year ago, a few months before Volkov came knocking, I was thinking of giving up the detective business. It was something I'd been mulling over for a couple of years, but I was getting ready to just shut up shop and quit completely. It was the people, I think. You know what it's like. When you're a private detective you deal with a lot of arseholes. Cheaters. Worse, their jealous spouses. Criminals. I did a bit of work for defence teams. These guys—and girls—most of them were guilty as all hell. Rapists, robbers, sons of bitches who'd gotten into an argument over nothing and ended up caving their best friend's head in with a ball-peen hammer. Real salt of the earth types."

An explosion sounded somewhere in the distance. A moment later, Tempest's victorious roar echoed over the hills. The clouds were turning orange. Fire in the city. I closed my eyes and kept dragging the sled.

"I had this fantasy—you'll laugh when you hear this—I had this fantasy of becoming a truck driver after I quit. No shit. I mean, what the hell do I know about driving trucks?" I shook my head. "But I could never get it out of my head. It seemed like a good job. Honest. I don't know what I'd do with an honest job, but there you go. But that's not the whole fantasy. There's this little town I know of, the sort of place you drive through, not to. You never would've heard of it. Anyway, there's this cafe in the town—it's pretty much the only thing there—and they make the best goddamn custard tart in the world. The other thing they have is this shelf of paperbacks—novels, you know—for customers to borrow and read. Now, I've read about two books my whole life since I left high school. But that's beside the point. So here's the fantasy. I'd be driving my truck on those long, lonely trips, and every time I went through that town I'd stop and go to that cafe. I'd get a coffee and a custard tart and I'd pick a book off the shelf. I'd sit there, eat my tart, drink my coffee, and—here's what makes the fantasy—I'd read one chapter of the book. Just one chapter, no more. Then I'd put the book back on the shelf and be on my way. Next time I was driving through the town, I'd get a tart and a coffee and pick up that book and read the next chapter. And so on and so on."

A gust of wind blew down the road, lashing my face with rain. I paused, shielding my face with my remaining coat sleeve, until the wind died down again. I wiped my face dry and kept walking.

"It's a stupid fantasy, I know. But it made me happy when I thought about it, even though I knew I'd never do it. I just figured it'd be a comfort to know that no matter where on the road I was, there'd always be something permanent in the world. That book, that next chapter, in that cafe." I laughed and shook my head. "How about that? Corny, right? I bet you've lost all respect for me now, huh, Healy. What do you say?"

But of course, Healy didn't say anything. Because Healy was dead. He'd been dead since I'd pulled him out of the car.

I dragged Healy and the sled to the side of the road. I wasn't going to leave him in the middle of the road for some panicking staff member in a car to run over. But I couldn't drag him anymore. I wasn't helping anyone.

Maybe I cried, I don't know. If I did, the rain washed the tears away quickly. I rested his arms on his chest, closed his eyes. It was the best I could do. Then I reached into his coat pockets to see what he had on him.

His wallet. I returned it to his pocket. I found something plastic in his outer pocket. I pulled it out into the light. His walkie-talkie. I switched it on. Static came through. It was working.

I slipped the walkie into my pocket and stood over Healy's body. I didn't know what to say, so I said nothing. What could I say that would make it better? What could I say that would strip away the guilt churning in my chest? Nothing. So I left him there and continued on down the road.

Fifteen minutes later the forest began to clear and the road began to rise. I followed it up. I could smell the salt of the sea now, and something thicker overlying it. Smoke, dust, fire, death. The rain lashed at me. I thrust my hands into my pockets, put my head down, and walked into the wind.

The rise topped out and the last of the trees gave way to grassland and rocky shores. I stopped, fished through my pockets, found the pack of Winfields I'd picked up at the hospital. I tore off the plastic, put a smoke between my lips, and cupped my hands around the lighter as I sparked the flame. I drew in a deep breath, thick with the smoke.

It wasn't as good as I remembered. But then, nothing ever was.

As I drew another lungful of smoke, I looked out over the scene of destruction laid before me. Tempest had crossed the water just down there, avoiding the bridge, taking a more direct route. I could follow where he made landfall again by the gouges carved in the quiet inlet beach favoured by sunbathers in nicer weather. The roads were cracked and broken where he'd headed inland. He hadn't stopped to flatten the surrounding suburbs and apartment buildings, only those that had been in his way. No, he'd made his way straight for the centre of the city.

Tempest was lit now by the flames of the city. He stood tall, proud, towering over the smaller buildings. Where earlier he'd attacked with precision, first killing Cunningham and then Healy, now he was a force of nature, a hurricane, a typhoon. With a kind of noble assurance, he charged the Media Division building. From here it looked like he was moving in slow motion, but I knew that was only the sense of scale screwing with my head. Over there, underneath him, he'd be moving faster than anyone would think possible. I knew. I'd seen it.

His bulk collided with the Media Division building full on. The first thing to go was the glass. A thousand windows shattered at once, tiny specks of glass glittering as they fell around him. For a moment it looked like the building would hold. It was strong, solid, built to survive earthquakes, tsunamis, anything nature could throw at it. But this wasn't natural.

The building seemed to bend at the centre, just a little.

Then it cracked. The sound was delayed in reaching me, but I shuddered at the tortured groan of the dying tower. The cracks ran diagonally down, away from Tempest. It had only been a few seconds since Tempest had slammed into it, and he was still moving. He shoved, putting his shoulder into it, and the building finally gave.

The top went first, the upper fifteen or twenty floors. They began to topple, and as they collapsed onto the lower floors those gave way as well. Thick clouds of dust billowed out of the tower as it collapsed. It only took another few seconds. And then the entire Media Division building was rubble.

Tempest tilted back his head and roared. The screeching, echoing sound sent goosebumps running down my arms. My hands shook as I took another drag of the cigarette.

As Tempest's roar died away, he lowered his head, looking around, as if for challengers. I could swear he could see me as his gaze slid across me. But that was just the fear talking.

An orange glow built in Tempest's mouth, casting each of his jagged teeth into silhouette. He snarled, stood up straight, flicked his tail back and forth. Then he pointed himself at the ruined Media Division building and opened his mouth so wide it looked like his jaw must've snapped off.

A jet of thick fire poured from his mouth like water. The fire collided with the ruined building and exploded out in every direction, flowing down streets and billowing back into the air. The flames rained on the nearby city buildings, those that hadn't already been destroyed. There were few left. Volkov's tower was one of the last remaining buildings in the central city, with its swooping "V" atop its roof. Tempest closed his mouth, let the fire fade, before turning to Volkov Tower.

He's saving it until last, I realised. *He wants Volkov to see. Just like he wants me to see.*

I finished my cigarette, stubbed it out on the ground. So that's how it was going to be. Fine. I pulled Healy's walkie-talkie out of my pocket and adjusted the dial to broadcast across all frequencies.

I depressed the button. "This is Escobar. Can anyone hear me?"

Silence, except for the crackle of static. I pressed the button again. "Repeat, this is Jay Escobar. Is anyone alive out there? Someone answer."

Quiet. Then a voice. I could barely make it against the crackling. "Boss, Jesus. It's Lindsey. You're alive? I thought he must've got you at the pit. I tried to reach you, but I couldn't get a response."

"It's good to hear your voice," I said. "My walkie was out. I'm looking at the city now. Our building...."

"Gone. He tore straight through it. What the fuck happened, Boss? Why is he free?" Her voice was strained.

I didn't have an answer for her. Was it me? Did I push Garcia too far? That shouldn't have been enough to break impulse control. But then, what the hell did I know?

"Is Healy with you?" she asked.

I closed my eyes, opened them again. "No. No, he's not."

She understood. "Shit."

"Who made it out of the building?"

"I was already out, heading back to Bio. I found Su-jin and Chiaki. Chiaki's pretty badly burnt. I don't know if she'll make it."

I tried not to picture Chiaki's soft skin bubbled and blistered. "All right. Who else?"

A pause. "No one else, Boss. I mean, maybe some of them made it out, but I don't think…." She sighed. "Maybe there's some more in the rubble. But I don't think anyone else survived."

I nodded, but I wasn't sure who I was nodding to. I watched Tempest across the city that separated us. That's who I was nodding to. Tempest.

Okay. Okay. I get it now. You want me to hate you? Okay.

"Where are you, Boss? A security detail went to try to get Volkov out, but I haven't been able to get in contact with them. I'm going to take the others to the port, get out of here. Can you make it to us?"

"You're not going anywhere, Fischer."

Tempest circled Volkov Tower, his tail flicking behind him. He casually sideswiped an adjacent office building and sent it tumbling to the ground.

"Boss?" Lindsey said. "What are you talking about?"

"We're not done yet," I said. "We have a job to do, Fischer."

"Boss, we've got to get out of here. I have to get to my girlfriend. I don't even know if she's still alive. We have to get off the island. Can't you see this? If he hits the ports we'll be trapped here with him."

"We're already trapped," I said. "We're trapped until we finish our job. The best thing you can do to help your girlfriend is to do your goddamn job. We're detectives, aren't we? Aren't we?" Silence on the other end. I smiled at the monster across the bay from me. "Someone killed Yllia. Killed her stone dead. We still have a job. Find her killer, find out how they killed her."

"Jesus fucking Christ," Lindsey said. "What the hell does that matter anymore?"

"It matters," I said, "because we're going to use that information. Stay alive, solve the case. Because we're going to kill him for this. For what he did to Healy, to Chiaki, to everyone. Tempest wants us to hate him. So we will. We'll hate him. We're going to find out his weakness. And we're going to kill him."

14

It had taken Volkov and his investors three years to get this city up and running. Tempest destroyed it in under an hour.

I watched him trudge through the centre of the city as I made my way across the bridge. He was proud of himself; I could tell by the way he thrust his chest out, challenging anyone to come take his kills away from him. The bridge trembled beneath me with every step Tempest took, even as far away as he was. He still circled Volkov building. Every now and then I'd see him thrust his claws down, probably crushing anyone trying to flee the building. He was big, but he was quick, and it seemed his eyesight was keen.

A little red light flashed in the sky, just above Volkov building. A helicopter's running light. As Tempest turned his back on his circuit around the building, the chopper began to rise.

Tempest's head snapped around and his massive arm shot out. The chopper swerved, evasive manoeuvers, but Tempest's claws closed on it, catching it like Mr Miyagi catches flies. Tempest roared, then brought the chopper up to his face, examining it.

He's looking for Volkov, I realised. Tempest turned the helicopter back and forth in his claws. Then, growing suddenly uninterested, he tossed it casually into the city ruins. The chopper spun end over end and disappeared out of my sight behind a half-demolished apartment building.

My head was finally clearing. I'd used the supplies in my meagre first aid kit to bandage my bitten hand. Now I was halfway across the bridge, staying in the shadow of the pylons. With every step, Tempest appeared to grow bigger, and the destruction ahead of me seemed worse. I could hear the crackle of the fires spreading through the ruins of the city, out to the suburbs that hadn't been as badly damaged.

I brought the walkie up. "You still there, Lindsey?"

"Yeah. But I'm starting to wonder why. We've taken shelter in Jiger Street Station. Chiaki's passed out. We got her patched up a bit, but she's not looking great."

"I know this is hard," I said. "It's not exactly a bag of laughs over here either. But I need you on your game. Sujin, too."

Lindsey was silent for a minute. When she came back through the static, I thought I heard a faint sobbing somewhere in the background. "What do you need?"

"Before Tempest broke impulse control, a witness placed Priya Dasari at the scene the night Yllia died."

"You think Yllia's own handler killed her?"

"Maybe."

"Where is she now?" Lindsey said.

"That's the thing. She was with Healy when Tempest

broke free. When I found him, she was gone. I saw foot-steps leading away. So my guess is she's alive. And you're going to find her."

"Great. Searching an entire destroyed city for one little Indian girl. What was that you were saying about a bucket of laughs?"

I approached a company sedan sitting abandoned on the bridge, its driver's door wide open. I peeked inside. Keys in the ignition. I got in and closed the door.

"There's a chance she went back to Psi Division," I said. "But I doubt it. She knows she can't hide there. She must know I'm after her. And if we don't find her, Tempest will come and take out Psi Division sooner or later. I think she's going to try to make a run for it. You hear if the airstrip's still running?"

"Word is Tempest flattened it on his way to the city."

That was about what I'd figured. "Then my guess is Dasari will head to the port. We'll have to stop her before she gets on a boat."

"I don't know about that, Boss."

"What's the problem?" I turned the key and brought the car to life. It was risky, taking a car into the city, and I'd probably have to abandon it when the roads became impassable. But we were operating on borrowed time.

"Maybe she's scared," Lindsey said. "Maybe she's plan-ning to run. But I don't think she'll go alone."

Of course. I should've thought of that. "You're right. Her family. Is the hospital still intact?" The hospital was outside the central city. There was a chance Tempest hadn't crushed it yet.

"Last I heard. We could also do with getting Chiaki some treatment."

"All right," I said as I put the car in drive and started driving towards the city. Tempest loomed large ahead of me. "You take Chiaki to the hospital. I'll meet you there. Put Su-jin on for a minute."

"Sure." The static returned for a moment, then Su-jin's voice came on.

"Mr Escobar," Su-jin said.

"How are you holding up?"

"We are not in a safe place. I don't think the station will remain intact if Tempest comes back this way."

I approached the end of the bridge and pulled off onto a side road, trying to keep as many buildings between myself and Tempest as possible. I drove carefully, slowly, so I didn't attract his attention.

"You won't be there long," I said. "I take it you didn't stop to let our favourite thug out of the tank before you evacuated?"

"Should I have?"

"To hell with him," I said. "I thought I'd let you know Cunningham's dead."

"That's...unfortunate."

"How do you figure?"

"I think the prisoner recognised him."

I scratched my beard. "Could be he'd been around when Cunningham was doing his story on the MPF."

"It's possible," Su-jin said. "But I believe there was something else. I got the impression that Cunningham was deliberately conducting the interrogation in a way that would not produce any useful information. If Cunningham was still alive, perhaps we could find out why. And what he knew."

"Shit," I said. "Well, that's a dead end now. Did you find out anything else from him or the thug before Tempest attacked?"

"The man was not talkative, even without Cunningham's influence. I don't believe he knew much more. But he let one thing slip. He and the one you shot, they worked on the loading docks. That was their cover. But the third man worked in Psi Division, one of the support teams. I was pulling the records when we had to evacuate."

"You're thinking the third man might know a little bit more about what they were doing."

"Yes. He was still unconscious in the hospital when Tempest attacked."

"Well, maybe we'll have to go wake him up."

"Do you want me to interrogate him?" she asked.

"No. Lindsey and I are on our way to the hospital anyway. I need you on something else. Head to Bio, or what's left of it. Find out who's alive and what they know. Gordon was supposed to be watching them, but who knows if he's still alive. We need to find out what killed Yllia and if we can do the same thing to Tempest." A thought occurred to me. "And if Dr Russell's alive, I'm going to want to talk to her. She worked with Volkov during the war. Maybe she can shed some light on this fiasco."

"I think we need to talk to Volkov himself."

I glanced out the window. As I drove, Tempest's massive form came into view in the gaps between apartment blocks. He bared his teeth at Volkov Tower, steam rising off his scaled body.

"You're welcome to try," I said. "Maybe the Alliance will send in a force in a day or so. If we're still alive by then, maybe Tempest will be distracted long enough for us to get into the building and ask Volkov some hard questions."

Su-jin was quiet for so long I thought something must be interfering with the transmission.

"Su-jin?" I asked.

"There may be another way we can distract him," she said carefully. "We would have to be careful. It may risk more civilian casualties."

"Come on, spill it."

"Is Psi Division still intact?"

"As far as I…." Something clicked in my head. I slammed on the brakes. I knew what she was getting at. She was right. It was stupid, dangerous. If it went wrong, it would go very wrong very fast. But it could be the key. It could end up saving what was left of the city, and it might distract Tempest long enough for me to get some alone time with Volkov. I pulled to the side of the road and brought the car around in a squealing U-turn. I didn't care how much attention I drew now.

"Tell Lindsey she'll have to go to the hospital without me. Keep me informed. And find Dr Russell."

I tossed the walkie onto the passenger seat and put my foot down, heading back towards the bridge. Tempest had stomped through the city completely unopposed. He'd killed my colleagues, he'd burned and crushed and eaten his way across the island and we couldn't do a damn thing to stop him.

Well, maybe it was time he fought someone his own size.

15

Psi Division was dark when I arrived—the power must've gone out. But the building had escaped Tempest's rampage intact. I banged on the glass door with my fist.

"Someone open this door or I shoot it open," I yelled. The lobby was dark, empty. Nothing moved.

All right, then. I took a step back, covered my eyes, and put two rounds through the glass. My ears rang at the gunshots. Spiderweb cracks appeared in the door. I slammed the butt of my gun into the broken glass. It shattered, raining glass into the entranceway and opening up a hole large enough for me to climb through. I pulled my coat over my head to protect myself from falling fragments as I stepped through, my shoes crunching on the glass.

I held the gun at my side as I made my way through the darkened corridors. "This is Jay Escobar," I called. "I know you're here! Your cars are all outside." Only my own echo answered me.

I scowled and tried to retrace the steps I'd taken through the building this morning. I found the quiet rooms and went one by one, throwing open the doors. Nothing.

"You little shits," I said. "Where are you hiding?"

I scratched my beard. *Calm down. Think like them.* Tempest's going crazy. When Yllia died, Curtis said several of the handlers felt echoes of the backlash. Maybe it was the same thing here. Or maybe they figured it wouldn't be long before Tempest paid them a visit. There was nowhere for them to run from here—the only port on the East Island was designed to bring food and supplies for the Maydays themselves, and those ships only came twice a week. If they wanted to escape the island, they'd have to cross the bridge and head for the Western Port like everyone else. So they had to be here. They must have a panic room. The basement?

I wandered the corridors until I found an elevator and a set of stairs. The elevator was down, so I hit the stairs. They went down about three times further than I expected. At the bottom, I was greeted with another corridor lit with red emergency lighting and a steel door like something you'd find on a Cold War fallout shelter.

I found the intercom beside the door. If the emergency lighting was on down here, I figured I could assume the intercom was powered as well. I thumbed the button.

"How's it going, everyone? Enjoying yourselves in there? It's Jay Escobar. I'm sure you know who I am by now. Seems we've got a bit of a situation above ground. Maybe you'd be so kind as to let me in so we can discuss it."

The reply was instantaneous. "Fuck you, Escobar."

I grinned. "Curtis. I don't know if you've lost your manners or found your balls. I'll give you a pass this time and put it down to fear. You should be scared, you know. You think this little cardboard box fort of yours is going to protect you when Tempest comes knocking? If you believe that, I guess you haven't seen what's become of the city. Let's just say the skyline's a lot clearer now."

"What do you want?"

"I want your people. I guess they're listening in on us, so I'll address them, if you don't mind. Tempest's tearing the city apart out there. Maybe the Alliance will come, but you know as well as I do they won't be able to do a damn thing to hurt him. I'm working on a plan that may take Tempest out of action. But until then, we need him distracted. And you guys in there are the only people in the world that possess any power that can stop him. I want you to stop hiding in this hole Curtis has stuck you in and help me. Get your Maydays and give Tempest a real fight. Let's go punch that big son of a bitch right in the face. Any volunteers?"

No reply for a few seconds. I thought I could hear angry whispering coming through the intercom. I stood back and checked my watch. The face was broken and the hands weren't moving. Goddamn it. An old girlfriend had given me this. Not the brightest girl, but tits like you wouldn't believe.

Something clunked. The shelter door swung open. A young, chubby Caucasian man and a muscular black woman stood in front of me. Behind them, another couple of dozen people huddled, sitting on the utilitarian bunk beds and standing in small groups. I saw Curtis, but he wouldn't meet my eyes.

"So," I said to the two in front of me. "You're it, huh?"

The woman nodded. "Seems that way."

"I'm Jay," I said. "I don't care what your names are. I want to know what you can give me."

The white kid pointed a thumb at himself. "How about the biggest, baddest motherfucker ever to stomp through the Americas. I control Nasir."

"Nasir, huh?" I turned to the woman. "And you?"

"Grotesque," she said.

I grinned. "Nasir and Grotesque versus Tempest. Wasn't that the title melee for last year's anniversary?"

"We won, as well," the kid said.

"Haven't you heard? That stuff's rigged. But let's go ask him if he wants a rematch."

It was beautiful, really. Magnificent. People use those sort of words to describe a sunset to the girl they're trying to screw. I should know, I'd done it myself a few times. But this, this was the real deal. Like if God Himself said "To hell with this," and came down to Earth to kick some arse.

Nasir stepped out of the inlet, his massive foot sinking into the soft earth. The seawater poured off him as he rose, mingling with the rain as it peppered the roof of my stolen car. His long arms swung in huge arcs as he took another step that carried him past the first block of water-side apartments. The road cracked and sunk as his foot came down. I raced along the bridge, trying to keep up with him. In the distance, Tempest's fire-lit silhouette stopped its endless circling and turned to face the approaching challenger. His claws flexed at his side.

"What do you think about that, huh?" I said through the windshield as the window wipers swung furiously back and forth.

Nasir's hands curled into fists as he strode towards the central city. Nasir's body was approximately humanoid, the only Mayday to resemble us in any way. If he was human-sized, he'd resemble a dwarf out of a fantasy movie: squat, heavy, muscular. Thighs like tree trunks and shoulders half again as wide as any man. But Nasir wasn't human-sized. Not even close. He was the tallest and heaviest of the Maydays, even taller than Tempest. What he lacked in speed and cunning, he made up for in pure momentum. His body was covered by brown skin the texture of rock. Angry red slashes striped his flank and his arms. His bullet-shaped head connected to his shoulders with no visible neck. Just more muscle. His eyes were narrow and slanted, but they had the same black sheen as Tempest's.

I pushed my foot to the floor and tore off the bridge and down the main street towards the city centre. Ahead of me, a black Range Rover roared along the road, matching pace with Nasir. Nasir's handler had convinced his driver to join him. In a normal melee, they'd be cutting through the ruins of one of the old cities together, the kid directing the fight while the driver kept them close enough to see but far enough away to stay alive. I guess this wasn't much different. Except there were people in this city.

The Range Rover took a sharp right, closing on Nasir. I kept on straight, letting the giant "V" atop Volkov Tower guide my way. The road was getting rougher. I slowed to ease around the rubble from a crumbling block of shops.

Nasir's strides lengthened. He was picking up speed. Something that big couldn't run, not really. But he didn't need to. His footsteps rumbled like thunder. The feeling vibrated through my chest like a heavy bass beat.

Tempest snorted and crouched, lowering himself into a fighting position. His mouth fell open and a warning roar screeched from his throat. Nasir kept on, silent. That had always been the most terrifying thing about him, or so said the survivors' reports. The silence. The other Maydays loved to roar, but not Nasir.

I dug my walkie out of my pocket. "Fischer, the cavalry's coming."

"I can see. Christ, the size of him. I never saw him during the war. This is all going to go downhill fast if they fight in the middle of the city."

"Don't worry, we just need to get his attention. You out of the central city yet?"

"Just arriving at the hospital with Chiaki," she said. "It's pretty crazy down here."

"Are they evacuating?"

"I guess you could call it that. You could also call it pants-shitting panic. I don't know how I'm going to find anyone in all this chaos."

"You'll figure it out." I leaned down to peer upwards through the windshield at the two monsters as Nasir closed on Tempest. "I bet Media Division's kicking themselves they're missing this."

"I think they're all dead, Boss."

"Yeah, well. Here we go. Stay safe."

"You too."

Tempest was still too close to Volkov Tower. I hoped Nasir's handler knew what he was doing. Tempest spread both his arms, bracing himself for the impact. Nasir twisted, swinging his fist, and charged.

The two giants slammed into each other. The steering wheel shuddered in my hands. I felt the impact rumble all the way from my feet to my skull. My ears rang like a bomb had gone off next to me.

Nasir swung, his fist colliding with Tempest's head. Tempest's flesh rippled beneath his scales. But he rolled with it. I didn't even see what he'd done until he'd done it. Tempest tucked his claws around Nasir's huge waist and swung, taking Nasir's momentum and flinging it past him. Tempest's legs flattened then jerked straight. In one smooth movement, Tempest hurled Nasir away to the north.

Nasir hit the ground like an earthquake. His arms flew out to the sides, but that didn't stop him rolling. There was just too much momentum in the throw. He tumbled, a wall of dust and rubble thrown up into the air. I saw him crash through a mall and two nearby apartment blocks before the cloud of dust and a wall of ruined buildings hid him from view.

I hope that was part of the plan. I didn't have a way to contact Nasir's handler, and it was probably better I didn't distract him anyway.

I was getting as close as I dared to Volkov Tower now. Tempest had taken a few steps away from it, his eyes fixed on the cloud hiding Nasir, but he was still between me and the entrance. I pulled over into an alley and got out. The stink of smoke and death was thick, choking. I held my handkerchief across my mouth and made my way down the abandoned street, using the shops and buildings to shield me from Tempest's eyes.

The opposite side of the street was almost completely rubble, but this side was more or less intact, apart from a few fallen signs and a car that'd been kicked through the window of a Thai restaurant. A scrabble of footsteps on stone came from behind me. I turned and spotted two bloodied and dirt-streaked women duck out of the shelter of a narrow apartment building and sprint down the road, away from the fighting. Hell if I know what took them so long to make a break for it. The rest of the city was dead or deserted.

A tense silence had fallen across the city. I passed a station wagon crushed in the centre of the road. Blood had leaked out through the crumpled doors and dried in pools on the road surface. If I squinted, I could just make out the twisted child-sized shapes in the back seat. The image of Healy's severed leg flashed in front of me.

So much death. Jesus, how had this happened? I tightened my hands into fists. The monsters were supposed to be under control. It was supposed to be over!

I shook my head, forced the panic and the rage and the nausea back down, locking them all deep inside myself. I glanced once more at the crushed car. Then I turned my eyes away and moved on.

I stopped at the end of the block and peered around the corner. Nasir was still hidden by the dust. Tempest was ahead of me, facing towards the north. He was close enough now that I had to crane my neck to look at him as he disappeared up into the sky. A sense of vertigo trembled at the edge of my mind as I stared up at him. The monster edged slowly back and forth, his head sweeping from side to side. He held his claws poised in front of him. But there was no sign of Nasir, not even the booming of his footsteps. He couldn't be down already. Maydays were made of tougher stuff than that.

Could I make it to Volkov Tower? I tried to gauge my chances. I was only a couple of blocks from the tower's entrance. But Tempest had turned those entire blocks to rubble. Broken water pipes sprayed water from what used to be restaurant kitchens, right next to fires slowly spreading through what remained of the buildings' wooden interiors. A few doorways and corners of buildings remained standing, the only cover between here and Volkov Tower's car park. I couldn't even make out the roads. Any cars that'd been parked around here were now buried. It'd be a hard two blocks to navigate. Climbing, clambering, and all the while completely exposed if Tempest glanced down and spotted me crawling like an insect through the rubble.

Tempest roared a challenge into the cloud of dust. I jammed my hands over my ears, trying to block out the screeching. Goddamn it, what was taking these handlers so long? We didn't need something flashy. We just needed Tempest away from Volkov Tower for a few minutes.

A footstep rumbled through my bones. Nasir must've gotten up. The ground rattled around me with another footfall. The vibration was too diffuse; I couldn't tell exactly where it was coming from. I peered around the corner of the building, staring into the clearing dust. Tempest screeched again and braced himself.

Dust swirled around Nasir as he stepped into view. Tempest flexed his claws in an obvious challenge. The ground shook again as Nasir stepped carefully forward. His hands were clenched into fists. The two monsters stared at each other across the ruined city blocks that separated them.

Tempest darted forward, skittering on his spider-like legs. Still too close for me to make a run for it. *Come on.*

Nasir raised his fists. Tempest darted forward, claws out.

And then Nasir opened his fists and threw two giant handfuls of dust and debris in Tempest's eyes.

It was a dirty trick. A human trick. I liked it. Clouds of dust puffed around Tempest and he reeled back, trying to get a view of Nasir again. And that was when Grotesque struck.

I'd heard Grotesque described as a gigantic crocodile before. I'd never really seen it—his snout was too flat, his tail too long and snake-like, arms and legs more like a tiger's than a reptile's. But seeing him come sprinting across the rubble on all fours, tail flicking back and forth as he moved, the comparison suddenly fit. His jaws sprung open, revealing layer after layer of piercing yellow teeth, made not to cut but to grab and hold on. His leathery skin was a pale greenish-yellow, the colour of sickness. On either side of the jagged spines on his back, large yellow pustules throbbed against his skin.

He darted out from between a pair of crumbling buildings, not twenty metres from me. I stumbled back as he stormed past, closing on Tempest's back. The rush of air following him carried his stink, the smell of rot. My guts clenched and I clapped my handkerchief back over my mouth. My eyes watered.

Tempest must've heard the charge. He started to turn, raising his claws in a defensive posture. But he was too slow. Grotesque leaped through the cloud of dust and spun. His tail snaked out, wrapped around three of Tempest's legs, and pulled tight. Tempest roared as he lost his balance. He swiped at Grotesque, but the slippery Mayday darted to the side, dragging Tempest with him.

Now. Go! As Nasir stomped back into the fray, I broke from my cover and rushed for Volkov Tower. The blood pounded in my ears as I scrambled through what used to be an electronics store's exterior wall, into an employee bathroom and out into the remains of the store floor. There was a crater where the store's entrance had been. I edged along the side of it, praying that the crumbling wall beside me didn't choose this moment to collapse on top of me.

Tempest roared in frustration. I glanced up to see Nasir slamming a heavy fist into Tempest's head as Grotesque continued to drag him away from the tower. For a moment, the blow seemed to daze Tempest. Then Tempest twisted, planting one set of claws in the ground.

Grotesque's muscles bulged, tail straining on Tempest's legs, but neither monster moved. Tempest got his remaining feet on the ground and swiped with his other set of claws. The claws sliced across Grotesque's tail, sending him hissing as his tail loosened. Tempest scrambled free and brought his other claws out of the ground, stabbing at

Nasir's shins as he backed away.

I clambered across a pile of broken bricks. Every move the monsters made caused the loose bricks to rattle and resettle. The Maydays were shifting their fight as Tempest moved back towards the tower. They were close enough now that I could throw a brick and hit Grotesque as he slithered up onto his back legs, tail flicking. One false move by the handlers and any of the Maydays could crush me, and they'd never even know. I used that encouraging thought to propel me on. Jesus Christ, what the hell did I think I was doing?

I slid down a short slope of rubble and planted my feet back on solid concrete. Only the car park separated me from Volkov Tower now. Tempest's bulk had turned most of the concrete to fractured slabs pointing up at angles, the cars parked there either crushed or thrown onto their sides. I took a breath, trying to keep my lungs from spasming at the thick taint of smoke and dust in the air. *Run for it.* Now!

I took a step forward. But at that second something squealed. I glanced to the side. Just in time to see Grotesque tumble through the air towards me.

I threw myself to the ground as Grotesque slammed into the concrete. The ground wave sent me flying into the air. For a moment I was suspended in space, my stomach doing flip-flops. Then I slammed into the bonnet of a crushed car. The air rushed out of my lungs and I lay there, gasping but unable to inhale. Grotesque squirmed himself back upright. Now he was close enough for me to poke with a long stick. I lay doubled over on the car's bonnet, watching through watering eyes as Grotesque's massive form rose above me.

Tempest was closing fast. His legs skittered across the car park, crushing all in his path. *Get up, you son of a bitch, get up.* I forced my arms away from my bruised gut and stumbled off the car. I could feel the wind from Grotesque's tail as it whipped above my head.

Tempest slowed his advance and snorted. I looked up at him from beside Grotesque's leg. His black eyes were fixed on me. His lips peeled back in that terrible smile.

Grotesque leaped forward, jaws snapping. Now was my chance. With the ground still shaking from the force of Grotesque's leap, I staggered forward. Tempest batted away Grotesque and jabbed his claws towards me. But at the same time, two massive hands appeared around Tempest's neck. The Mayday roared as Nasir tightened his fists and dragged him backwards. Tempest's legs scrambled wildly, flinging debris and bits of cars towards me. The front end of a minivan bounced off Grotesque's knee and crashed past me. There was nothing else for it. I put my head down and ran.

Tempest twisted free of Nasir's grip and reached for me again. But Grotesque leaped forward, spinning, wrapping his tail around Tempest's waist and clamping jaws down on his shoulder. Tempest threw his head back and forth as he growled. The orange glow of fire grew bright in his open mouth. He was going to fry me alive.

Nasir brought both fists slamming down on Tempest's head. The fire in his mouth died. I sprinted across the car park, jumping from plate to plate of fragmented concrete.

I could make out figures in Security uniforms behind the glass doors at the entrance to Volkov Tower. I waved my arms at them.

"Open the fucking doors!" I hollered.

I don't think they could hear me over the cacophony of roars and thunderclap punches, but they understood what I was saying. And they weren't in any hurry to obey.

One of the Maydays slammed to the ground somewhere to my right. The resulting quake jerked my feet from under me. I landed on my hands and knees, pain burning up my arms, then I was up and running again. The Security guys shared a glance and engaged in a discussion.

I gave my input by pointing both my identification and my gun in their direction. Volkov Tower's entrance might've been bulletproof—I wouldn't put it past the paranoid old man—but I don't think the Security guys stopped to consider that. Their eyes widened and one of them fumbled a key into the lock at the base of the glass doors.

The doors opened for me and I flew inside, feeling every cigarette I'd ever smoked. The two Security guys slammed the doors closed behind me as Nasir crashed to the ground outside, Tempest atop him. All three of us backed away from the door as the giants struggled in the car park.

I put my hands on my knees and doubled over, gasping for breath. When my lungs stopped burning, I said, "Nice of you to let me in."

"Mr Escobar," one of them said. "I didn't see it was you at first."

"Sure you didn't. It's Jackson, right?"

"Yes, sir."

I stood and put my hands on my flanks, stretching. I could feel every scrape and bruise on me, from the fingermarks on my throat to the torn skin on my knees. I was too out of shape for this bullshit.

"Volkov," I said. "Where's Volkov?"

"Still in his office. He wouldn't leave. We've got most of the staff gathered—"

"I don't give a shit," I said. "I guess the elevators are down?"

"Yes, sir."

"Then point me to the stairs."

16

I walked past the empty reception desk and shoved open the doors to Volkov's office. Volkov had his back to me, a thick cloud of cigarette smoke around his head. The filing cabinets along one side of the room were all flung open, their contents spread across the desk. Volkov rubbed his bald head as he shoved papers aside. He snatched a folder from under a stack, flicked it open, and started scribbling something on it. On the desk, atop an open book of his own writing, lay a heavy pistol.

"Planning on going down with the ship, Professor?" I said as I strode into the room.

Volkov jerked around, his hand going for the gun. He stopped when he saw me, then turned his back and continued to pore over his notes.

"I thought you would be on a ship by now," Volkov said. He stubbed out a cigarette on the edge of his desk and drew another one from his pocket. "I'm rather busy, Mr Escobar."

Out the wall-spanning window behind him, a blur of bodies and claws went hurtling past. Grotesque slammed into the ground outside and the whole tower shook. Dust puffed down from the ceiling tiles and a stack of Volkov's papers slipped off the edge of his desk, scattering across the floor.

"I won't take up much of your time. But we need to talk." I sat down on one of the couches and grabbed the half-empty pitcher of water off the coffee table. I didn't bother with a glass, just gulped it down straight from the pitcher. My throat had been killing me. I put the pitcher down and wiped my mouth with my hands. I could taste the blood on them. "I guess everything's gone tits up. Care to explain how this is possible?"

"I'm trying to fix it. You're not helping."

"I disagree," I said. "I think I'm the only person on this damn island who's got a chance of stopping all this."

"And how do you propose to do that, Mr Escobar?"

"Easy. Kill Tempest. The same way someone killed Yllia."

Volkov froze. His head twitched towards me. He glanced at his pistol resting on the desk.

I reached into my pocket and drew my revolver, letting it rest in my lap. Letting him see it. Just so he didn't do anything stupid. Sure, I was mad at Volkov. His tech was supposed to be foolproof. It was supposed to keep us safe from the Maydays. The Alliance had bet on it, I'd bet on it. And now here we were, with Tempest stampeding through the city. My people dead. Healy dead. But that didn't mean I was going to shoot Volkov.

Probably. I was still thinking about it.

Volkov turned slowly. He didn't look at the gun again. Probably for the best. "Tempest is Volkov company property."

I laughed a bitter laugh. "Ah, go fuck yourself. Soon Tempest will be the only bit of Volkov property left. Have you looked out the window? He wants you, you know. He's waiting for you to go outside."

Volkov sniffed, cast a glance out the window. Outside, Tempest delivered a spinning blow to Grotesque, sending the reptilian Mayday crashing to the ground. He moved in for another attack, but just then one of the pustules on Grotesque's flank bulged and burst. Thick yellow liquid splashed out with the force of a fire hose. Tempest roared and backed away from the toxic liquid.

I got up and went to stand beside Volkov. "I'm here to ask you a few questions. Then I'll be on my way."

"You work for me."

"That's right. And you hired me to do a job. I'd like to see it through. So I'd appreciate it if you answered my questions. If not, well, I figure I'll shoot you in the head right now and toss your body out the window for Tempest to enjoy. You can consider that my resignation."

Volkov turned on me. "You threaten me?"

I put the barrel of my revolver between his eyes, right on that thick monobrow. "Yeah. I threaten you."

He glared at me. He didn't seem particularly scared.

"Very well," he said around his cigarette. "Ask your questions."

I lowered the gun. "Thanks, Boss. Appreciate it. First, you want to tell me why they targeted Yllia? Assuming they had the ability to kill any Mayday, why go after her?"

"How would I know?"

"Speculate. Could it have anything to do with Irkutsk?"

His cheek twitched. It wasn't much, but it was enough. "What do you know of Irkutsk?"

"I know your lab was there when Yllia attacked. I know she came directly for you. I know you're still alive, which is an impressive feat when you're in the middle of a Mayday attack. And I know you finished developing the LIM prototype soon after. What I'm a little fuzzy on is how that all fits together."

Volkov chewed it over a few seconds. I gestured impatiently.

"We're on the clock, Professor."

"You still work for this company. You are bound by your non-disclosure agreement to keep anything I say now between us." I smirked and opened my mouth, but he cut me off. "Yes, even during extreme circumstances such as these. Do you agree, Mr Escobar?"

I threw up my hands. "Sure, why not."

"Prior to Yllia's attack on Irkutsk, our research was going nowhere. We were investigating potential bioweapons for use against the Maydays. Parasites, mostly."

"What about the LIM?" I said.

"There was no LIM. Not yet. The Alliance was considering pulling our funding. Then Yllia attacked." He closed his eyes. "We lost most of our people that day. Many before we even knew what was happening. Scientists, lab assistants, they just started killing themselves, all at once. Throwing themselves off catwalks, slitting their own throats with broken glassware. It was unbelievable. We had no defence against a Mayday, no bunker. We were a small group, operating out of an underground lab. When she came down and used her plasma to blow a hole in our ceiling, I was sure we would all die that day."

"And yet here you are."

"Yes," he said. "Here I am. We did what we could to hold Yllia off. More of us died. But during the attack, something happened. I will not bore you with the science. You would not understand it. But the key point is this. When Yllia left, we had the building blocks of a rudimentary LIM system."

I scratched my beard with the barrel of my revolver. "Spell it out nice and slow for me."

"Yllia has powerful psychic abilities, yes? The ability to manipulate us."

It dawned on me. "And you took that somehow? You, what, reverse-engineered her powers? Is that what you're telling me?"

"Yes, Mr Escobar. My impulse control technology is based on Yllia's abilities. We had the prototype functional in a month. Soon after, we captured Serraton in Laos. And then Grotesque, and Nasir, and so on, until we had them all under control."

"Fascinating." I watched through the window for a few seconds as Nasir shoved Tempest back, before Tempest ducked under his arms and sunk his claws deep into Nasir's side. "Doesn't tell me why Yllia was targeted, though. I assume this won't stop you making the LIM."

"No. But…." He frowned and sucked on his cigarette.

My gaze slid back to the window. "Tempest breaking impulse control. It's connected."

"I didn't think this would happen. I still do not understand why Yllia's death has caused the LIM's impulse control to weaken. But, yes, it appears so. I suspect Yllia's presence on the island generated a level of latent psychic activity that boosted the strength of the LIMs. I must find a way to replicate that activity so I may recapture Tempest. A task which you seem intent on interrupting."

"You really think you can pull that off before Tempest gets impatient and knocks this building to the ground? Stay here, run away, shuffle papers, I don't care. As long as you answer my questions first. And I've got a pressing one. If Tempest's broken impulse control, does that mean the others will go as well?"

"It is possible."

I turned away, running a hand through my hair. "Jesus. We're not just going to have Tempest stomping around. We're going to lose control of all of them."

"I will find a way to improve the LIMs," Volkov said. "I can maintain order."

I laughed. "Sure you can. Sure. The Alliance is going to have your head. But I guess that's not my problem. Here's what I know. Yllia's handler was seen at Yllia's pit around the time she died. Could she have any legitimate reason for being there?"

"During the night? Not to my knowledge. This is Miss Dasari, correct? Who saw her there?"

I waved my hand. "Not important. I've got my people picking her up as soon as they find her. We know some MPF splinter group was interested in her. For what, it's not clear. But a handful of them have infiltrated the island. It's not really a reach to think that maybe they killed Yllia so the Maydays would be free of impulse control."

"That is not possible," Volkov said. "Not even I knew the effect Yllia's death would have on the LIM systems. And very few know how the LIM was developed."

"How few?"

"Myself. And Catherine."

"Catherine? Dr Russell?"

"Yes. But I cannot believe that she would be involved—"

I held up my hand. "Leave the disbelief to me, Professor." I dug the walkie-talkie out of my pocket and turned my back to Volkov. "Su-jin. Come in, you there?"

It was a few seconds before the reply came. "I am still alive, but if these Maydays continue fighting I may not remain that way."

"Have you found Dr Russell?"

"The Biology building's upper floors are demolished. I'm trying to gain access to the basement laboratories. If she is alive, I believe this is where I will find her. She has no family on the island. Nowhere else to go."

"Great," I said. "If and when you find her, take her into custody and put the screws on her." I relayed the information I'd gathered from Volkov. "If she's got ties to this MPF group, I want to know."

Su-jin acknowledged the order and I turned back to Volkov.

"You're making a mistake," he said. "If I am unable to improve the LIM, Catherine may be our only hope."

"I'll take the risk."

Volkov moved to the window and stared out. I stayed

where I was, thinking. I needed that murder weapon. If Dr Russell knew what killed Yllia, maybe I could use it against Tempest. But if the secret was buried here among Volkov's papers, I couldn't see it.

My walkie crackled again. "Boss."

"Lindsey." My heart pounded. "Have you got Dasari?"

"I saw her. It's madness here. She slipped through the crowd and made for the wards."

"Fantastic. Great job. Keep an eye on her and don't let her leave. Break her legs if you have to. I'll be there as soon as I can."

"Roger, Boss."

"How's Chiaki?"

"It's...not looking good."

I closed my eyes, my fist tightening around the walkie. "All right. Keep Dasari in sight."

I tucked my walkie into my pocket and returned to the coffee table to finish off the water pitcher. This was it. That bitch had screwed me around long enough. She was going to tell me how she killed Yllia. And then this miserable goddamn day could be over.

I smiled to myself and glanced at Volkov. He was staring out the window. The Maydays had moved out of sight, but I could still hear them fighting. Grotesque was making a horrible squealing hissing sound that was accompanied by repeated thuds that shook the foundations of the building. I'd almost feel sorry for Grotesque if he wasn't a mass murdering monster.

"Well, if I don't see you again, it's been a pleasure, Professor," I said.

He turned back to me. The lines on his face were deeper than I remembered. "This company will endure. This, all this destruction, it is tragic. But it will not be our demise. Finish your job, Mr Escobar. Find out what happened, and your place here will be assured. I am putting a great deal of faith in you and your team. But if you attempt to destroy any of the company's...*assets*...I will not be so grateful."

"Me and my team?" I said. "Do you even hear yourself? My team? My team is dead. Your asset killed them." I jabbed my finger towards the window. "It's not a fucking photocopier. It's a monster. And if I can put it down, I—"

A black eye appeared in the window behind Volkov. A reptilian eyelid blinked closed and open again, focussing on me. The words caught in my throat.

Volkov stared at me for a moment, puzzled. He turned towards the window. Grotesque's gaze moved to Volkov. The monster let out a delighted hiss.

Fuck. Grotesque was free.

Volkov took a step back. That was as far as he got. Grotesque's paw smashed through the window, firing shards of glass through the room. I grunted and toppled backwards, shielding my eyes as a flurry of tiny pains prickled my bare skin.

When I opened my eyes, Volkov was gone. I thought he'd been eaten. Then I saw Grotesque slithering away, a tiny figure clutched in his paw.

My head pounded. *Not again. Jesus.* I pushed myself to my feet and stumbled across Volkov's office on rubber legs. The rain was coming straight in, hammering my face, stinging the new cuts that had appeared. Half the office floor was gone; the desk now teetered on the edge of a drop down to the next level. I shivered in the sudden wind.

Nasir lay on the rubble of the city as Tempest rained blows down on him. Grotesque approached the fighting Maydays, and Tempest's attack ceased. Grotesque raised Volkov. An offering. I guess Tempest had finally lost patience.

Tempest puffed out his chest. I swear he was grinning at me. He tilted his head back and let loose a victorious, screeching roar. I stood in numb horror, watching. I knew I should move, should get the hell out of here, but my legs were frozen.

With the same surprising dexterity he'd displayed when catching the helicopter, Tempest reached out and pinched Volkov between his claws. I couldn't even see Volkov now, he was so far away, but I thought I could feel an echo of his terror.

Grotesque bounded on Nasir while Tempest went to work on Volkov. The smoke and distance made it unclear exactly what Tempest was doing with his claws. I was glad. I could see the glee on Tempest's alien face. An expression for me and those of us remaining. I got the feeling that Volkov's torment was as much for my benefit as for Tempest's. A message.

You're next.

17

I took the stairs down from Volkov's office, trying to hold my lunch in. The Security guys unlocked the front door for me. They asked me what'd happened; they'd heard something smashing and were worried the building was going to come down. I snarled something incomprehensible at them and ran for it.

Thick smoke enveloped me as soon as I was outside. The ground beneath my feet was even more broken and unstable now. At least Tempest had lost interest in the building now that he had his hands on Volkov.

It cost me fifteen minutes and a couple of new scrapes on my forearms to get through the rubble and back to the car. Thick soot coated the windows now. I started it up and turned towards the hospital, running the window wipers as fast as I could to keep off the twin problems of soot and rain. A flash of lightning lit the clouds, followed a few seconds later by the hammering of thunder. Just what I needed.

My walkie crackled. "Boss, where the hell are you?" Lindsey said. "We've got fires spreading this way. Everyone's abandoning ship. Dasari's got the mother walking. I think she's getting ready to run for it."

"Stop her," I barked into the walkie. "I'm three minutes away. Stop her now."

"What about the family? The mother and child?"

"Get them out of the way. Lock them in a cupboard. I don't care."

"Boss, did you not hear me say that there's fire heading this way? I'm not locking some woman and her grandson up to let them burn to death."

"Get Dasari!" I yelled. "I don't care what else you do, but get Dasari."

I jammed the walkie back into my pocket and put my foot down. The orange glow of fire was off to my right, spreading through rubble and the remains of the tightly packed suburban homes. The rain was no longer enough to slow the fire's creeping advance.

I checked the rearview mirror. Three giant figures stood against the broken skyline. The fighting had stopped. All three monsters were free of impulse control now. I wondered if the two handlers were still alive. I doubted it. As I watched, Nasir cocked back his massive fist and threw a punch at Volkov Tower. Dust puffed up from the building. Nasir wound up and delivered another blow.

The building trembled. Then it began to collapse, the huge "V" toppling to the earth. Grotesque scratched at the air and hissed with delight. My grip tightened on the wheel. Panic crept through my muscles, my veins. My skin seemed to tingle. *There's no stopping them.*

Movement in front of me drew my attention back to the road. I jammed on the brakes as a scattered crowd of bloody and dirty people appeared in my headlights. No one even seemed to notice me as I brought the car screeching to a halt. A few of them carried bundles or bags, but most just clutched family members as they ran as fast as the crowd allowed. I spotted one young man in the crowd, spinning around, panicked eyes searching for a lost loved one. He cupped his hands around his mouth and yelled something, but no one took any notice.

I edged forward in the car for thirty seconds, leaning on the horn. It was hopeless. I got out and shoved my way through the crowd. I contemplated firing a couple of shots into the air to clear the way, but decided against it. These people were wild, panicked. I didn't know whether the Maydays' attack had left them so shellshocked that the gunshots would mean nothing, or whether it'd start a stampede. I relied on my bulk to push my way through.

The crowd cleared enough for me to get a good view of the hospital. Dim lights came from the windows; emergency power, I guessed. Three ambulances were parked haphazardly in the emergency bay, nurses and paramedics loading people on gurneys into them. I didn't know what they hoped to achieve. The hospital wasn't big, but surely they had more bedbound patients than they could possibly hope to evacuate. And even if they did get them away, where would they go? They'd have to skirt the edges of the city to get to the ports. It'd be a buffet line for the Maydays.

Not my problem. I shoved my way through the car park, making for the main entrance. There were as many people trying to get in, carrying wounded family members, as there were trying to evacuate. The hospital staff were struggling valiantly to maintain order, but you don't reason with desperate people.

The begging and sobs of the crowd were so loud it took me several seconds to realise my pocket was yelling at me. I pressed my hand over one ear and pulled out my walkie.

"Boss! Boss!" Lindsey said.

"What is it?"

"We've got a problem. Dasari must've seen me. She made a run for it. I couldn't get through the crowd. I'm going to lose her."

"Goddamn it! What direction was she heading?"

"North side. Emergency exit."

I broke into a run. "I'm going to head her off. Get your arse moving and make sure she doesn't double back."

I jammed the walkie back in my pocket without waiting for a response and elbowed a balding man out of my way.

I sprinted around the side of the hospital's northern wing, dodging several parked cars. The crowd thinned to nothing. I scanned the side of the building. There was the emergency exit, or one of them, at least. Hell if I knew how many there were. I made for it.

The door swung open. Priya Dasari appeared in the entrance, dragging the boy by his hand. Her mother was a step behind. I slipped my hand into my pocket, touched my gun.

Priya's head swivelled, scanning the car park. Her clothing was ripped and she bore a few new scrapes across one side of her face. She didn't see me at first, coming at her from beside a long line of staff cars. Then her gaze snapped back to me and I saw the whites of her eyes grow.

I slowed from a run to a walk. I held my left hand out, palm toward her. "Don't even think about it."

Her gaze darted around. A trapped rat, that was what she reminded me of. She pulled the boy behind her and put out her arm as if to protect her mother. The older woman's face was near black from her bruises. Her gait was unsteady and she looked dazed, like she'd just come off a three-day bender.

Priya backed away. "I just want to get my family to safety."

"Admirable," I said. "Stay where you are. Stop, I said." I pulled the gun from my pocket and held it by my side.

Her eyes went to it. She stopped.

"I don't know what you think I did, but my family—"

"I don't have a problem with your family. They're free to go. You, you're coming with me."

Priya shook her head and started backing away again. I advanced to match pace. The boy was staring at me, eyes wide. Dried tears made rivers on his cheeks. He looked blank, far away. The thousand-yard stare.

"My mother is hurt, drugged," Priya said. "They need me to look after them. Let me get them to the boat."

"No time, sweetheart. They'll be looked after if you come with me now. If you run, I'll shoot. I'll be aiming for you, not them. But I'm not a great shot."

I saw movement behind Priya and her family. Lindsey emerged from an exit further down the side of the building. She saw me, met my gaze, and nodded. She crept towards Priya.

"Let them go back inside," I said. "The hospital staff will take care of them."

Priya's face fell. She knew I had her. She had more to lose than me. Her eyes went to the city behind me, where the thump of giant footsteps punctuated the crackle of approaching fire. She closed her eyes, opened them again. She knelt down and zipped up the last couple of inches of her boy's jacket as she spoke to him. He didn't look like he was taking in what she was saying. She pushed his hand into the older woman's, then stood and said something in Hindi to her. Priya's mother nodded blankly. With a small push, Priya directed them back into the hospital. They disappeared through the emergency exit.

Priya stared at me, naked hate on her face. Then she turned to run.

Her first step carried her right into Lindsey. She stumbled, trying to sidestep, but Lindsey was ready for her. Lindsey put out her arms and wrapped the smaller woman in a bear hug, pinning her arms to the side. Priya struggled and swore, but it did her no good.

"Fuck you!" Priya shouted. She kicked at Lindsey, to no avail. "If they die, I'll kill you."

I slipped my gun back into my pocket and walked over to them. Lindsey kicked Priya's legs out from under her and forced her to her knees, still holding her arms in place.

"She's a fighter, huh?" I said as I stood over Priya.

Lindsey looked at me as she held the struggling handler. "You know the hospital's not going to be able to evacuate those two. Neither of them looked like they knew what was going on."

I shrugged. Priya glared at me and I met her sneer with one of my own. "Don't give me that look. You were at Yllia's pit when she died. You killed her. You weakened the LIMs so Tempest could break free. Do you know how many of my people are dead now? Do you?" I grabbed her by the chin. "Look at me. If your family die, it's because of you."

She spat, the saliva landing on the lapel of my coat. "Me? I don't remember that night, okay? But you. I told you not to push Miguel."

"Jesus, not this bullshit again."

Lindsey frowned. "What's she talking about?"

"He caused this," Priya said. She must've seen the disbelieving smirk on my face. "Yes, you piece of shit. Maybe Yllia's death weakened the LIMs. But it was still enough. There was time, time to bolster the impulse control. Until you came along. You made Miguel push Tempest too far. You pushed inside his head. You made him kneel!"

I shook my head. "Shut her up," I said to Lindsey.

"Big man," Priya said. "Don't you want her to hear the truth? Did it make you feel good, pushing Tempest around like that? What did you think would happen? You see this, this fire, this destruction? You did this. You. All these people dead. All because you wanted to be the big man. My family might die. And it's your fault."

I licked my lips. Lindsey was staring at me. I shook my head again. "She's screwing with us. Come on, let's her back to the car."

But Lindsey didn't move. "You had Tempest's handler interrogate him?"

"Tempest was our best witness," I said. I glanced back

at the city. The monster's silhouette stomped across the island, heading towards the bridge. *He's going to break Serraton's impulse control. Then they'll all be free.*

"Help me," Priya said to Lindsey. "Get my mother and son to a boat. Please. They won't survive."

"Stay where you are, Fischer," I said. I wasn't liking the look in Lindsey's eyes. She didn't believe this bullshit, did she?

Did I?

I replayed the interrogation of Tempest in my mind. I'd been so excited, so thrilled. And that thrill had drowned out the tightness around my neck and the squirming anxiety in my stomach. But that wasn't why I did it. I had to get that information somehow. He was our best chance of a break in the case.

But what if Priya was right? What if Yllia's death had set the trap, and I'd been the one to spring it? If I'd taken my time, played it safe, could I have prevented this from happening? Would Tempest still be in his pit, still under control?

"Boss?" Lindsey said.

I pulled myself out of my swirling thoughts to find her looking at me.

"Is it true?" she said.

I glanced back at the city. "I...I don't know."

Lindsey's face darkened. I could see the exact moment when she turned against me.

"Lindsey," I said holding out my hands. "Wait."

But she didn't. She released Priya and turned her back, heading into the hospital after the older woman and the boy.

I darted forward and grabbed Priya before the handler could make a run for it. "Fischer! Get back here. We're not done yet. Fischer! What about the job? What about Chiaki?"

"Chiaki's dead," she said over her shoulder. Then she was through the doorway and gone.

My collar was tightening around my throat. I could feel fingers there, pressing. *No.* It was all in my head. I hauled Priya to her feet.

"It wasn't my fault," I said.

"Are you sure about that?"

I bared my teeth and dragged her into the hospital. "Fuck this. It's time you finally talk."

18

I slammed Priya up against the wall, my fists gripping her shirt. "Answers," I said. "No more evading. What were you doing at Yllia's pit on the night she died?"

"I don't know."

"Bullshit."

She wriggled, trying to push me away, but I wasn't going anywhere. "I didn't know I'd been there. But I knew I'd been somewhere."

"What the hell are you talking about?"

"I blacked out. Last thing I remember I was getting ready to go to bed. When I came to, I was still in my room, but I was dressed and there was mud on my shoes."

I scoffed. "Come on."

"I'm telling you the truth."

"Yeah, well, you'll forgive me if I don't put much faith in what you call truth."

She scowled. "You wanted answers, so I'm giving them to you."

"Why didn't you mention this before?"

"Because of this right here. Because you're a violent thug. Because I knew you wouldn't believe me. Because

I didn't know what'd happened. Because I didn't want to put myself under suspicion. Why does anyone lie to a detective?"

"Usually because they're guilty," I said. "All right, go on then. Let me hear this story of yours."

"I've told you it. I don't remember the exact time when I blacked out, but I must've lost about an hour and a half. Psi Division would've been winding down, it would have been easy for me to get out without someone seeing me. When I came to my keys were in my pocket, so maybe I drove somewhere."

"Somewhere like Yllia's pit," I said sceptically.

"Maybe. Are you satisfied?"

"Not yet. You say you can't remember anything. You don't remember going to Yllia's pit. You don't remember killing her."

She closed her eyes. "All I remember was waking up in my room. Mud on my shoes and trousers. And I found this bit of glass on my sleeve. That's it. That's all I remember."

"Glass. What sort of glass?"

She shrugged. "I don't know. Glass."

"Like from a beer bottle? A window? A car?"

"I don't think it was from a window. It was curved. Clear. Not like a beer bottle, I don't think."

"Like what, then? A test tube?"

She shrugged again. "Maybe. Why?"

I thought back to the glass fragment I'd found at Yllia's watchtower. Could it be the same? It was a stretch, but maybe she was telling the truth.

"All right," I said. "You've got my attention. What happened after that?"

"I put my clothes in the wash, got ready for bed again. I didn't want to tell anyone I'd been sleepwalking. It was embarrassing. Maybe twenty minutes passed. And then I felt Yllia break impulse control."

"Your headache, you mean?"

She nodded. "I was telling the truth about that. The pain was blinding. I didn't know what'd happened until my head cleared enough to hear what my assistant was telling me."

I studied her. She seemed sincere, but how could I tell? She was a slippery one. Maybe she was telling the truth, maybe not. Maybe she was still holding back more.

"This morning." I checked my watch. It hadn't spontaneously repaired itself. "Or yesterday morning, maybe. Whatever. When I came to Psi Division and you wanted to come with me to Yllia's pit. Why?"

She licked her lips. "I…I wanted to know. I thought that if I went there I might remember where I'd been."

"You thought you might have killed her."

"I didn't know what to think. But I didn't understand it. I'd never done anything like that before. Why today, of all days?"

I finally released my hold on her shirt, but I blocked her path so she couldn't get away. I tapped my lip. It still sounded like bullshit. A blackout? It was absurd.

Then again, maybe it wasn't. I'd seen Garcia turn into the raving mind-slave of Tempest just a couple of hours ago. Maybe these handlers were susceptible to some kind of outside influence.

But that still left the big question. "How?" I said. "If you killed Yllia, how'd you do it?"

"I don't know."

"Come on, there must be something. You did it somehow."

"I don't know if I did or not."

I waved my hand. "Fine. You *allegedly* did it. I don't think you throttled her with your bare hands. How, then?"

"I don't know, okay?" She rubbed her face with her hands. "Why do you still care? Look what you've done to this city. What *we*'ve done." Her eyes were wet. "We're already dead."

"Not yet. Not if we kill them first."

She blinked, stared at me. She looked confused for a second. Then understanding dawned on her face.

"You want to save your family?" I said. "You want to save yourself?"

"Yes."

"Then I have someone I want you to talk to."

I kicked open the locked hospital door and stepped into the small private room. Both the thug's wrists were cuffed to the bed rails. There were no doctors around, no nurses, no security. They'd all abandoned him. All he had to entertain himself was a window looking out over the destroyed city. But lucky him. I'd dropped by to say hello.

The thug stared at me through unfocussed eyes. I could tell he didn't recognise me. He tried to raise his head from the pillow, but he was weak. A bandage covered his forehead and right eye. Some of the hair above his brow had been shaved off by the medical staff.

I tapped my forehead. "Sorry about that," I said loudly as I came in and stood over him. "I've never been pistol-whipped, but I imagine it must sting like hell, right?"

His eyes widened as he figured out who I was. His hands jerked up, only to be caught by the handcuff chains. "Hey!" he yelled past me. "Help!"

"They're long gone, pal. I don't think they'd even hear a gunshot." I slipped the gun out of my pocket and pressed the barrel against his knee. "Should we find out?"

His face drained of colour. He was a heavy guy, not as muscular as his friend I'd interrogated back in the tank, but fatter.

I glanced behind me as Priya entered the room. She stopped, staring at him.

"Recognise this guy?" I said.

She nodded. "Leo Corman. He's Miguel's main hazard driver."

"Well, he's also one of the guys who was beating up your mother."

Her gaze flashed to me and then back to him. Her face went hard. I gave the guy a sneer. Just the sight of him was making my head pound.

"I think you've just lost yourself an ally," I said. "Now, I don't have much time. There's a fire heading this way. And I figure one Mayday or another will come stomping through here in the next half hour. So I'd like you to answer my questions as quickly and concisely as possible. Okay?"

Corman chewed his lip, his eyes fixed on the gun

pointed at his knee.

"You were trying to get to Miss Dasari here," I said. "Why?"

He looked at Priya. His cuffed hands spread in a pleading gesture. "Priya, don't let this guy—"

"Hey!" I ground the gun barrel into his kneecap. "You're talking to me, not her. Why were you trying to get to her?"

"I don't know what you're talking about."

"Bullshit. Tell me."

"I…I can't," he said.

I snarled. "We don't have time for this, Corman. Tell me."

"No. You don't understand." He was scared. But not of me.

"I'm going to count to three," I said. I glanced at Priya. "Any objections?"

Her eyes had gone dark. "Are you sure it was him? Are you sure he was the one hurting my mother?"

"Why don't you ask him?"

She met his eyes. "Priya..." he said.

I looked at her. She said nothing.

"There we go," I said to Corman. "No objections from the crowd. Tell me what I want to know and I'll let you go. I'm giving you one more chance. Don't make me do this."

"I can't," he said.

I slugged him across the face and brought the gun barrel back to his knee. "One."

He spat blood at me. "He'll kill me."

"I'll kill you. Two." I pulled back the revolver's hammer.

"Priya, please," he begged. But Priya just stared back

at him.

A Mayday footstep landed somewhere nearby.

I paused an extra half second. *Answer, you son of a bitch.* But he just looked up at me, eyes wide. I glanced at Priya. She opened her mouth. But she didn't stop me.

"Three," I said.

And I pulled the trigger.

Blood and bone fragments splattered across my hand. The crack of the gunshot rang in my ears. Then came the screaming.

I stood there for a second, my ears ringing, the gun trembling in my hands. I shook my head, grabbed the writhing, screaming Corman by his shoulders, and shoved the gun barrel under his chin. "Answer the fucking question or it's your head next. Why were you trying to get to her?"

His eyes were wide and staring at the ceiling. His hands opened and closed into fists, trying to grab his crippled knee, but the cuffs held him in place. I watched him writhe for a second, dark satisfaction pumping through me.

Priya grabbed my arm, tried to pull me away. "That's enough! He's going to go into shock."

I shoved her back and pressed the barrel of the gun against Corman's forehead. My finger itched on the trigger.

"Who's your boss?" I yelled in his face. "Who gives you orders? Tell me!"

"Garcia!" he screamed.

I bared my teeth. *Miguel Garcia.*

If Garcia was running the MPF splinter group, that meant he'd killed Yllia to free the Maydays. That slimy bastard. I had to find him. I'd left him beaten on top of the watchtower at Tempest's pit. Was he still alive?

Corman's screaming quietened. His eyes were slipping closed. I slapped his face. "Hey. Wake up. I'm not done with you yet. Why were you after Priya? What does Garcia want with her? How'd you people kill Yllia? Hey!"

I smacked him across the mouth again. His head snapped limply to the side. He was out.

"Goddamn it!" I roared. "Wake up!"

"Stop it," Priya said. She tugged on my gun arm, pulling me back. "He's unconscious."

My breathing was fast and shallow. The shakes were hitting me. Around me, the walls seemed to pulse slightly. I glanced at the hole I'd blown in Corman's knee. Blood pulsed out, turning the sheets a brownish red. My stomach turned. I looked down at my gun hand, saw the blood splattered there. I hurriedly tucked my gun back in my pocket and grabbed some paper towels from the dispenser by the sink in the corner. I tried the tap, but no water came out. I settled for trying to clean the blood off my hands with the paper towels. I couldn't get the stain out.

Thumping made the windows rattle. For a single, wild moment I thought it was my own heartbeat. Then I realised it was footsteps. I glanced towards the window and saw Nasir closing on the hospital.

"Come on," I said. My voice was hoarse. "Time to go."

"What about Corman?"

I didn't look at him. "What about him? You saw what he did to your mother. Don't pretend you've just grown a conscience."

"He'll die if we leave him here," she said. But she sounded like she wasn't sure if that was a good thing or a bad thing.

It didn't matter. I grabbed her arm and pulled her out of the room. "He's already dead."

19

I shoved Priya into the passenger seat and climbed behind the wheel. The loose change in the ash tray rattled in time with Nasir's footsteps. The stolen car started first try. I pulled a U-turn and ducked down a side street, carrying us away from the Mayday's advance. I watched his silhouette in the mirror as we drove away. He didn't give chase. He continued on his way to the hospital. The screams followed us for a few seconds, then we were too far away. I breathed a sigh.

"I thought we were just going to talk to Corman," Priya said.

"He was stalling," I said. "If you care so much, why didn't you stop me?"

She hesitated. "I don't know."

"I think I know."

"Where are you taking me?" she said.

"Wherever I go."

"My family—"

"Lindsey will take care of your family."

"If she's anything like you, I don't know if I believe that," she said.

I let a grim smile twist my face. "She's not like me. She's got morals."

We fell silent. I drove towards the bridge. Ahead, on the East Island, I could see Tempest heading for the far side. Heading for Serraton's pit. As I pulled onto the bridge, I briefly saw Grotesque's spines carving through the water before disappearing from sight. He was swimming north, towards the mainland. Or maybe to intercept an Alliance fleet. Surely they must've heard by now. They'd be mobilising. Not that it would do any good.

I drove with only the parking lights on to avoid attracting Tempest's attention. I shouldn't have bothered; he never looked in our direction. As I drove along a familiar stretch of road, I spotted a shadow lying on the side of the road. Priya saw it too.

"Stop," she said. "I think that was a person."

"It was. He's dead."

"How do you know? Go back. He might've been—"

"He's dead," I said, harder this time. "You should know. You left him there when you ran away."

She fell quiet.

I pulled into the demolished car park at Tempest's pit and opened the car door. "Come on."

She came without protest. We fought our way through the rubble at the base of the wall and climbed the spiral staircase to the viewing platform at the top of the watchtower. Panting, I emerged onto the platform with my gun by my side.

Garcia was gone.

I kicked the wall where he'd been. *Goddamn it. God*

fucking damn it. I felt drained after my interrogation of Corman. Numb. My face felt scratchy. I needed sleep. I was a different man than I'd been when I woke up this morning, and I wasn't sure I liked who I'd become.

I put my gun away, then dug my cigarettes out of my pocket and put one between my lips. Priya was staring out over the city. I offered her the pack.

"I quit," she said.

"Me too."

She drew a cigarette and I lit them both. We leaned against the railing.

"Do you have a family?" she asked.

"Nope."

"I didn't think so."

"What's that supposed to mean?"

She shook her head and said nothing.

"Where would Garcia go?" I asked after a few minutes. "Psi Division?"

"I don't know. I don't think so. He would know you'd look for him there."

That was what I'd figured. Maybe he was already making his escape now the Maydays were free. Maybe he was hiding in a hole somewhere. If I had a day and a phone and some more people to help me track him, I'd find him no problem. But it was just me and a broken city now.

"What kind of guy is Garcia? Does he have friends? Family?"

Priya bit her lip. "I didn't know him well. He's only been here two years or so. I don't think he had family on the island. None of us really have friends. Psi Division is isolating. There's a certain amount of collegial friendliness between us all, but that's it."

"What about lovers? Did he have any?"

"I didn't exactly put a spy camera in his room," she said.

"That's a shame. I would've." I stubbed my cigarette out on the railing and flicked the butt into the pit. "Did you ever sleep with him?"

"Fuck you."

"Is that a yes?"

"It's a no. What's wrong with you?"

"My mother never hugged me," I said. My walkie-talkie came to life.

"Mr Escobar," Su-jin said.

I jerked the walkie from my pocket. "It's me," I said. "Have…have you talked to Lindsey?"

"She said she was going to try to find her partner and evacuate with Miss Dasari's family."

I licked my lips. "Did she say anything about me?"

"She said some things. I will not repeat them."

"And you're still here?"

"The job is not finished. Tempest still stands."

I allowed myself to breathe. I wasn't alone. Not completely. "Then we've got work to do. What did you call about?"

"Dr Russell. I got into Bio. She's not here."

"Shit. We need her, Su-jin."

"I know. That is why I've been talking to the surviving biologists. One of them saw her loading sampling instruments into one of the division's vehicles soon after

Tempest's attack. The scientist tried to ask her where she was going. She wouldn't say. But the scientist says there is only one possible use for that equipment."

"She's going to Yllia's pit," I said.

"Yes."

I glanced at Priya. She'd overheard the conversation.

"I'm on my way," I said. "Stay in Bio, see what you can find out. We need that murder weapon. And keep your ear to the ground about Miguel Garcia, Tempest's handler. He's connected to all this." I put away the walkie and turned to Priya. "You're coming with me."

She took a last lungful of smoke and stubbed out her cigarette. "Let's get on with it, then."

The wind had taken hold of one side of the white tent covering Yllia's body. It whipped back and forth, dancing in the rain. When it billowed up, Yllia's rear legs came into view, limp and damp with the rain. The smell was as strong as it had ever been. I held my handkerchief over my mouth and squelched through the mud. Priya grunted as the mud sucked her foot in. I offered her my hand and pulled. Her foot came loose with a wet sucking sound. We pressed on and ducked inside the tent's entrance.

Electric lanterns cast Yllia's flank into orange light. The wind blew waves through Yllia's fur every time it came whistling through the tent. The fur was even more limp now, revealing the skin beneath as dry and desiccated.

Priya touched my arm and pointed towards Yllia's head. I followed her gaze and saw a figure in a plastic poncho toiling under the light of a lantern. The woman was struggling with something that looked like an oversized leafblower with a drill bit on the end. As we watched, she plunged it into the underside of Yllia's chin, driving it upwards. A grinding, whirring sound came a moment later. The noise covered our footsteps as we trod over to her.

Dr Russell's normally well-kept blond hair was pressed to her cheeks in damp clumps. Her face was drawn, her eyes sunken. Her gaze swung towards us as we approached. She gasped and took a step back, leaving her contraption buried in Yllia's thick flesh.

"Burning the midnight oil, huh?" I said, my hands in my pockets. I grinned up at the rain leaking through a tear in the tent. "Nice night for it."

Her gaze darted to Priya then back to me. "What are you doing here, Escobar?"

"Looking for you, actually. A little bird told me I might find you here." I cast a look over the machinery sticking into Yllia's chin. "I have to admit, though, I'm a little confused about what you're doing. I knew I should've spent biology class listening to the teacher rather than flirting with the girl sitting in front of me. You should've seen her, though. She had one of those short bob hairstyles—you know what the fashion was in those days. And her legs, my God." I whistled. "But there you go. That's a lesson, I suppose. Don't pay attention in class and you end up like me, trudging around in the mud, getting strangled, roughing up folks for information. You know what I did before I came here? Shot a guy right in the knee because he didn't tell me what I wanted to know." I shook my head. "Listen to me, going on. So, what's happening with you?"

She gave me a hard look and turned back to her contraption. She flicked a switch and the whirring became a
slurping sound. "I don't have time for this. I have to get
this done."

I strolled closer, putting myself in her space. "Don't
you just hate that, when you're trying to do your work and
some arsehole just won't stop talking to you? Yak yak yak.
Drives me crazy. But humour me."

"Escobar—"

"What the fuck are you doing here, Catherine?"

She glared at me. "I'm collecting samples."

"Why?"

"Because we didn't get the right ones this morning."

I glanced at Priya, to see if that meant anything to her.
She shrugged. I turned back to Catherine. "Okay. Let's try
a different question. What do you know about the LIM
systems?"

"I know everything about them."

I strolled around behind her. "Good. Then you know
they were based on Yllia's psychic powers." She was silent.
"Of course you do. You were there at Irkutsk, weren't you?"

She made a frustrated noise. "Yes, I was. Now why
don't you ask Volkov about this?"

"Volkov's dead, Catherine."

She froze, eyes staring straight ahead.

"Yeah," I said. "I was there. Grotesque plucked him
right out of the tower. I guess Tempest had something of
a grudge against him, what with all the mind control and
slavery and all that. I'll tell you, Tempest took his time killing him." I held my fingers up like claws. "He had him like

this, you see. And he was doing this—"

"Enough," she said.

"Just stabbing him, over and over again, like—"

"Enough!" She whirled on me. "Be quiet."

I grinned cruelly. It felt good to get a reaction out of her. I leaned over her and got in her face. "You think you'll die better than Volkov? Or do you think you'll survive? Is that it? You won't. We're all dead, Catherine. Unless we do something about this little problem. I'm trying to stop him. I *need* to stop him. I need to finish this case. So I'd appreciate it if you stop jerking me around and answer my goddamn questions."

She stared at me. I stared back. She broke eye contact first. My grin widened.

"Do you know who Miguel Garcia is?" I asked.

Dr Russell kept her eyes on Yllia as she nodded.

"I believe he's the leader of an MPF splinter group based on the island. I believe he was responsible for Yllia's death." I studied her face. Something had changed behind her eyes when I mentioned Garcia. Just a flicker. But I went for it, trusting my gut. "I know you didn't want to work with him, Catherine. Did he threaten you?"

She reached up, tucking a lock of damp hair behind her ear with trembling fingers. She still wouldn't meet my gaze. "He had pictures of my husband and children. Surveillance photos, you understand? The message was clear."

"When was this? Before you started working here?"

She nodded. "He wanted me to pull strings with Volkov, get myself a job in the Biology Division. I suppose he knew

Volkov would put me in charge. He knew our connection."

"I suppose he did." I straightened, gave her a little space. I flashed a smile at Priya that she didn't return. "Once you were working here, what did he want from you?"

"Access. Access to the infant."

"Infant?" What the hell would Garcia want with a baby? I glanced at Priya, looking to see if this made any more sense to her.

Then I remembered something she'd said, something she'd seen in her vision last time we were at the pit. *The little one.* "An infant Mayday," I said slowly. "Are you saying you have an infant Mayday?"

Dr Russell nodded. She flicked a couple of switches on her sampling machine. The sucking ceased, leaving only the pounding of rain on the plastic tent. It bothered me a little that I hadn't heard any Mayday footsteps for a while now. But I could only focus on one thing at a time. Dr Russell tucked her arms around herself, as if she'd only just noticed the cold.

"Eleven years ago," she said, "before the end of the war, I was helping Volkov track Yllia's movements across Eurasia and North America with a small research team. Other Maydays moved around the globe based on opportunity and convenience. By the end some of the attacks could be predicted. But Yllia's movements were more unique. We were sure there was a pattern."

"Didn't she notice you following her?" I asked.

"We suspected she did. But she never attacked."

Priya spoke up. "You would've been no more than a curiosity to her. She wouldn't consider you either a threat or a good target."

Dr Russell nodded. "After a few months, we stumbled across a certain location in Siberia that she always returned to. We hypothesised that it was her nest. When she went on a raid of eastern China, we took a chance and moved in to investigate. We found a huge underground cave. And in the cave, we found the infant."

"You think it was Yllia's child?"

"It seems that way," she said. "The infant is not much bigger than a dog. But when we found it, it was trapped in some sort of gelatinous pouch." She put her fist in her hand, modelling it. "We thought it was dead. We loaded it up and drove it back to our research base in Irkutsk for study. But once we got it back and started running tests on it, we realised it wasn't dead. It was frozen. Some kind of stasis. We did tests on the pouch, trying to estimate its age. It sounds ridiculous, and even at the time we couldn't believe it. But we estimated that it was at least four billion years old."

"Billion with a 'B'?"

She nodded. "Older than the earliest evidence we have of life on Earth."

"All right," I said. "That's impressive and all. But what the hell does it have to do with anything?"

A blast of wind ripped through the tent, sending another section of it flapping into the sky. Through the gap I could see the silhouette of another Mayday moving through the forest. Serraton. He was free.

"We began studying the infant intensively," Dr Russell said. "Unlike the other Maydays, this one was vulnerable to our instrumentation. We were able to take samples and do imaging on it. X-rays, MRI. For the first time we could gather some idea of the Maydays' anatomy and physiology. We wanted to keep the project a secret until we knew what we were working with. We hoped to use that information to discover a weakness. And we did." She glanced at the instrument sticking out of Yllia. "A parasite. The infant was carrying a colony of parasites. Some sort of worm. The infant seemed to show signs of brain degradation as a result of the infection. But the gelatinous pouch had frozen the parasites as well as the infant. We suspected that any attempts to revive the infant would allow the parasites to quickly destroy the host."

"So it was like Walt Disney."

Dr Russell's brow furrowed. "What?"

"You never heard that rumour? They say Walt Disney was cryogenically frozen and stored under Disneyland to be thawed out when they created a cure for lung cancer."

"That's absurd."

I held up my hands. "I'm not the one claiming to have found a frozen Mayday older than life itself."

She gave me one of those looks. "Well, that was essentially our hypothesis. That the infant was preserved in stasis to prevent the parasite from killing it. The gelatinous pouch that enclosed it was of organic origin. It seemed that the infant had secreted the gel and put itself into stasis in response to an outside stimulus. We'd developed a way to reverse the stasis, but we weren't prepared to use it yet. We wanted more time to study the parasites. We suspected they may also be dangerous to adult Maydays."

"Hang on," I said. "You're saying monsters that can withstand everything we ever threw at them, up to and including nuclear blasts, are vulnerable to some little worm? I find that a little hard to believe."

"Believe what you want. The parasite was unlike anything we'd found in nature. It appeared perfectly adapted to infecting Maydays. Our initial investigations suggested that it was so specialised it would pose no risk to humans. We had begun preparations to extract some of the parasites for study, to try to replicate them for use as a weapon. And that was when Yllia attacked our lab.

"She came right for us, ignoring the other civilian targets. She knew what we had. I was standing there, watching my colleagues slit their throats, watching them burn in Yllia's plasma, watching—" Her voice cracked. "I lost Volkov in the chaos. I thought he was dead. I thought we were all going to die. Yllia's eyes were looking down at me, and she saw me. I felt a...a pressure in my mind. All my own thoughts and fears being crushed under the weight of Yllia's mind. My legs started carrying me up to the edge of a catwalk. I climbed up onto the railing, looked down at the fall below. I knew I was going to die, but I felt... nothing."

A Mayday's footsteps rumbled in the distance. Dr Russell clutched herself tighter. She looked as tired as I felt.

"What stopped you?" I said.

"Yllia did. She released me. The pressure left my mind. Suddenly, I could control myself again. I climbed back onto safe ground. I didn't know what had happened until I looked over the edge of the catwalk and saw Volkov on the floor below, standing next to our containment chamber for the infant. He'd punched in the instructions to start the process of bringing the infant out of stasis. And now he held a gun to his own head. If he killed himself, there would be no way to stop the infant from coming out of stasis."

"And then the infant would be eaten by parasites," I said. I scratched my beard. I had to give it to Volkov, he had balls. Well, he used to. "So Volkov blackmailed Yllia into leaving you alone?"

"Yes. I thought that was where he stopped. I found out later Yllia was communicating with him psychically. Volkov wasn't content with letting us survive. He'd seen an opportunity."

Priya got it first. "Information," she said slowly. "Impulse control. Yllia told him how to do it."

Dr Russell nodded.

"Jesus," I said. "Now that's what I call intellectual plagiarism. Yllia told him how he could capture the Maydays to stop him killing her child. I bet the other Maydays couldn't've been pleased."

"We kept the infant as insurance," Dr Russell said. "After the war, Volkov and I had a falling out. This…spectacle of his disturbed me. I thought the Maydays were too dangerous to be used as entertainment. Volkov brought the infant to the island where he could continue to study it. I think one of the conditions Yllia had for the information she divulged was that the infant remained alive and nearby, where she could be assured of its survival. He kept up the research on the infant almost singlehandedly, while

I returned home."

"Until Garcia contacted you, wanting access to the infant." I said. "Why?" And then it clicked. "The parasite. That's the murder weapon, isn't it? Garcia didn't want the infant. He wanted the parasites. So he could kill Yllia and free the Maydays." I chewed my lip. "That's it. That's the answer. We need to get back to your lab and get more of them. More parasites. We can kill Tempest. We can kill them all."

Dr Russell licked her lips. She wouldn't meet my eyes. "We extracted all the parasites from the infant. We were unable to replicate them. And when he threatened my family I…I gave them all to Garcia."

I turned in place. "Fuck. Fuck!" I growled. "Why didn't you tell me about this before? We could've done something! Look at me, damn it!" I grabbed her by the arm and forced her gaze to meet mine.

"I didn't know," she said, her voice cracking. "I didn't think this would happen. I thought he was trying to sabotage the company. I thought he wanted to euthanise the Maydays. I didn't know he wanted to free them. My family…."

I dry-washed my face with my hands. Goddamn it.

"I'm trying to make it right," she said. She jabbed her finger at the sampling instrument. "There must be parasites in Yllia. They killed her, so they have to be here. I thought our samples this morning would capture some. But, I don't know, maybe they don't replicate as well in adults as they did in the infant. Maybe they cause death too fast. But there has to be some, somewhere. I'm going to find them."

"You better, Doc. Because if you can't—"

"Escobar!" Priya called. But her voice came from far away, dampened by rain and wind. I spun around. Where the hell had she gone?

She called again. Her voice was coming from outside the tent. "Escobar, quickly!"

I sloshed through the mud, back through the tent's entrance and into the driving rain. Priya's small form was almost invisible in the darkness.

"Don't you ever run away from me again, Dasari," I said. "What is—?"

A crack of lightning ripped through the sky, illuminating the hills and forest around the pit for a moment. I froze, the afterimage seared into my retinas. I turned slowly in place. On the hills around us, three Maydays stood motionless. Nasir. Serraton. Tempest.

And they were watching us.

20

I heard Dr Russell squelch through the mud and push through the tent flap behind me. She gasped.

"Catherine," I said over my shoulder in a low voice. "Get back inside. Find us those parasites." When I didn't hear her moving, I glanced back. "Now, Doctor."

She nodded without looking at me and backed slowly inside. I turned my attention forwards again. Priya was a few feet in front of me, frozen like me.

"Priya." I held my hand out, beckoned. "Come on. Slowly."

Priya kept her eyes on the Maydays around us as she stepped back and put her hand in mine. Her palm was clammy with sweat and rain.

Another ripple of lightning rolled across the clouds. Serraton was edging forward to our left. Like Grotesque, Serraton was almost reptilian in nature, but his slender body and long, thin limbs were more reminiscent of a snake or a Chinese dragon. A long tail ending in a fin swept back and forth behind him, while his narrow snout formed a blade that ended in a sharp, curved point. He lacked the weight of the heavier Maydays, but during the war he'd loved using surprise to launch his attack, frequently slipping undetected through shallow harbours before making landfall, or on a few occasions digging his way through softer earth to burst out in the middle of a city, consuming terrified civilians as they tried to flee from a monster they couldn't keep track of.

I pulled Priya back. Serraton fell to all fours, nimble like a cat, and started forward.

Tempest roared. The screeching, tortured sound froze Serraton in his tracks. The slender Mayday tossed his head and glared at us with his big black eyes. A blue frill flicked open from the sides of his neck and he growled threateningly. But he didn't take another step.

"They're not attacking," I said.

"It's Yllia," Priya said. "They're afraid she's infected."

"Then why the hell are they all here? Don't they have better things to do? They're free, Volkov's dead, why don't they bugger off to stomp some other city?"

"Maybe they think we're a threat."

I stared at Tempest across the forest that separated us. He snorted, steam rising from his nostrils. *Is that it? Are you scared, big guy? How does it feel?*

"You reckon that fire-breathing attack of his can reach us from there?" I asked.

"I don't know. I don't think so. Maybe he could start a forest fire, but it's so wet I don't know if it would catch."

"Let's hope you're right." Serraton was on all fours, straining like a dog on an invisible leash. "And let's hope he can keep that one under control."

"We've got to get out of here," Priya said.

"You won't hear me arguing." I ran through the scenarios in my head. They had us pretty much boxed in. We'd have to go straight through them to get back towards the city. That wasn't going to end well. We could retreat further east, but Grotesque was still unaccounted for. He could be circling around behind us as we stood here, just waiting for us to run.

I couldn't see a way out. The skin of my throat itched, tightened. I forced myself to breathe. I couldn't panic. But this was terrifying. We weren't anonymous souls running around a city as a Mayday stomped blindly through. Tempest had made this personal. He knew who we were, who I was. And he was hunting us.

I tugged Priya's hand. "Let's go back inside. I think we've got a bit of time before they get too impatient and try to burn us out."

She nodded and we backed away together. It didn't look like she had any better ideas. Maybe she didn't like me, and maybe I didn't trust her, but neither of those feelings would stop us being crushed beneath a Mayday's foot. We had to stick together, for now at least.

We slipped inside. When my eye contact with Tempest was broken by the white tent plastic, I turned and started trudging as fast as I could through the mud. "How's it coming, Catherine?"

Dr Russell slipped a glass container out of the base of her sampling machine and held it up to the light of an electric lantern. Thick brown sludge sloshed around inside.

"I can't get deep enough," she said. "I'm not hitting neural tissue."

"Well, hurry it up," I said. "Our friends are waiting."

She flicked a switch, starting the drill again, and pulled the machine out of the underside of Yllia's chin. The whirring machine splattered a small amount of sludge in the mud as it came out. She switched off the machine, loaded a new vial into it, and took a step back, studying Yllia's corpse.

"Give me a boost up," she said. "I'm going to climb onto the side of her head and try to get in that way."

I looked up at the corpse. Sounded like a good way to fall off and break a leg, but it wasn't my leg.

"Sure thing," I said. I went over and cupped my hands to give her a foothold. The smell of Yllia's corpse was almost overpowering this close. Dr Russell leaned the sampling machine against Yllia's fur and put her foot in my hands. She wasn't that heavy, which was good because I was running low on energy. I hefted her up and she grabbed hold of Yllia's thick fur further up the side of the Mayday's neck. She still had a fair climb to get onto level ground, but at least the Mayday had sunk into the mud somewhat and her flesh had continued to deflate, making the climb a little shorter. When Dr Russell had a stable hold on the corpse, I grabbed the sampling machine and passed it up to her. She slung it over her shoulder by its strap and started climbing.

"Look at that," I said, stepping back and watching her go. "Pretty nimble. You ever do rock-climbing?"

"Shut up, Escobar," she shouted back down. "How about instead of staring at my butt, you work out how we're going to get out of here. Even if I get something, I'll need to head back to Bio before we can put it to any use."

It wasn't a bad suggestion. I jerked my head at Priya and put as much distance as I could between me and the corpse. I peeked out the edge of the tent. The Maydays were still out there, waiting. For some reason, it was more disconcerting to see them motionless than it had been to watch them destroying the city.

Priya came alongside me. "What are we going to do?"

"If we run, we die. If we stay, we live for a while, until we die." I shook my head. "We need a distraction."

"Are the Alliance sending a response?"

"Probably. Eventually. The Alliance has been running on a skeleton crew for the last decade. I wouldn't hold your breath for an intervention before Tempest runs out of patience." I'd seen exactly how long the Mayday had waited before plucking Volkov out of the tower. Maybe he'd wait longer knowing that his life could be at risk. But he was cunning. I didn't want to hang around and see what plots he could concoct.

No, we needed to come up with something ourselves. Take different cars and split up? No, the Maydays could easily kill all three of us. Take our chances retreating east? But then how the hell were we going to get back to Bio?

We needed to divert their attention. Distract them, blind them, trick them, confuse them. Something.

Wait. "This morning," I said. "When you mind melded with Yllia and made everyone's brains leak out their ears. The Maydays all started roaring. They felt it too, right?"

She nodded uncertainly. "I guess."

"Do it again."

"What?"

"That's our distraction. We blow their goddamn minds out."

"That knocked everyone out last time," she said.

"So do it different. Make it affect them more than us. I don't know, I'm not the goddamn psychic."

She screwed up her face. "I might be able to do it. *Might*. But even if I can direct it away from you, it's still going to affect me. I'll be out cold as soon as I do it. Then what?"

"Then I carry you when we run for it."

She quirked her eyebrow.

"Trust me, sweetheart," I said. "You're still a suspect in this whole shitstorm. You'll be coming with me if I have to drag your unconscious arse all the way back to Bio myself."

"Do you know what kind of pain you're asking me to endure?"

"I'm not asking."

She sneered. She really needed to stop doing that. It wasn't a good look for her.

"All right," she said. "Fine. If I do this, what do I get out of it?"

"You get to live a little while longer."

She shook her head. "That's not good enough. I'm taking the risk. I'm putting myself through the pain. I want something out of it."

"Like what?"

"You stop threatening me. We see this through to the end. Whatever that end is. But I'm not your prisoner anymore, or your hostage. I don't know what I did when I blacked out last night. Maybe I'm partly to blame for all this. So are you. If she's telling the truth, so is she." Priya

CHRIS STRANGE

pointed at Dr Russell as the biologist reached the top of Yllia's head and began preparing her machine. "So we make it right. Together."

"That's a real nice speech," I said.

"Is that a yes?"

I grinned. I still didn't trust her. But at least this kept her under my nose. What did I have to lose? I stuck out my hand. "Sure thing. Partner."

She grasped my hand and we shook like a couple of old pals. I showed her my teeth and she showed me hers. The handshake lasted a hair too long. She was dangerous, this one.

We let go and she said, "I'm going over to Yllia's head to prepare."

I nodded. "Just don't blow your wad too early. I'll keep watch."

Priya trudged away through the mud. I glanced up at Dr Russell as she drove the sampling machine into Yllia's ear canal and started the suction. I didn't trust Russell any more than I did the handler. How come the women I encountered in this job never lived up to the *femmes fatales* in movies? I got all the distrust and none of the sex. It was a crying shame.

I peeked out the tent flap. My eyes had adjusted to the light from the electric lanterns, making it appear even darker outside. I squinted into the night and the rain. Another flash of lightning lit up the sky. I caught a glimpse of fallen trees and upturned dirt on the left side of the hill. The ground rumbled beneath my feet. My heart stopped.

I ducked back inside and cupped my hands around my

mouth. "Ladies, we may want to hurry this up," I called. "Small problem. Serraton's gone."

"How is that a problem?" Dr Russell yelled back over the whine of her machine.

"Because that sound…" I pointed down at my feet. "… that rumbling, that's not thunder. Serraton's digging. He's coming for us."

21

I ran back to Yllia's corpse, slipping in the mud. "You nearly done there, Doc?"

She was examining another glass vial. "I've definitely got brain tissue this time. I'll have to get it back to the lab before I can say whether we've captured any parasites. If I just had a little more time—"

"You don't. You'll have to make do. Get your arse down here."

She tucked the vial into her pocket and started to scramble back down.

The mud beneath my feet was rippling with the low rumbling coming from deep beneath us. How far away was Serraton? Where would he break the surface?

"Are you sure you can pull this off, Priya?" I yelled.

"No," she said. "Are you sure you can get us out of here if I can?"

"Sure I'm sure," I lied. I breathed through my mouth to try to keep Yllia's stench from making me retch. Dr Russell was edging down Yllia's neck. Beneath us, the rumbling grew louder.

"Catherine," I called up. "Let's go. We're out of time."

She glanced down. "I'm going to jump."

"What?"

"Catch me."

She let go of Yllia's fur and jumped. My guts twisted up as I lurched forward and stuck my arms out. *She's fucking crazy.*

Dr Russell slammed into me. I wrapped my arms around her as we toppled into the mud. She wasn't a big lady, but I tell you, when she hit me I swear one of my lungs collapsed.

She panted and picked herself up. "Thanks."

"What the hell is wrong with—"

A scratching noise rattled through my bones. I glanced to the side, near Yllia's flank. A sinkhole was appearing in the mud. The sharp point of Serraton's snout stabbed up through the ground. A moment later, a spray of water shot from the snout, dousing Yllia's side. Yllia's fur began to wilt and turn black where it was hit. The air tasted sharp.

It wasn't water. It was acid.

"Priya!" I screamed as I staggered up, slipping through the mud. "Now! Do it now!"

Priya's small form was staring past me at the snout, her eyes wide.

"Priya!" I yelled.

She snapped out of it and pressed herself against Yllia's nose. I ran towards her.

Something black and heavy slammed into my mind. I thought I'd be prepared this time. I wasn't. Every nerve ending in my body was on fire. Images flashed before my eyes, but this time they were incoherent, just a smear of colours skipping across time and space.

Then, slowly, it began to fade. I blinked the tears out of my eyes and brought the world back into focus. I was on my hands and knees in the mud, my muscles quivering. My brain was sparking but nothing was happening. *Get up, Escobar. Get the fuck up.* I planted my feet and stood, still shaking.

And then the air erupted in a cacophony of tortured screaming.

I jammed my hands over my ears and squeezed my eyes shut, but I could feel the screeching bouncing around inside my skull. The Maydays. They were pissed off. Now was my chance. I had to go.

I forced my eyes open and found Dr Russell curled up in the mud a couple of metres away from me. I stumbled over and grabbed her arm. Her eyes opened into slits.

"Up!" I yelled. My voice was drowned out by the monsters' screaming. Dr Russell stared at me, dazed. I grabbed her and hauled her to her feet. I pointed. "Get to the car."

She sure as hell couldn't hear me, but I think she got the picture. She stumbled towards the tent flap.

Priya. Where was Priya? My vision was fuzzy. Something buzzed in my head, bouncing around like a mosquito stuck inside my skull. I trudged through the mud as fast as I could. I glanced behind me. Serraton's snout slammed about in its hole, making a horrible creaking noise as it screamed. Acid sprayed intermittently from the snout, causing massive blisters to form on Yllia wherever it touched bare flesh. Serraton had been trying to destroy Yllia's body before the infection could spread. Or maybe he'd just been trying to kill us. Whatever the case, we needed to get out of here.

My vision focussed long enough for me to make out a small figure in the mud in the shadow of Yllia's nose. I rushed over, knelt down. Priya. She was breathing. Good enough for me. Ignoring my trembling muscles, I pulled her into a fireman's carry and staggered towards the exit.

I emerged from the tent. Tempest and Nasir were on the hills. Nasir was down on one knee, fists driven into the hillside as he shook his massive head back and forth. Tempest crouched, legs curled and kicking like a spider in a cloud of bug spray. He howled into the rain.

Priya had done it. Now we just had to make use of the distraction. I pushed my screaming legs on and carried Priya out into the car park. Dr Russell waved frantically at me from beside the stolen car. She shouted something I couldn't hear.

I shifted Priya's weight and tossed Dr Russell the keys. "Get the back door!" I pointed and she figured it out. She opened the back door and I tossed Priya down in the back seat. I grabbed the keys out of the door and climbed into the driver's seat. Dr Russell got into the passenger seat next to me. I jammed the keys in the ignition and started the engine.

"Is she all right?" Dr Russell yelled, nodding at Priya.

"She's alive." *For now*, I added silently. I stared at the monsters on the hilltop. I swallowed and put my foot down.

We tore away into the rain. Dr Russell gripped the side of her seat and the handhold above the door. We followed the winding road up the hill, the two Maydays growing larger ahead of us. I prayed neither of them were standing on the road.

I glanced back at Priya. She flopped around in the back seat as I brought the car skidding around a tight turn. I should've buckled her in. Too late now. In the rearview mirror, I could see the white tent over Yllia's body begin to collapse, a hole growing in the centre as Serraton's acid ate away the plastic.

"Look out!" Dr Russell screamed.

My attention snapped back to the road as the shadow of one of Tempest's legs loomed above us. I tugged on the wheel and brought the car sliding around to the right as the monstrous leg slammed into the ground to our left. A pair of trees snapped under Tempest's weight. Splinters pelted the window. The car bounced as the groundwave rippled beneath us. The road cracked and opened up. I set my teeth and gripped the wheel as the tyres went bounding over the cracks.

I risked a glance to the left. Tempest was staggering, tearing up the ground around him. Maybe he knew we were here, maybe not. But either way all twelve of his legs were flailing, slamming into the dirt all around us. I hit the brakes and pulled the wheel around the other way, fighting the car as another scaled leg kicked out, skimming the air above the car. I jammed my foot back on the accelerator. The tyres squealed, desperately trying to gain some grip on a wet patch of road. Then we hit another crack and the tyre caught and we were off again.

I looked to my right. Nasir was rising, a giant against a ripple of lightning. He swung his massive fists in an arc around him, carving a swathe of trees from the landscape. But they all landed well clear of us. I forced a breath between my teeth and fought to stay on the road.

"How are we looking?" I said. The roars of the Maydays had faded, leaving a pain behind like someone had taken a wire brush to my ear canals.

Dr Russell was pressed against the seat, the tendons in her neck pulled tight like the cables of a suspension bridge. She turned stiffly around to look out the rear window. "Serraton's up."

"Chasing us?"

"No. He's burning Yllia's body. We're not going to have anything left to take samples from."

"You've got your sample. It'll have to be enough. The others?"

"They're angry."

"No shit," I said. "Do they know where we are?"

"I don't think so. I think we're all right."

I took a deep breath and let it out slowly. My hands wouldn't release their death grip on the steering wheel. I kept throwing glances in the rearview mirror, waiting for Tempest to turn and chase us, but it never happened. We took the winding road down the other side of the hill and headed for the bridge. The broken city appeared ahead of us. Fires still flickered in the rubble. I couldn't see any Maydays stalking amongst the ruins. We were clear.

I slowed the car as I took us across the bridge. "Check on her," I said, jerking my head to the back seat.

Dr Russell unbuckled her seatbelt and climbed over the centre console into the back. I glanced in the mirror as

I drove. Dr Russell wasn't a medical doctor, but her biology background probably meant she'd be more use than me.

"She seems all right physically, but I can't get her to come around," Dr Russell said.

"She'll be okay," I said with more confidence than I felt.

"That…that whatever it was. The psychic bomb. That was her both times?"

"Yup. Her and Yllia."

"When it happened this morning, or yesterday morning, I saw something. A world like ours, but ancient. Impossibly ancient. With thousands of Maydays."

"Yeah," I said. "I saw it too."

"It had to be Earth. The Maydays used to rule here."

"So it seems." I was having a hard time giving a shit. I wasn't much interested in ancient biology or where the Maydays came from. I wanted to see Tempest on the ground with parasites eating into his brain. That would make me a very happy man indeed.

"I have a hypothesis," she said, apparently unconcerned by my lack of interest. "The way the Maydays appeared, we always suspected they must have been with us a long time. Subterranean, or at the depths of the oceans. Our visions back that up. Thousands of them occupied the Earth before life as we know it arose. Perhaps they evolved on Earth, perhaps they had another origin. But at some stage during their reign, this parasite must've started to infect them. When we found the infant in Siberia, we thought it must've been a rare disease among Maydays. But what if it wasn't? What if it was a plague, an epidemic, something that devastated the population. What if these Maydays are the only ones who survived?"

Despite myself, something she said triggered a memory. "Earlier this evening, when Tempest first broke impulse control, I think he was somehow controlling Garcia. He said something." I tried to remember the words he'd spoken as he raged at me. "He said something about how he saved his people."

"I doubt the Maydays had any concept of medicine or disease," Dr Russell said. "They were probably essentially invincible until the parasite started to kill them. Maybe it spread across the population before most of them knew what was happening." She paused. "When a highly infectious disease strikes, it may be necessary to quarantine or isolate the infected individuals."

"But what do you do when most of the population is infected?" I said.

"You isolate the uninfected. Keep them away from the infection. I think that's what happened. The few uninfected Maydays buried themselves, put themselves in stasis, like the infant. It was a natural defence mechanism. Perhaps they'd encountered a similar disease previously in their history. They let their infected brethren die on the surface, let the years pass so that the parasites would have no more live hosts and would die out."

I nodded. It made sense. It was your basic nuclear fallout vault idea. Preserve a portion of the population while the nuclear winter raged overheard. In a few decades' time, when it was safe to emerge again, they could open the vault and return to the surface. Most of the population would die, but the species would live on. Except....

"Why put the infant into stasis?" I said. "It was infected. All that does is risk the uninfected Maydays when they come out of stasis. They should've let it die on the surface."

"Isn't it obvious?" a weak voice drifted out of the back seat. I glanced back to see Priya's eyes half-opened, her hand massaging her forehead.

"Morning, sleepyhead," I said. "Told you I wouldn't leave you there. Isn't what obvious?"

"Yllia put the infant into stasis for the same reason she relented when Volkov threatened it. She didn't want to leave her child to die."

"Well, ain't that touching," I said. "The mass murdering monster has a heart of gold after all."

The roads got rough around Bio Division, but I was able to drive the car almost to the front door. Well, what was left of it.

I'd radioed ahead and filled Su-jin in on everything, so she was waiting for us as I pulled up. I hadn't seen her since before Tempest broke impulse control, so it was a shock when I saw how she'd fared. Her clothes, normally neat and business-like, were torn and stained with blood. Her left arm was in a makeshift sling. Her hair looked like it had been singed by fire. She'd taken a hell of a beating, especially for someone her age. But she still moved confidently as I got out and helped Priya out of the car.

"You all right?" I asked Su-jin.

She gave a single curt nod. Her gaze drifted away from me, keeping a cautious eye on the horizon. We hadn't seen the Maydays again, but we could still hear the footsteps.

Behind Su-jin, Bio Division had been reduced to a few piles of debris and dust. The building had once had four floors aboveground. Now only the basement labs remained.

"Through here," Su-jin said.

Dr Russell followed the Korean investigator while Priya and I took the rear. After a few steps, Priya shook me off and began to walk on her own, a little unsteadily at first. But if she wanted to prove how tough she was, it was no skin off my nose.

Su-jin led us around the side of the building and clambered over a fallen chunk of floor tiling into the twisted ruins of the building. Glass crunched underfoot as we navigated the maze of rubble to reach an emergency stairwell in the rear of the building. As we descended the stairs, Su-jin pulled a torch from her pocket and lit the way.

I don't know how many floors we went down. I was too busy trying not to fall and break my neck in the flickering darkness to keep track. But finally we emerged into a corridor that led through what I guessed was some sort of decontamination room—which we ignored—and into a long room broken up by wide laboratory benches. On each bench, instruments and bottled chemicals sat in racks above computers and notebooks. Electric lanterns had been set up on every third bench or so, giving the place just enough light to see by. Whispered conversations reached us from the end of the room. A handful of scientists were deep in conversation alongside a bank of refrigerators and large box-like machines I didn't recognise.

"That's it?" I said. "That's everyone from Bio?"

"There were more," Dr Russell said. "Most of the survivors fled to their homes or the port. A few remained."

"To help?" I said. "Or because they were too scared to run for it?"

Dr Russell said nothing. The group of scientists looked up as we approached.

"You're alive," one of the women said to Dr Russell, stating the obvious. "We thought…."

Dr Russell held up the vial containing Yllia's brain matter. "We need to process this as quickly as possible. With refrigeration down we might not have much time. We're going to need whatever emergency power we can generate to power the instruments."

A couple of the younger scientists looked confused, but the woman who'd spoken quickly took the vial and got to work. I guessed knowledge of the infant and the parasite was restricted to a few of the senior biologists.

Something rumbled far above us in the city. A Mayday returning. I wondered if the port had survived. Had Lindsey got away? I glanced at Priya and saw her looking into the middle distance. She was probably wondering the same thing about her family.

Exhaustion settled over me in an instant, weighing me down. I shook my head. I wanted to sit down, close my eyes, but I couldn't afford to. We were way outside my field of expertise now. But we still had work to do.

I opened my mouth to talk to Priya, but when I looked at her again the words stuck in my throat. Her face had drained of colour again. She swayed on her feet, her eyes lidded. Her knees buckled.

I darted forward and caught her before she hit the

ground. Su-jin came to my aid a moment later. Between us, we laid the handler down on the cool linoleum floor. The scientists' conversations hushed.

"Is there water here?" I asked Su-jin.

"I will find some." Su-jin stood and hurried away. I glanced up and saw Dr Russell and the other biologists staring.

"Get on with it," I snapped. "We've got a monster to deal with, remember?"

The scientists looked away and I returned my attention to Priya. Her eyes were partly open, but her gaze was unfocussed. I snapped my fingers in front of her face.

"Dasari. Over here. Look at me, damn it. You alive?"

She mumbled something incoherent. I heard footsteps behind me and Su-jin crouched on the other side of Priya holding a beaker full of water. "Drink," she said, holding it to Priya's lips. The handler sipped the water, spluttered, and sipped again.

Su-jin glanced at me. "What is wrong with her?"

I shook my head. "I had to push her hard to get us out of a tight spot."

"I'll be okay," Priya mumbled. "Just need to rest."

Someone brought a bundled lab coat and put it under her head as a pillow. This was a pain in the arse. I couldn't afford to have her die yet. She knew more about the psychology of Maydays than all of us. If Dr Russell got us the parasites, we still needed to deliver them to Tempest and his buddies without getting killed ourselves. I was running low on ideas.

"How long until you'll know if you've got something?"

I said to Dr Russell as she hurried past and slid the vial into one of the machines.

"A few minutes. If we have parasites, we can try to culture them using some of the infant's tissue. But I don't know how long they'll survive without a true host."

Something thumped overhead. Dust spilled from the ceiling tiles. Everyone went quiet.

"It's Tempest," Priya whispered.

"How do you know?"

"He's looking for us. He's afraid." There was a hiss and a crackling. "He's trying to burn us out."

Couldn't we get a minute to breathe? "Catherine?" I hissed.

"I'll know in a minute."

"I had another vision," Priya said.

"What? When?" I said, my voice low. Could Tempest hear us down here?

Priya's eyes were focussed on the ceiling. Some of the colour had returned to her face, but she still looked half-dead. "Before. At the pit. I remember what happened the night I blacked out."

"Great," I whispered. "You can tell me later. For now, shut up."

If she heard me, she didn't pay any attention. "I can see it. But it's like I'm looking at myself from outside. I found the parasites in a small freezer in Miguel's quarters. I don't know how I knew they were there, but I did. He was out somewhere. I went in, took the vial, and left Psi Division. I had my car keys. I drove to Yllia's pit." She closed her eyes, shook her head. "Why did I do that? I wasn't questioning it at the time. It was like I wasn't there."

Another giant footstep made the basement shudder. I tried again to shush Priya, but it was no good.

"Yllia was waiting for me. It was raining, but she was out of her shelter. I went up into the watchtower. I had to break the lock. I didn't have my card. When I got to the top, she crawled over. She came to me. She knew what I had in my hands." Priya lifted her arms, looked at her palms. She tightened her hands into fists and returned them to her sides. "She brought her face right up against the watchtower. I was close enough to touch her. There was a pressure on my mind. Like she was trying to tell me something. A message, but not with words. A chemical message. And then she sat back and I...I broke the vial over the railing. And she let me infect her." She shook her head again. "She *made* me infect her."

Tempest roared above us, the sound muffled by the earth separating him from us. But my attention was now fixed solely on Priya.

"Are you saying Yllia was controlling you?" I said.

"I...I think so."

I took her shoulder. "You're saying she made you kill her. You're saying she committed suicide. Is that what you're saying?"

Priya nodded slowly.

"Bullshit," I said. "That doesn't make any sense."

"It's what I saw."

"Then either your vision was wrong or you're lying. Since we're one big happy family now, I'll give you the benefit of the doubt and say you're confused." I looked up.

"Catherine? Give me something here."

She'd taken the vial from the machine. Where before the fluid inside was murky and grey, now the majority of it appeared to run clear while a thick layer of matter clung to the bottom of the vial. She'd extracted a small sample of the fluid and was now examining it on a slide under a microscope. I waited impatiently while she stared through the eyepieces.

"We have them."

I stood up and heaved a deep breath. "Thank Christ. Get it ready to go. We're getting out of here." I looked down at Priya. "Can you stand?"

"I think so."

"I got a feeling we're going to need your help out there. But I can't have you passing out."

She planted her hands and got to her feet without help. "I'm fine. And you're right. You won't be able to do this without me."

"We'll see. Go get yourself ready to go." I turned to Su-jin as Priya made for the bathrooms at the end of the lab. "You up for this?"

Su-jin nodded. "All the Maydays are free now. It will not be enough to kill only Tempest."

"One at a time," I said. "Tempest first. For what he did to us, our people. Okay?"

Su-jin nodded again, her eyes steely. "Tempest will fall."

I clapped her on her good shoulder and gave her a grim smile. As I was about to turn away, her gaze slipped past me and her eyes widened.

A strangled cry echoed through the lab. I spun, my

hand going for the revolver in my pocket.

"Don't," a voice commanded. "Don't, Escobar."

Priya stood in shadow at the end of the lab, frozen. Someone stood behind her. One arm was wrapped around Priya's upper chest. The other pressed a slender knife against the handler's throat.

I froze, my hand halfway to my pocket. The figure urged Priya to take a step forward. He came out of the shadow, the broken lenses of his glasses catching the light of an electric lantern. Behind the frames, Miguel Garcia stared at me.

"Let's all be very, very calm," he said. "And let's discuss these parasites of yours."

22

Time seemed to slow down. I was aware of Su-jin and Dr Russell and the scientists behind me, but they seemed far away.

Garcia kept his eyes fixed on me. His face was blotched with purple bruises, dried blood still smeared across his upper lip. He had two shiners from the beating I'd given him. He must've put his nose back in place, but it was swollen and angry where I'd broken it. His forehead and cheeks gleamed with sweat.

"Hands behind your head, Escobar," he said. There was none of the manic, alien snarling coming from him now. This was the real Garcia, not Tempest speaking through him. I wasn't sure I liked him any better this way.

I hesitated, then slowly raised my arms and wrapped them around the back of my neck. Even if I could get to my gun without him opening up Priya's throat, I wasn't a good enough shot to hit him with Priya in between us. Not with the way my hands were shaking.

I wanted to say something, something sharp and scathing that would at least let me pretend I had control of the situation. But my throat had closed up and I couldn't think. I didn't trust Priya, but I had to admit I'd developed a grudging respect for her. However temporary our alliance, she'd saved us at Yllia's pit. I couldn't do it. I couldn't risk her.

"Good," Garcia said. "Okay." He was nervous. That made me nervous. I would've preferred him to have steady hands with that knife against Priya's throat. His gaze moved away from me. "Dr Russell. I thought our warning would have been enough. We're disappointed to see you here."

Moving my head as little as possible, I glanced back at Dr Russell. The whites of her eyes matched the paleness of her skin. She stood frozen, staring straight ahead.

"Come here, Doctor," Garcia said. He nodded at the floor in front of him. "Stand over there."

Dr Russell walked mechanically forward. As she passed, I opened my mouth to speak. But nothing came out. She moved forward until she was a few feet in front of Priya and Garcia.

"Stop," Garcia said. "There's good. That's them there, isn't it?" He nodded at her hands. "The parasites."

She looked down at the vial as if she was seeing it for the first time.

"There's a bottle over there," Garcia said. "H-two-S-O-four. That's sulfuric acid, right?"

She nodded.

"Pour the parasites in there."

Dr Russell's back went stiff and she shook her head.

Garcia's grip tightened on Priya. "Do it! You have to do it."

I finally found my voice. "Don't. Catherine, you can't."

"Shut up, Escobar," Garcia snarled. "Just shut the fuck up. Do it, Doctor." He lowered his voice. "You know what will happen if you don't."

Dr Russell stared at Garcia. "No. You can't."

He took a step back and to the side, dragging Priya with him. Priya's eyes were wide. She looked to me, but I had nothing to offer. As Garcia turned, he revealed a small backpack on his back.

"Do you see that in the side pocket?" he said.

"A phone." Dr Russell's voice was meek.

"A satellite phone," Garcia corrected her. "It has a wireless relay with a transmitter aboveground. Take it."

"No." She shook her head.

"Take it!"

Trembling, she reached out and took the phone from the backpack's pocket.

"There's a call on hold," he said. "Maybe your family can make you see reason."

"Please," she said. "Don't do this."

"Answer the phone."

She turned, glanced at me. Then she pressed a button on the phone and held it to her ear. "Hello?"

The lab was quiet enough that I could hear the murmur of a voice coming through the phone. I think it said, "Honey."

Then a gunshot cracked on the other end of the line. Dr Russell screamed and dropped the phone. She backed away, staring at the phone on the floor as if it was a rattlesnake. "No."

"That was your husband," Garcia said. His eyes were wide, mad. "You understand now? You understand how serious we are?"

Dr Russell's free hand was in her hair, rubbing her face. She was hyperventilating.

"You still have three children, Doctor," Garcia said. "Do you want them to be next? Do you?"

She shook her head back and forth. "Oh God. Oh God. No."

"Then take the acid and pour in the parasites."

Her spine went limp. She'd been broken. She reached for the bottle of acid on the shelf above one of the lab benches.

I put my arms down and dug my hand in my pocket. Garcia's attention was focussed on Dr Russell. By the time he snarled a warning, I'd already drawn the gun.

I aimed down the sights at Dr Russell. "Don't. Don't move, Catherine. I can't let you do that. I can't. I'm sorry."

Priya cried out. Out of the corner of my eye I could see a line of blood trickling down her throat where Garcia had dug the knife in.

"Put the gun down, Escobar!" Garcia yelled. "Put it down! Shoot her and I'll kill Dasari."

I blinked the sweat out of my eyes. Blood rushed in my ears. "I can't. This is all we have. We have to kill Tempest. We have to. You know that, Catherine."

"He has my family!" she screamed. "My family, you understand? My husband—" She cut off with a choking sound and buried her face in her hands.

I tried to keep my hands steady, but they wouldn't stop

shaking. It wasn't about us, or Dr Russell's family. We had a job to do. We had to kill him. He couldn't get away with this. He couldn't live. I wouldn't allow it.

"It's over, Escobar," Garcia said. "Put it down."

"Why?" I said. "Why the hell should I? If we don't kill him we're all dead. Don't you understand that, you crazy bastard? Can't you see what you've done? You freed him. Is this what the MPF wants? Do they want to see the world destroyed? Why would you do this?"

"I want to live," Garcia said. "I don't have a choice."

"What are you talking about? You did all of this."

"It wasn't me," he said. "I did what I had to do to survive. It was him. He made me."

Him. Even as he said it, I knew who he meant. And another chunk of the puzzle fell into place.

I licked my lips and lowered the gun a few inches. "Miguel. Let's talk about this. How long has Tempest been threatening you?"

"The time for talking is over. If I don't call off my man in the next two minutes, Dr Russell's oldest child will die. Maxie, isn't it?"

Dr Russell's gaze swung wildly from me to the bottle of sulfuric acid. I steadied my aim on her and forced calm into my voice. "It's all right, Miguel. Just calm down. I know you weren't to blame for this. Tempest manipulated you into it all, didn't he? We can make him pay for what he did to you, what he did to all of us. We can end this. You don't have to be afraid."

His mouth split in a black smile. "You have no idea. None." He drew the blade slowly across Priya's throat, just

enough to leave a thin scratch. She grimaced. The bruises
on my own neck started itching. "Put the gun down."

"I can't. Miguel, listen, we can—"

He snarled and turned his attention back to Dr Russell.
"One minute left until little Maxie's brains are on the wall,
Doctor. Do it now!"

"I will shoot you dead, Catherine," I said. "So help me
God, I'll do it."

She looked at me through wet, hollow eyes. And I knew
I'd lost. She picked up the bottle of acid and took out the
stopper.

I moved my finger to the trigger, began to squeeze.
Black dots appeared in my vision. I was holding my breath.
My collar tightened around my neck.

Dr Russell opened the vial. The incident at the hospital flashed in my mind. My finger pulling the trigger, the
thug's choked scream as I blew his knee apart. I couldn't
breathe.

I had to do it. I had to do it to save us.

Dr Russell looked at me. "I'm sorry," she said.

She upended the vial into the acid.

My arms dropped limply to my side, the gun dangling
from my fingers. I couldn't do it.

A thin layer of bubbles appeared on the surface of the
fluid, vapour rising off. I could smell the sharp scent. Then
the acid settled, and it was over.

Tempest stomped overhead. He knew. The bastard
knew. He'd won. Serraton had destroyed Yllia's body.
Those parasites were all we had left.

The tension drained out of Garcia's face. He gave a

loose smile, but kept the blade on Priya's throat. "Good. Hand me the phone."

Dr Russell, still shaking, put the bottle of acid down on the bench next to Garcia, picked up the phone, and held it out. Garcia grabbed it with the arm across Priya's chest and awkwardly pressed a couple of buttons.

"Call it off," he said into the phone. He hung up and looked at Dr Russell. "Put it back in my backpack."

She took the phone and he turned to give her access to the pack. Woodenly, she slipped it back into the pocket.

Garcia spun and plunged the knife into Dr Russell's upper thigh.

She didn't scream, not right away. She just stared down at her leg as Garcia jerked the knife back out. Blood began to bubble out of the hole in her trousers. I stood, frozen, watching it happen. We all did.

Garcia tugged Priya back and slashed at Dr Russell's face. The biologist cried out and jumped back instinctively. As her wounded leg touched the ground, it gave. She stumbled back and fell. Only then did she start to scream.

The sound of her pain jerked me from my stupor. I took a step forward. Out of the corner of my eye I could see Su-jin moving with me.

At the same moment, Garcia spun back, keeping Priya off balance. He grabbed the bottle of acid and hurled it towards us. The glass shattered on the linoleum, spilling the pungent fluid across the floor.

Dr Russell shuffled away from the growing pool, even as blood trickled from between her fingers. Su-jin and I backed away as glass and acid flowed towards us. The pool was too wide to jump. And in that moment's hesitation, Garcia brought the knife back to Priya's throat and dragged her out of the lab with him.

The acidic vapour burned my eyes and nostrils as I backed up. I didn't know how strong the acid was, whether it would eat right through my shoes. But Garcia was getting away with Priya.

One of the other biologists was faster thinking than me. He rushed forward, arm across his mouth and nose, and upended a bottle of thick white powder onto the acid flowing towards us. The powder began to soak up the acid. Another scientist dug in a cupboard and came out thrusting masks and goggles into our hands. I put my gun away, then pulled on the mask and goggles and heaved myself up onto a lab bench, climbing over it to reach Dr Russell.

"Up you get." I dropped down onto a clean bit of floor, stuck my hands under her armpits, and pulled her up onto the bench. She cried out in pain as I moved her. Her eyes were red and watering.

The scientist handing out the protective gear climbed over the bench beside me and tossed me another mask and goggles. I put them on Dr Russell and held her still.

"Did you get any on you?" I said. "Catherine, look at me."

Her lips were peeled back in a grimace. "No. I don't think so. Jesus."

The biologists helped me lower her to the floor. Su-jin appeared alongside with a first aid kit she'd found. She pulled back Dr Russell's hands and tore her trousers open around the knife cut to better examine the wound.

"I think it is not arterial," Su-jin said.

"Have you got this?" I asked.

She glanced at me from behind her goggles and nodded.

I stood up, pointing my finger at the small group. "None of you go too far."

I didn't wait for an answer. I drew my revolver again, darted across the powder soaking up the acid, and ran for the stairs.

As soon as I was clear of the fumes I pulled off the mask and goggles. My feet pounded on the stairs as I ran in near total darkness.

I burst out of the stairwell and looked back and forth. I was momentarily disoriented. Rain hit me, trickling down through the demolished floors of Bio Division. I looked up.

Tempest was stomping away, his twelve legs carrying him quickly across the ruins. I swear to God, he was strutting.

"Hey!" I screamed. "Hey! Fuck you, you hear me? Fuck you!"

The monster continued on his path through the city. I don't think he even heard me.

I gritted my teeth and clenched my fist. I spun in place. Garcia. I couldn't kill Tempest, but I could kill Garcia. I just had to find him.

I clambered through the rubble, out to the street. Empty. I went around the other side of the building. No one there. Nothing but rain and smoke and the stench of death.

He was gone.

23

I slouched back into the lab, picking up my mask and goggles on the way. One of the scientists was sweeping the swollen powder from the spill area. The rest of the group had gathered at the far end of the lab, away from the fumes. Su-jin was putting the finishing touches on a bandage wrapped around Dr Russell's thigh wound. The biologist was looking a little pale, but she was alert. She glanced at me as I came in, then looked away, eyes downcast.

I couldn't find it in myself to be angry at her. I hadn't been able to shoot her, and I didn't even care about her all that much. How could I expect her to sacrifice the rest of her family?

Su-jin glanced up and gave me a questioning look. I shook my head once. She got the picture. We were screwed.

None of the other scientists met my eye. I could tell they were scared of me. Suited me fine. I wasn't in much of a talking mood anyway.

When Su-jin finished bandaging Dr Russell, she came over and leaned beside me on a lab bench. The sling on her arm was now stained with the biologist's blood.

"He got away," I said quietly, so only Su-jin would hear.

"He must've had a car to get Dasari out of the area so fast."

"We can find him," Su-jin said.

I shook my head. "Why bother?"

"He had a reason for taking the handler. We need to understand why—"

"Jesus," I said. "Drop it, will you? It's done. Don't you see?" I waved my hand at the patch of acid-soaked powder in the corner. "That was all we had. You understand that? We have nothing that will kill Tempest now. The war is going to begin again. And we already lost it. Right here, in this room."

"You are a soldier then?"

"What?" Sometimes Su-jin's English was a bit off.

"Are you a soldier?"

"Of course I'm not."

"Then why do you care about war? War is not your business."

I sighed. "Jesus. Let it go, Su-jin." I dug the pack of smokes out of my pocket and put one between my lips.

Su-jin grabbed it out of my mouth and tossed it into the corner.

I slammed my fist down. "Goddamn it. What? What do you want from me?"

"I want you to do your job, detective."

I tilted my head back and silently asked God to strike me down and save me from this bullshit. "You're going to give me the same speech I gave Lindsey, is that it? Guess what, Su-jin? Lindsey fucked off. You know why?" I tapped the side of her skull. "Because she's the only one of us that has any damn brains."

Su-jin's good arm darted up and snatched my finger as I tapped her temple once more. She twisted and pulled it down, almost to the point of breaking. I grunted. Her face remained calm, but her voice took on a metallic edge.

"You are a pathetic man," she said. "A poser. You care for yourself, for glory, for congratulations. I have always disliked you." She released my finger. "But today you showed one aspect of yourself I can respect. Tempest killed our people. Good people, good detectives. Do you know what happens when a police detective is killed in the line of duty? Every police officer in the city will help hunt down the person responsible. They do not stop until they find that person. That person will learn what it means to kill a policeman. Tempest needs to learn what happens when he kills our people. The other Maydays, they are nothing. We break Tempest, they will fall."

I stared at her a few moments. She'd just spoken more words to me in the last minute than I got in a typical month. And each one was a perfectly aimed punch in the gut.

"I'm a mess, Su-jin. I've nearly died too many times today. I'm not the man to do this."

"You are nobody," she said. "You do not matter. How can any of us matter when we face something like this? Your fears, your morals, none of it is important. It only matters that we do our jobs. We must finish what we have started."

"How?" I raised my hands. "Tell me how, tell me what to do, and I'll do it."

"Why do you not listen? A soldier says: 'Tell me what

to do.' A detective finds the answer himself. Whatever else you are, you are a detective. So am I."

"What else is there to find out? We know Tempest used Garcia to threaten Dr Russell and get access to the parasites. Dasari says she killed Yllia, but I don't believe it. It had to be Garcia. He killed Yllia to free the other Maydays. The parasites were the one advantage we had. No more."

"There are loose ends," Su-jin said.

"There's always loose ends. Sometimes some bits of a case just don't make sense."

"Why did Garcia take Dasari?"

"Jesus, how should I know? Did you see the guy? He was three smokes short of a full pack. She was probably just a hostage to him."

Su-jin shook her head. "I think he needs her for something. Or Tempest does."

"Like what?"

"Information, perhaps."

"She doesn't know jack. No more than any of us. Certainly no more than Garcia and Tempest. They've been playing us from the start. We never had a chance. Dasari was always a tool. She was a tool for Volkov and she was a tool for me. And if by some twist of fate she was telling the truth, she was a tool for Yllia. She was Yllia's noose."

"So perhaps she is a tool for Tempest," Su-jin said.

"What kind of tool? She's only ever been a handler. She told me that herself. What use would Tempest have for a handler? It's not like she has any connection to the other Maydays. She was groomed specifically for Yllia. And Yllia is dead."

Something sparked in my brain, two ideas connecting. Yes, Yllia was dead. But....

I glanced at Dr Russell on the floor. The idea grew. I turned it this way and that in my head, testing it for holes.

"What is it?" Su-jin said.

I rubbed my face, feeling the scratch of my beard on my palm. "If Yllia killed herself like Dasari said she did, then that wasn't part of Tempest's plan. He didn't predict it. He seems to have a certain amount of control over the other Maydays, right? But Yllia, she was unpredictable. Maybe her suicide wasn't supposed to happen. If I hadn't gone to his pit and antagonised him, it might have taken him weeks to break impulse control, if he could do it at all. Volkov might have figured out a way to patch the holes by then. Maybe he wants to make sure impulse control can't be re-established. Maybe Priya's the key."

"How?"

"There's still one Mayday that's not free." I looked at Dr Russell through the small crowd gathered around her.

"The infant," Su-jin said.

I nodded. "We still hold it. If I'm right, that's where Garcia will be going. To retrieve the infant. The parasites have been removed. It only needs to be released from stasis."

"It is Yllia's infant. Tempest will not care about it."

"No. That's *exactly* why he'll care about it. Yllia's psychic powers were the key to the Maydays' capture. If the infant shares some of the mother's powers, maybe with Priya's help we can bring it under our control. Maybe we can use it against him."

Su-jin's eyes narrowed and a small, vicious smile touched her lips. "Good work, detective."

I grinned and touched her good shoulder. "Can I count on your help?"

"As I said, we must finish the job we started. We have a lesson to teach Tempest."

I nodded, then turned and walked towards the small crowd. The scientists parted until I stood over Dr Russell.

"I take it you told Garcia everything you knew about the parasite, the infant, all of that," I said to her.

She looked away. "Essentially."

"So he knows where the infant is now?"

"Well, not quite."

I raised my eyebrows.

"I had it moved," she said. "As soon as Yllia's body was found. He believes it is still in the chamber on the northeast coast. An old submarine base used by the Alliance during the war."

"So where is it really?"

"Below us. In this building."

I glanced at Su-jin. "This is going to be the first place they come looking once they realise it's not where they think it is."

Su-jin nodded her agreement.

"Can we move it?" I asked Dr Russell.

"It will fit in the car."

I pressed the stolen car keys into Su-jin's hand. "Get the geeks to help you. Get it away from here. Tempest's pit. Take it there. Son of a bitch won't look there. He probably never wants to see the place again."

"What will you do?"

"I'm going to intercept Garcia. We can't let him keep his hands on Dasari."

Su-jin nodded. "She would be better dead than in their hands."

I made no comment on that.

"You should not try to do this alone," she said.

"I know. I'm going to make a call. It's a long shot, but…." I shrugged.

"Very well. Good hunting," she said.

I turned my back and made for the door.

"Escobar," Dr Russell called.

I turned and found her sitting up. Her eyes were wet but her face was hard.

"If you find Garcia," she said, "kill him. Kill that bastard."

I nodded and left without another word.

I left my stolen car for the others and found another abandoned car three blocks away. There was a crack that ran the whole length of the windscreen, but I figured I couldn't be picky.

Tempest's shadow loomed through the smoke and dust, away to the north-east, near the shipping port. He made a pretty good landmark. I started the car and headed towards him. As I drove, I pulled out the walkie-talkie and held it on top of the steering wheel. I steeled myself, adjusted the frequency, and pressed the transmit button. The static cut out, leaving a quiet hiss in place.

"Lindsey, it's Escobar. I hope you're out there. If you're

there, pick up."

I released the button and waited. Only static hissed back at me.

"All right," I said into the walkie. "Just listen then. I don't think you're dead. And I don't think you left the island. So just listen."

I edged the car between a crushed bus and the fallen wall of a small office block. The Maydays had really done a number on this part of town.

"I screwed up," I said. "I know that. All this, this destruction, I'm responsible. I thought I could handle it. I've done terrible things today. Things I can't...." I closed my eyes for a moment and shook my head. "It doesn't matter. I can't make it right. But I can finish it. Su-jin helped me see that. There's a chance, Lindsey. A chance for us to spit in Tempest's eye. One last kick in the balls. But I need your help. Please."

Silence. I waited a minute, two. All the while driving closer to Tempest as he stalked back and forth through the smoke. A devil walking the Earth. A monster that should've died four billion years ago. A colossal son of a bitch.

"All right," I said. "Maybe you're not interested in revenge. But I know you've got people you care about. People you want to protect. Your girlfriend, right? I don't think I ever asked her name. And I'm not going to now. You know why? Because I'm an arsehole. I'm not a good man. I'm not a nice man. I'm a thug, a snoop, a manipulative bastard. I'm a coward. So to hell with me. Don't help me. Help your girlfriend. Help the people still remaining. I'm not your boss anymore. We don't have to be friends. But we have to do our jobs. That's still important. Isn't it?"

The crackle of static returned. I waited. Tempest stomped northward. I knew Garcia would be close by. They'd be nearly at the old sub base. If they didn't find the infant, what would they do? Would they risk keeping Priya alive?

The walkie stayed silent. I sighed and put it on the passenger seat. Okay. It looked like I was doing this myself. I didn't rate my chances. But my path was set now.

A beep cut through the walkie's static. A distant voice spoke.

"I found my girlfriend," Lindsey said. "She's okay. We had a cat as well. But he…."

I picked up the walkie. "Fuck Maydays."

"Yeah," she said. "Fuck 'em. What do you need?"

24

The gates at the shipping port were ripped off their rails. I drove over the cracked concrete, past a crane and between stacks of shipping containers. The light of my headlights glistened off the rough seas ahead. Flotsam was scattered amongst the waves, gleaming every time a new flash of lightning rolled across the sky. A freighter was tilted over to one side, its cargo tossing in the waves as the ship slowly sank. Closer in, oil spills burned with flame that the rain couldn't dampen.

I stopped the car and got out. A moment later, Lindsey stepped out of the shadow of a stack of containers. Together, we sat down on the hood of the car and watched the burning waves.

"One of the passenger ships got out," she said. "Then some of the freighters tried to load up with passengers and make it away. Grotesque intercepted them offshore. Just wrapped his tail around them and snapped them, one at a time, then swam around, swallowing survivors as they tried to swim back to shore. It was awful."

I nodded. "I take it no one else tried to sail a boat out."

"Some people scattered back into the city. Said they

were going to find places to wait it out until help came. The rest are all around the waterfront, hiding in the underground stations, waiting until they think it's safe. Every now and then, just when it looks like the coast might be clear, someone spots Grotesque's spines carving through the water. He wants us to know he's out there. He always was a sadistic bastard."

"Any idea where the other Maydays are?"

"Last I heard Nasir was on the East Island. Someone said he hit Psi Division."

I scratched my beard. "Maybe they were holding off until they knew Priya wasn't there. I saw a crushed SUV on the way here. It belonged to Grotesque's handler. I sent those handlers into the city, just to give me a distraction to get to Volkov. Now they're dead too. Another waste."

"Serraton was last seen leaving the island. Someone had a radio, it said an Alliance evacuation fleet was being sent from Japan. Serraton's probably gone to intercept it."

"Probably. I'd say we're alone out here."

"I'd say so," Lindsey said, her eyes fixed on the water.

I glanced to my right, squinting into the rain. Tempest waded through the water less than half a kilometre away, every movement of his legs sending waves crashing against the coast and the shipping ports. His claws cut lines through the sea. He was growing impatient. Funny, how I could tell that. I felt like I was getting to know him. An old friend.

"Garcia?" I asked.

"I saw him go in ten minutes ago," Lindsey said. "I didn't even know that old sub base existed. But it's not hard to find when you know where to look."

"You can handle your half?"

"My half's fine," she said. "You'll be the first to get killed if anything goes wrong."

"Don't remind me. I'll make us switch." I took my revolver out of my pocket, checked it was loaded. "Is your girlfriend somewhere safe?"

"She's looking after the Dasaris. She's quite taken with the boy. She always wanted kids."

"You didn't?"

"We'll see." She looked past me at Tempest. "He's moving. Are we done with all this sappy shit?"

I grinned. "Don't I even get a hug?"

She slid off the car bonnet and started walking away. "Don't fuck up, Boss."

"I told you," I said. "I'm not your boss anymore."

She slipped back into the darkness and disappeared. I sat there another few seconds, willing my heart to stop pounding. Then I gave up, tucked the gun back in my pocket, and walked over to the gantry crane.

The crane was still intact amongst the toppled containers. It was the sort of crane that ran on wheels to move containers around the port and onto the backs of trucks. All the taller cranes made for unloading ships were lying in crumpled heaps on the concrete or snapped off at the base and sunken beneath the waves. But this one would work fine.

I climbed the stairway to the top and stood alongside the driver's cab. I was close to the waterfront. The extra height gave me a good view of the wreckage on the sea. I spent a couple of seconds searching the waves for Grotesque's spines, but I didn't see him. I figured he'd be further west, patrolling the other end of the bay where most of the island's passenger ships launched from. Suited me fine. I could do without the interruption.

I turned back towards the east and slipped a cigarette between my lips. Tempest splashed through the water, forcing a wave before him. He snorted and flexed his claws. He hadn't seen me yet. He was distracted, waiting for Garcia to retrieve the infant. I wondered if he knew yet, if he suspected that the infant wasn't there. I smiled at the thought as I lit my smoke. Then, just as Tempest began to turn to pace away from me again, I pulled the revolver out of my pocket and fired it twice into the air.

The crack of the gunshot was swallowed by the wind and the sea. For a moment, I was afraid he hadn't heard it. Then he slowed, his muscles rippling. He turned towards me. I fired once more for good measure. His black eyes snapped towards the muzzle flash. I slipped the gun back in my pocket and waved.

Tempest let out a screeching growl and gnashed his jagged teeth. His eyes glanced down and to his left, where I knew the old submarine dock was hidden in a hollow in the coastline. Scaled lips pulled back in an alien snarl. He came for me.

I forced my feet to stay still, even though every fibre of my being told me to run. Tempest seemed to grow as he rushed towards me. The wave he pushed ahead of him splashed up onto the concrete of the pier and flooded the ground beneath me. The rumbling of his footsteps through the sea made the crane rattle. Another stack of containers crashed onto the pier behind me. Lightning flashed across the sky, but I was already in Tempest's shadow.

Tempest slammed his claws down. His left set pierced the concrete pier to my right. His other claws wrapped around one of the gantry crane's legs and squeezed. The crane let out a groan of tortured metal. Tempest brought his face down and breathed hot, putrid air across me. Thick saliva dripped from the ends of his uneven teeth, raining down on me. His tongue slipped out and tasted the air around me. I looked into his eyes and saw the rage there, the cruel intelligence.

It was the most terrifying thing I had ever experienced.

I painted a false grin to my face and plucked the cigarette from my mouth, moving slowly and carefully so as not to betray the pounding of my heart. I exhaled a thin stream of smoke in his general direction and raised my hands above my head.

"Ooga booga boo," I shouted, waving my hands in the air. He let out a low growl. I smiled and lowered my hands. "See, aren't we both such scary guys. You and I have a lot in common, you know that?"

He showed me his teeth. They were nice teeth, I'll give him that.

"Yeah," I said. "You understand me, don't you?" I took a slow drag of my cigarette. "Trouble is, I don't speak Mayday. Shame, really. Some say French is the language of love, but they've never heard your dulcet tones. Why don't you get your ol' pal Garcia up here and we'll have a chat. I've got some things I want to discuss."

Tempest slid his claws out of the concrete and brought them up. He pointed the tip of the middle one at me and moved it slowly towards my chest until I could see the individual drops of rain dripping off the serrated point. He could skewer me like a butterfly in an entomologist's display cabinet. I stood my ground.

"I wouldn't kill me if I were you," I said. "Seeing as I suspect Mr Garcia is having a little trouble locating the infant right now."

The claw stopped. Tempest's tongue rolled across the tips of his teeth. I smiled up into his black eyes.

"And don't go thinking you can use those little claws of yours to get the answer out of me. I clean forgot where it was taken. But don't worry. I can find out." I pulled the walkie-talkie from my pocket. "I've got people to keep track of these things for me. Though if I were to get startled, well, I might just end up dropping this…" I dangled the walkie over the end of the railing. "And then where would we be?" I raised my finger. "Oh yeah, one other thing. If I don't make a certain call in fifteen minutes, my people are going to bury that infant and let it suffocate. Guess where I got that idea?"

Tempest glared at me, sizing me off. He backed off a few inches.

"That's better. I'm guessing you have ways of communicating with Garcia. How about you get him up here?"

He did nothing, but I had to guess he'd be able to use the LIM to contact Garcia.

I nodded to myself. "I've been thinking about that name Dr Russell uses. The infant. Kind of cold, isn't it? I don't know what you call it. Little baby Mayday? You reckon it's a boy or a girl? Does it have a little Mayday penis?" I tilted my head to the side as if I could see between Tempest's legs. "You Maydays don't really have much in the way of genitalia, do you? Funny that. I'm so much smaller than you, but at least I've got a big swinging dick. Not like you. Poor little dickless Tempest." I stroked my beard. "That's another thing. How do you guys even have babies? I never noticed any of you getting frisky with each other since I've been here. I bet you do some sort of asexual reproduction, don't you? Tough break."

I took another drag and snapped my fingers.

"That's it, isn't it? That's why you're so mad. You can't get any pussy. It all makes sense now. This one time, I didn't get laid for five and a half months. Five and a half fucking months. Longest five and a half months of my life. Of course I was jerking it every day, sometimes twice, you know, but it's just not the same. I started going a bit stir crazy. Getting angry at people for no reason. I look back, and I'm ashamed of how rude I was to everyone. Then one day I convinced my secretary to come home with me and then…." I snapped my fingers again. "Back to normal. Just like that. I tell you, there's nothing in this world that makes you feel more alive than pussy."

I leaned closer to him and lowered my voice. "You know, I could help you out. I've got this system. Guaranteed to make any woman fall for you. You know, things to say to them that'll make their panties drop. I learned it from this book. I can't remember the name, but I know I've got a copy of it somewhere. Tell you what, you stop this whole mass destruction thing, and I'll lend you the book. No, wait, I'll do you one better. I'll buy you your own copy. You'll have so much pussy you won't know what to do with it. Shaved pussy, hairy pussy, young pussy, old pussy. Even surgically enhanced pussy—have you heard about that?" I shook my head. "Don't ask me how that works. You never know what they're going to come up with next, do you? Anyway, how's that sound? Do we have a deal?"

Tempest continued to stare at me in silence. Every long breath he let out burned away a few more of my nostril hairs. I held up my hands in mock surrender.

"All right, all right. I was just kidding. Let's be serious now. Look, this is my serious face. Here's the real deal. You and all your Mayday friends piss off to the deepest hole you can find and you stay there until the end of time. Either that, or we finish this little pissing contest, and when I win, you'll be my puppet. I will put you back under impulse control and make it my life's goal to ensure that you don't spend a single second without feeling the humiliation of knowing that I beat you. And when I die, my kid will spend his life torturing you. And when he dies, his kid will do the same. And on and on and on until the sun explodes and swallows this planet and takes you with it. How's that for a deal?"

Tempest's lips stretched into a grin. He leaned forward and gnashed his teeth in front of me.

I shrugged. "Suit yourself." Footsteps clanged on the stairs behind me. "Looks like the translator's arrived." I turned as Garcia reached the top of the stairs and stood facing me across the short gangway. "Mr Garcia. Thanks for coming on such short notice. Where's Dasari?"

"Somewhere safe," he said. He was panting a little bit—I guess he'd run here. Rain had plastered his hair to his forehead. I noticed he kept his eyes focussed on me, not looking at Tempest. And it wasn't like Tempest was easy to miss. "Where is the infant?"

"Relax, Miguel. There's no rush." I pulled the cigarette pack from my pocket and held it out. "Smoke?"

He didn't move.

I shrugged, slipped the pack back in my pocket. I dangled the walkie in my left hand, making it obvious that I'd toss it if he tried anything. He held his knife down by his side. He hadn't cleaned the blood off it yet. Sloppy.

"Okay," I said. "The way I see it, we've both got things the other wants." I turned to Tempest. "Isn't that right? I've got the infant. You've got Dasari. Maybe we can do a little trade."

"Why?" Garcia said. "We will find the infant eventually. We know it's on the island. We have all the time in the world."

"See, there's where you're wrong. As I was explaining to your boss, my people want to do some very cruel things to the infant. They're not very fond of Maydays, baby or not. Now, the parasites are gone, but I'm willing to bet that there are other ways we can kill such a small and vulnerable Mayday, especially one that is currently in stasis. Suffocation, for example."

"What makes you think we care about the infant?"

I jerked my thumb at Tempest. "How about the fact that this big bastard over here hasn't eaten me yet." I glanced at the Mayday. "Come on, you're not fooling anybody. So let's do a little horse trading."

Tempest growled. Garcia put his hand to his head like he was getting a migraine. "You cannot have Dasari."

"How come? One of you got a crush on her?"

"You cannot have her," Garcia said.

"All right, relax, pal. Jeez, you guys are real ballbusters. Why don't you give me your offer. What's the infant worth to you?"

Garcia and Tempest went quiet for a few seconds. I took a last couple of puffs on my smoke and stubbed it out on the railing.

"Tempest will allow you to live," Garcia said. "For now."

"That's it? That's your deal? I always intended to live." I turned to address Tempest. "I mean, I get it. You hate me *so much*. I remember your little speech. But give me a break."

"What do you suggest?" Garcia said.

I scratched my beard. "You let everyone on this island get off alive. Call off your little dog." I pointed into the sea. "The one swimming out there, knocking over boats. Let all us little humans get to the mainland and spread out. That's as low as I'll go."

Garcia narrowed his eyes at me. "You're not going to try to stop the Maydays from attacking other locations?"

"Why bother?" I shrugged. "I already tried it with the big guy and he didn't take. I'm not Alliance, I'm not some hero. I'm a company man. You agree to leave this company alone, you can have the infant."

"One day, Tempest will find you."

"Then good luck to him," I said. "I'm planning to go somewhere I'll never ever be found. This is a big planet. So what do you say? Do we have a deal?"

Garcia went silent once again, his eyes looking through me. I glanced over the edge of the gantry crane. Shadows moved across the pier.

I looked back as Garcia focussed his gaze on me once more. I couldn't read the expression on his face. He nodded once. "Very well. It's a deal."

I stuck out my hand at Tempest. "Shake on it." The Mayday just glared at me. "What? All right, fine." I withdrew my hand.

At the same time, the walkie bleeped in my other hand. I held up a finger.

"Excuse me," I said to Garcia and Tempest. I spoke into the walkie. "Yes?"

"I've got her," Lindsey said.

"Great."

Garcia gave me a confused look. I smiled at him.

"Deal's off," I said.

Then I pulled out my gun and shot the fucker in the head.

25

Garcia's head snapped back, a thin trail of blood spraying into the air. He toppled backwards, arm tangling in the crane's railing as he fell.

Tempest's claws jerked away and the Mayday screeched. The sound rattled my bones. Tempest's eyes closed and he stumbled back drunkenly. I guess that mental snapback Priya talked about went both ways.

I was already moving before Garcia was all the way down. I dashed for the stairs and hurried down them three at a time, my legs wobbling and my ears aching in response to Tempest's roar.

My shoes hit concrete and I ran for the container stacks. I was halfway there when Tempest stopped screaming and I felt his weight shift behind me. Another wave of water splashed across the pier, soaking my shoes. I risked a glance back. He was mounting the pier. And his black eyes were fixed on me.

The sight of those eyes made my stomach turn cold. I was prey, pure and simple. I turned my eyes forward and willed my legs to run faster.

One of Tempest's feet hit the pier behind me. Concrete

crunched and a crack appeared to my left. I dodged to the right and made it between two stacks of containers.

Tempest screeched. I glanced back again as he swiped his claws. A stack of containers toppled behind me. Hollow clanging filled the air as the pile crashed into the concrete and sent the next row falling.

Something heavy slammed into my back. I went down hard, putting my arm out to break my fall. My open palm connected with the concrete. I felt a bone crack in my wrist. Sickening pain roared up my arm. My gun went skidding across the concrete, out of sight.

I bit my tongue to stifle a cry. *Move, damn it!* Clutching my broken wrist, I scrambled to my feet and kept moving.

I took a sharp left, pausing behind a fallen container, and peeked out. Tempest continued to stomp forwards. His head swept to the right, searching for me.

I took my chance and darted around the side of the container, doubling back. A leg passed above me and slammed down on the next container over. The container groaned as it was crushed beneath the Mayday's bulk. I kept going, sticking to the shadow. And then I was under him.

The view from beneath Tempest wasn't an improvement. All twelve legs moved with alien efficiency. I couldn't keep my eyes on all of them at once. If just one of them landed on me, I was done.

Tempest stopped. I did too. My arm throbbed so bad it was making me woozy. I was almost directly beneath the middle of his abdomen, legs all around me. His short tail swiped back and forth in front of me. His arms hung down at his side, claws opening and closing.

I held my breath as he turned towards the water. Maybe he was wondering if I'd tried to swim for it. He took a step forward, then changed his mind and started to turn back.

I took three quick steps and ducked inside a fallen container. Boxes of dried food had spilled out the opening. I stepped over them, trying not to cause a crunch, and pressed myself into the darkness.

Tempest's frustrated growls were punctuated by the thudding of footfalls as he moved. Out of the crack in the open container doors I could see a thick, scaled leg swing past, dripping rainwater across the pier.

A few seconds passed. I could hear Tempest moving about, but the echo inside the container made it difficult to tell exactly where the monster was. Part of me wanted to run, but that would've been suicide.

Tempest screeched somewhere outside. I put my good arm over my head, trying to cover my ears. When the screeching stopped, a crackling sound followed. An orange glow reflected off the rain-slicked concrete outside. Fire. Tempest was trying to flush me out. But his first gout of flame had been directed elsewhere. I took a breath and risked a glance out of the container.

Tempest was further down the pier, bathing it with fire. He was facing away from me. This was my chance. I waited until he reared back to breathe another cone of fire onto the pier, then I ducked out of the container and ran for the road.

I paused beside a truck cab, checked I was clear, then ran the rest of the way. Every step sent another jolt of pain up my arm. When I hit the cover of a port warehouse, I caught my breath, put my good hand against the wall, and retched. Acid stung my throat and prickled the backs of my eyes. The fire in my wrist burned on. I couldn't get the sight of Garcia out of my head, the red blossom appearing in the centre of his face, tearing his nose apart and driving into his brain. He wasn't the first person I'd killed today. I didn't regret it. But that didn't stop the darkness from churning in my stomach.

When the nausea passed, I stood up and took a few more breaths. I took out the walkie and spoke into it. "Lindsey, I'm clear for now. Where are you?"

"Seafood Heaven."

"Roger. Pick me up some prawns. I'm starving."

I peeked out and made sure Tempest wasn't looking my way. Satisfied, I stepped out of the shadows and jogged back across the street and down a couple of alleys.

Seafood Heaven used to be a waterfront restaurant popular with the younger crowd on the island. It was looking a little worse for wear now, though. The car sat in the car park, headlights off. I checked for Tempest once more, then crossed the car park and got into the passenger seat.

"You all right?" Lindsey asked from behind the wheel.

"No," I said. "I'm pretty far from all right." I held my wrist tight against my body, unwilling to look at it too closely.

Lindsey gave it a look. "Is it broken?"

"Of course it is," I said.

I twisted to face the back seat. Priya sat there, eyes closed. I couldn't tell if she was dozing, unconscious, or just resting her eyes. She bore a couple of new bruises on her arm and that nasty-looking scratch on her neck, but other than that she didn't seem too badly injured. I sat back as Lindsey pulled slowly out of the car park.

"Any trouble getting her out?" I asked.

Lindsey shook her head. "She was tied up in a locked bathroom in the base."

Priya stirred in the back seat. "What happened to Garcia?" she said.

I turned around again to address her. "Dead."

Priya nodded.

"Are you okay?" I asked.

"I'm fine."

"Did Garcia say anything? Did he say what he wanted with you?"

"He said he was sorry that he had to do this."

"What an arsehole," I said.

"Where are we going?"

"To introduce you to a new friend."

While Lindsey drove, I fashioned myself a sling from an old t-shirt the car's previous owner had left in a gym bag in the back seat. I can't say it helped much, but Lindsey's driving wasn't doing me any favours.

We paused when we came to the bridge. If we were going to get ambushed on the way back to Tempest's pit, this would be where a Mayday would hit us. After a few minutes watching from beneath the shadow of a seaside tree, we decided to risk it. We could hear Nasir stomping around the East Island somewhere, and Tempest was just visible in the firelight behind us, combing through the wreckage of the West Island. He was agitated, that I could tell. Without Garcia, his link to us was severed. He was too big to search for the infant himself with any efficiency. We had him stumped.

Lindsey started the car again and we drove across the bridge, headlights off. We all kept our eyes glued to the water, expecting to see Grotesque or Serraton rise out of the waves, but we made it to the other side unhindered. Relieved, we continued on to Tempest's pit.

A small group of people were gathered in the darkness of the car park at the pit, near the destroyed remains of the gate. We pulled up nearby and got out. No lights here, nothing but the lightning. The group was bigger than I expected. It wasn't until I got closer and my eyes adjusted to the dark that I saw why.

Su-jin was here, along with a biologist who was offering a shoulder to the wounded Dr Russell. But two extra faces had joined the group. One I recognised instantly. The white kid who was Nasir's handler. His eyes were less playful than they had been earlier in the evening. He had the same look of suppressed pain that Priya had borne when I first met her, the pain of breaking impulse control. I gave the kid a nod.

"I thought you were dead," I said.

"I could say the same about you."

I looked at the other man present, a dark-skinned, middle-aged man whose ethnicity I couldn't place. It took me a moment before I recognised him from my visit to Psi Division.

"You're another handler?" I asked.

The man nodded. "I used to control Serraton."

"You're a bit late to the party," I said. I glanced at Su-jin. "How'd we pick up these strays?"

"We drove past Psi Division on the way here," Su-jin said. "It was destroyed, as we suspected, but these two were alive and hiding. They waved us down and asked to come with us."

"Might as well die together, I guess."

Priya exchanged greetings with her colleagues while I looked over my shoulder at the forest. Nasir's footsteps made the ground vibrate with every step. But he was a ways away. He didn't know where we were. Not yet, anyway. But we had to get on with it.

"Did you get the infant out?" I asked.

Su-jin nodded and led me to the back of a station wagon. Black rubbish bags had been taped in place over the rear windows, blocking the interior from view. Su-jin slid a key into the boot and opened the back of the station wagon.

I don't know what I was expecting. Something bigger, maybe, like an overgrown insect large enough to chew someone's head off. What I got was a naked grey slug about the size of a Dachshund. Two big black eyes stared out one end, just above a large proboscis like you see on close-up images of fly mouths. The rest of its body was segmented into six sections, growing smaller along the infant's length. It had no legs, no arms, no tail, no nothing. It was just a smaller, slimier Jabba the Hutt.

"Ugly son of a bitch, isn't it?" I said to no one in particular.

Priya came alongside me and quietly observed it. The infant was contained in a perspex container about the size of a large fish tank. It was completely submerged in a viscous, greyish-green fluid contained within some kind of translucent pouch. An old laptop was connected to the tank via a jerry-rigged interface. Behind the tank, a couple of large batteries were hooked up to keep the electronics working.

"Is it still alive?" Priya asked.

Dr Russell hobbled over to us and sat down on the lip of the station wagon's boot to examine the laptop's display. "All vitals remain unchanged. It doesn't seem to have been affected by being moved around."

"And the parasites are definitely gone?" I said.

Dr Russell nodded. "The infected area was removed surgically months ago. The parasites had walled themselves off in a section of the infant's brain while they replicated, presumably to avoid any attack by the host's immune system. We can drain the fluid. It should release the infant from stasis."

I glanced at Priya. She was still staring at the creature, her expression unreadable.

"What do you think?" I said.

"I don't know," Priya said. "I was never trained for anything like this. My LIM probably won't—"

"Priya. Shut up. We all know this is a long shot. This is the beginning and end of my brilliant plan to save us all and stop that bastard out there. I'm asking if you can try."

She nodded. "I can try."

I patted her shoulder and turned to Dr Russell. "You

heard her. Time's a-wastin'. Wake it up."

"You understand that we know very little about this thing?" Dr Russell said. "We don't know if it's dangerous. As far as we know it bears no microorganisms that may be harmful to humans. We can't be sure, though. We never found obvious poison glands or any other defence mechanisms, but most of its anatomy and physiology is still a mystery to us. "

I turned around and addressed Su-jin and the others. "You all hear that? Anyone who's scared, feel free to get lost."

There was silence for a moment. Then Nasir's handler spoke up. "Where the hell else are we supposed to go?"

"Exactly," I said. I looked to Dr Russell. "Do it."

26

The process took ten minutes. We all stood around and watched the infant as the tank hummed. A thin tube siphoned the viscous liquid out of the pouch onto the broken concrete. I could feel the heat coming off the tank. In the distance, I thought I could hear Nasir stomping slowly closer. Every now and then, Tempest roared to the sky. Someone had left the car radio on, the only sound a slow crackle. I thought I might hear something, some message, maybe word from the Alliance fleet. But we were alone out here in the middle of the sea. Serraton and Grotesque would see to that.

Rain and wind lashed us. We huddled together for warmth, passing around a half-stale packet of biscuits someone found in a car. No one spoke. I was so tired I could fall asleep on my feet. I just might have if it hadn't been for the throbbing pain in my broken arm. I found some Panadol in the glove box of my stolen car. It didn't help much.

The last of the fluid drained from the tank. Nothing happened. I lit up a couple of smokes and gave one to Priya. We smoked them to the butt and I reached into the packet to get another couple.

Then the infant twitched.

We all froze. The movement had been so small I don't think anyone was too sure they'd even seen it. I returned the cigarette pack to my pocket and stared at the creature so hard I should've been able to see through it.

A ripple shuddered down the creature's body. No doubt about it this time. One by one, the segments of the infant's body expanded and contracted. It twisted slowly around. And it looked at us.

My good hand edged towards my pocket, then I remembered I'd lost my gun running from Tempest. Not that I thought the thing was actually dangerous, or even particularly scary. But it was weird. I didn't like weird.

Dr Russell unsealed the front of the tank and pulled it open. The infant just stared. It made a slight hissing sound as it breathed, more like an asthmatic kid than a threatened snake. Its proboscis twitched from side to side as it tasted the air.

"Is it just me, or does it look a bit dopey?" I whispered. I don't know why I was whispering. I guess I didn't want to spook the damn thing.

Dr Russell studied the creature for a few moments, then checked the laptop's readout. "As far as I can tell it doesn't seem to be in any distress. Not that I really know what I'm looking at. This is the first time we've brought it out of stasis."

"That makes this an auspicious moment. Anyone want to make a speech? Introduce ourselves? Give it a bottle of wine and a bouquet of flowers? No?" I glanced at Priya.

"Then I guess it's your move."

Priya nodded, inhaled, and stepped forward. She took a moment to free her damp hair and pull it back into a tighter ponytail. I didn't think she had any more of an idea what she was supposed to do than I did.

She put out a hand and reached for the creature. The infant just watched, unmoving. Its smooth skin was still greasy with the fluid that'd drained from the tank. The idea of touching the thing made me squeamish. But Priya rested her hand on the back of its slug-like body. Its flesh rippled, but it didn't move. I noticed now it had a strange smell to it, somehow fishy and earthy at the same time.

I waited. A few seconds passed while Priya stood there, eyes closed. I didn't know what would come from this. All I knew was that Tempest wanted to use Priya and the infant. And if he wanted it, I wanted it too.

Priya's forehead creased as she screwed her eyes shut even tighter. She was in pain, that much was obvious. But I didn't want to say anything in case I distracted her.

"Something's wrong," she said.

"The LIM?" Dr Russell said.

Priya gave a short shake of her head. "The LIM's working. Barely. I can make the connection. Its mind is similar enough to Yllia's. Not the same. There's something else here as well. But there's a space. Emptiness. The infant's mind is incomplete. There's nothing for me to grab hold of."

"It could be the damage done by the parasites," Dr Russell said. "We saw significant atrophy in part of the brain. Yllia mustn't have known the extent of it."

"So it's retarded," I said. "Great. Fantastic. Where does that leave us?"

Priya's face tightened, creases forming on her forehead. "I can feel that it's alive. Some of its responses are there, some of its instincts. But there's no higher thoughts, no curiosity, no complex emotion. No personality."

"We don't need to know if it's marriage material," I said. "Can you control it? Can we use it?"

Priya was quiet for a few moments. Then she slowly shook her head. "No."

I turned away and threw a kick at the door of the nearest car. "Fuck. Fucking hell." I ran my good hand across my cheeks. The others all seemed to slump, as if they'd all just realised how tired they were.

That was it. We were done. I looked to Su-jin. She met my eyes, her face holding the same determined expression she'd kept up the whole night. But the strength had gone out of her spine. She suddenly looked every one of her years, with a few more piled on top.

Lindsey turned away from the group and headed back towards the car.

"Hey," I said. "Fischer. Where do you think you're going?" I ran after her.

"Back to my girlfriend. I should've stayed with her."

"Like hell you are. Get back here. Fischer, I said get back here." I grabbed her arm.

She turned, grabbed me by the neck, and threw me up against the side of the car. Pain roared through my broken wrist. Her eyes were bloodshot and burning. She was stronger than I expected. Her nostrils flared as she stared me down.

Priya called out, breaking the staring contest. "Can you people keep it down? I'm trying to concentrate. I think I've got something."

Lindsey's hand loosened on my neck. I took the chance to throw her off me and stalk back towards the station wagon. "What?"

"I can't control the infant, not like I could control Yllia. But it shares traits with Yllia. I can feel the latent psychic power there. The problem is that it's unfocussed. I think I can boost it, like I did at Yllia's body."

"All right," I said. "What does that get us?"

"I may be able to get the background level of psychic activity on the island up to the level it was when Yllia was alive. It may be enough to resonate with the LIMs of the remaining handlers."

I took a second to make sure she was saying what I thought she was saying. My heart started hammering. "You mean we'll be able to get the Maydays back under impulse control."

"I think so. Maybe. But both Tempest's and Grotesque's handlers are dead."

I turned to Dr Russell. "Can you make new LIMs? Make some more people handlers?"

She chewed her lip. "Perhaps. But it will take a few months. We lost so many of our records when the Bio and Psi Divisions were destroyed. I can probably work with a team to develop new LIMs from first principles, but Volkov was always the expert."

"But we can do it," I said. "We can get Nasir and

Serraton under control, at least." I turned to the two remaining handlers. "Right?"

"We can give it a shot, I guess," Nasir's handler said.

"I don't know how stable the control will be," Priya said. "The infant's not in good shape."

Lindsey had wandered back over to the group, and now she spoke up. "Before we do this, what are the risks?"

"I don't know," Priya said. "It may be dangerous for me and the other handlers. I've never dealt with something like this before. Other than that, it's too hard to tell. We don't know exactly what Tempest had in mind for the infant. It's possible there will be effects we haven't accounted for."

"We can't dwell on the maybes," I said. "We all know we're out of time. One of them will find us soon, and then we're all dead. Help's not coming, not while the Maydays are free. I say we do this. Get back control of Nasir and Serraton. Use them to keep Tempest and Grotesque distracted. Maybe buy us enough time to get an evacuation fleet here. Get the survivors off the island." I met Lindsey's eyes. "Get the people we care about out of here. Then we let the good doctor here get to work. In six months all four of these big bastards will be back under our thumbs. And we can get on with getting therapy for all this bullshit. All right?"

Everyone looked at each other or at the ground, but no one said anything.

"Okay, how about this," I said. "Does anyone have a better plan? Anyone? Anyone at all?"

I looked at Lindsey. She shook her head slowly. The two

handlers looked resigned to it. I nodded and turned back to the car, back to Priya and Dr Russell.

I lowered my voice. "As for the three of us, we don't really have much choice, do we? You were right, Priya, what you said at Yllia's pit. We all fucked up. We're each a little bit responsible for what happened here. We have to do this. Agreed?"

Priya nodded, her eyes still closed. With a slight grimace of pain, Dr Russell pushed herself up, leaning on the station wagon for support. "Can I talk to you a second?"

I offered her my shoulder and we moved around to the front of the station wagon, just far enough that if we kept our voices down we wouldn't be heard. "I heard what happened with Garcia," she said. "You shot him."

I said nothing, waiting.

"I should thank you," she said.

"It wasn't for you. It wasn't for Dasari either. That was between me and him. He made me responsible for the deaths of my people. I'm not a good man. But they were. So the bastard had to die."

She nodded. "But it hurts you, doesn't it?"

"Lady, everything about this day hurts me."

"Are you always like this?"

"Only on work days. On weekends I sit on the couch and cry at sappy movies and eat low-fat ice cream."

That got a smile out of her. "Where do they teach you those stupid hardboiled detective lines?"

"There was a booklet. Came with the hat."

"You lost your hat."

"Yeah. It was a good hat. Are you ready?"

She nodded. "You realise this isn't going to work?"

"Of course it's not. Did you listen to the plan? It's the flimsiest piece of shit I've ever heard."

"Just making sure you knew. Tempest and Grotesque versus Nasir and Serraton? We're going to be torn apart."

We turned and I helped her to the back of the station wagon. The two handlers had found cars. The biologist who'd accompanied Dr Russell was going to drive for Serraton's handler. The other kid, Nasir's handler, insisted on driving himself. "My last driver smashed us into the back of a bus earlier this evening. Useless. And he was trained. I'm not trusting any of you with my life." He eyed our injuries. "Especially not looking like that."

The handlers got in their cars and drove off. Nasir would be easy enough to find; his footsteps still boomed across the island every few seconds. The other guy might have a little bit more trouble tracking down Serraton. With a bit of luck the Mayday was still hunting ships offshore.

Those of us who remained gathered around Priya and the infant for a few minutes. I stood with Su-jin and Lindsey, feeling out of my depth. All three of us investigators had nothing to offer besides moral support. Lindsey found a bottle of water in the station wagon. We shared it around. I put another cigarette in my mouth, but the look Su-jin gave me made me grin sheepishly and slide the smoke back into the pack.

"All right," I said. "That should be long enough for the handlers to get in position."

Dr Russell examined the laptop. "I think we're ready when you are," she said to Priya.

Priya nodded. "Okay. I'm going to try to boost the infant's psychic signal."

I braced myself in case we had a repeat of Priya's psychic bomb at Yllia's pit, but it didn't even tickle. It wasn't particularly interesting to watch. We had no way of telling if it was working. A squiggly line on Dr Russell's laptop got a bit more squiggly, but that was about it.

I was about ready to go for a little walk around the nearby cars to see if I couldn't find an umbrella. Then Priya gasped. We all froze and turned back towards her. The infant was waving its bulbous head slowly back and forth. Dr Russell had her nose right up against the laptop display, pulling up certain windows and rearranging them on the screen.

"What is it?" I said.

"The power is pulsing," Dr Russell said. "It's strong. As strong as Yllia's was. More, maybe. Unrestrained."

It took me a moment to realise I hadn't heard Nasir's footsteps in the last few seconds. Was it done? Had we got him back under impulse control?

In the distance, Tempest let loose a screeching cry. One I hadn't heard before. Not frustrated, not filled with battle-rage.

It was delight.

"No," Priya said, her voice rising. She seemed frozen in place, only her lips moving. "No, no, no."

I rushed over. "What is it? What's happening?"

"He knows," she said. Her eyes opened and turned to me. Then past me, to the west. To Tempest. "He knows where we are."

27

"Get in the car," I said.

No one moved. They all stared towards the rapidly approaching footsteps.

"Get in the fucking car!" I yelled. I went for the driver's door, tried to reach for the handle with my broken arm, and changed my mind. "Lindsey, you're driving."

Lindsey swept past me and started the car. I ran around the other side and helped Dr Russell into the back seat. I turned back for Priya.

"I have to keep contact with the infant," she said.

"To hell with that," I said. "Whatever you're doing, stop it. It's bringing Tempest right to us."

I reached for her arm, but she flinched away. "It's too late. If I let go, the others won't be able to recapture Nasir and Serraton. Tempest knows where the infant is now. I don't know how, but he knows. There's some connection—"

"Fine," I said. "Bring the ugly thing with you."

I reached into the back of the station wagon and touched the infant. Tiny flickers of electricity seemed to hum through my fingers. My palm sunk into the slimy, fleshy skin. I took some of the weight with my good arm and Priya took the rest. Together, we lifted it out of the empty tank and carried it around to the back seat. As Priya sat down, the infant rested in her lap like the ugliest cat I'd ever seen. Its breathing seemed to get louder.

I slammed the door, ran to the back and shut the boot, then jumped into the front passenger seat. I had enough time to put on my seatbelt before Tempest's head appeared over the tree line in the distance. My heart stopped.

Lindsey slammed the car into reverse and put her foot down. The station wagon's tyres squealed on the rain-slicked concrete for a moment. Then the rubber caught and I was thrown forwards as the car hurtled backwards across the broken ground.

"We can't outrun him," Dr Russell said. "We have to hide."

"There's nowhere to hide," I said. Lindsey spun the car, put it in drive, and took off onto the road. I kept my eyes on the side mirror. Tempest carved a swathe through the forest, scattering trees like they were toothpicks. "Keep driving."

"It's what I'm doing, isn't it?" Lindsey snapped. She tugged hard on the wheel to take a corner. We were forced to follow the winding, narrow roads across the island. Tempest wasn't. He continued straight for us, each step of his twelve legs bringing him closer.

Lindsey's driving was taking us further east, further inland. The car climbed up the increasingly steep roads, winding around the low mountain, carrying us past a river swollen with rainwater.

"This doesn't make any sense," Priya said.

I was half-listening as I watched Tempest grow larger in the mirror. "What doesn't?"

"This connection I have to Tempest through the infant. I can't break it. Why is it only Tempest? Why not the other Maydays as well?"

Lindsey threw the car into another turn. We slid along the outside of the bend, one tyre skimming the edge of the road. A monstrous foot slammed into the road fifty metres back, cracking the surface.

"Faster, Lindsey. Faster," I said.

"I swear to God, Boss, one of these days I'm going to—"

A claw fell from the sky and skewered the road right in front of us. Lindsey slammed on the brakes and pulled us around. The car slid to the right, past the claw. It skimmed along the outside of the car with a nails-on-chalkboard sound, shearing off the side mirror. I was close enough to see the grain of Tempest's claw as we flew past.

The road darkened around us. He was directly above us. I jerked forward, staring up through the windshield. Tempest's claws were poised above us, the points glittering. I held my breath.

A copse of trees disappeared to my left, crushed beneath a massive brown foot slashed with red. Nasir.

Tempest screeched and turned as Nasir threw his colossal fist. The ground shuddered beneath us. The car was filled with a sound like a sonic boom as the punch connected.

Somehow, Lindsey kept control of the car. Another of Tempest's legs slammed down on the road as Nasir's punch threw him back, but Lindsey guided the car around it, skidding onto the dirt at the side of the road. Then we were back on the road and out of there.

I twisted in my seat to watch the monsters fight. I didn't know where the handler was, but he couldn't be far away. Nasir raised both his fists and brought them crashing down on Tempest's back. Tempest took the blow. He sunk into the ground and stabbed downwards with his claws. The giant blades slid into the soft earth on either side of Nasir's feet, pinning the monster to the ground. Then Tempest looked up, roared, and breathed a gout of flame straight into Nasir's face.

Nasir swung his arms furiously. But he was blinded by the flames. He couldn't land more than glancing blows against Tempest. I could see the corded muscles of his thighs straining as he tried to kick free of Tempest's claws.

I saw the mistake an instant before Tempest took advantage of it. As Nasir tried to fight free, Tempest slid his claws out of the ground and swiped. The movement caught Nasir off-balance. He swung his arms wildly, but it was no good. He toppled.

The Mayday crashed into the ground. I could actually see the shockwave of dust as it rippled out. The car jumped on the road, skidding on the wet surface. Tempest didn't take time to kick his opponent while he was down. He turned back towards us, roared, and charged.

Dr Russell moaned in despair. The Mayday would be on us again in less than a minute. Nasir wouldn't be able to catch up. We were dead.

"Priya," I said. "There has to be something you can do. Distract him. Blow his mind. Something."

Her face was lined, her skin growing pale. "He's…he's talking to me. He's mocking us. I can't get him out of my head."

"Ignore him." I reached back, grabbed her by the arm. "If you want to listen to a bastard, listen to me. Are you listening?"

Her forehead creased with pain. "Yes."

"So he's talking. You know why? Because we made him mad. We fucked with him. Now he wants to show us what a big mean scary monster he is. I've seen it a million times before. You know what I'm talking about, don't you, Su-jin?"

Su-jin nodded. "A suspect may stay silent if you ask him questions, if you push him, if you hurt him. But if you anger him, he won't be able to stay quiet. He'll get angrier and angrier and then he'll break."

"Exactly," I said. "You hear that? This is good. We've got him talking. We've got him ranting and raving in the interview room. He's ours now. We can make him say whatever we want. Filter out all the shit, all the insults. Look for something we can use. Some way we can distract him."

"I can't!" Priya said. "I can't get him to be quiet. Why won't he be quiet? It hurts so much."

I ran my hands through my hair and stared out the back window. Tempest was closing. Lindsey was pushing the car to its limits. It wasn't going to be enough. Tempest screeched, his huge mouth split in a wide grin. Steam billowed from between his teeth, trailing behind him. There was no careful intelligence in his eyes now. Just the thrill of the chase. The animal rage.

A moment of calm settled over me. No, not calm. The terror faded, pushed to the side by a stronger emotion. My own anger, cool and sharp like a knife. I was tired of being chased around like a cockroach on the kitchen floor. He wanted to yell and scream and rage? Fine. I'd put up with worse. That was my job. Get to the truth. No matter who stood in the way throwing tantrums.

"Let me talk to him," I said. "Can you do that? Let me talk to the fucker."

"I...." Priya frowned.

"I what? Can you do it or not?"

Lindsey glanced at me. "Boss, are you sure—?"

"Shut up." I squeezed Priya's arm. "Priya?"

"I think I can do it," she said, so quiet I could barely hear. "It will hurt. It will hurt both of us."

"I can take it," I said. "Can you? Can you take it for your family?"

"Don't you fucking talk to me about my family," she snarled. "I would do anything for them."

"Then shut up and plug me in."

Her eyes snapped open. She stared at me for a split second. Then she grabbed my hand and pressed it against the fleshy body of the infant.

The burning started in my teeth. Like they were being twisted and pulled out one by one. The ache spread to my jaw, up to my temples, behind my eyes. My vision went black. There were needles in my lips, jammed in my ears.

I tell you, she wasn't kidding about the pain.

I swam in darkness, my whole world agony. I could feel

other presences, other minds, voices coming to me from across the blackness. After a moment, I realised one of the voices was mine.

Focus, you son of a bitch. Forget the pain. Get out of the dark. Get in his face. Get in his head.

I forced the pain down, crushed it beneath tightened fists and clenched teeth. So he wanted to play? All right. I'd been playing this game a long time.

I moved through the blackness. It was thick, clinging to my mind with dark strands. I put my head down and forced my way through, towards the voices. I could hear them properly now. One voice, soft, swirling with fear that bordered on panic. And another. A voice that sounded like a six-year-old's first try on a violin. I could taste the bile coming off it. The language it spoke wasn't English, but somehow I understood it perfectly. I kicked free of the last strands of darkness.

And found myself floating above the world.

I had to admit, it wasn't what I expected. I was no longer inside my own head. I was somewhere else, some shared consciousness built by me and Priya and Tempest, all anchored in the damaged mind of the infant. The island was spread out below me, flickering in and out of existence. I was aware of a car cutting through the forest. It tasted like prey. No, that wasn't my thought. It was hard to separate the words swirling around me. *Concentrate. Remember who you are. Remember why you're here. Remember what he did.*

The voices quietened, separated. I looked around the twisting dream world. A monster skittered across the island, smashing trees before him. His claws snapped open and closed as he gained on the car. He opened his mouth, roaring. But in the roar were words. Insults, hate, taunts. All in a stream so thick I could barely decipher them. Yeah, he was mad all right. I grinned even though I didn't have a mouth.

"Run, run, run, as fast as you can," I called through the ether. "You lose something, big guy?"

The monster kept on, kept running. But something ghostly twitched towards me. An indistinguishable form, a black cloud the size of a skyscraper. Blank eyes stared out from the centre of the form. A mouth gaped. A squealing noise came out. I could understand what it said.

"You." I heard it inside my head. I wondered if this was what the other Maydays heard when they communicated with each other.

"That's right," I said. "Me. Escobar. I'd give you one of my cards, but I seem to have misplaced them."

The form snarled and turned away from me. He was ignoring me. I didn't like being ignored.

I flickered out from my position above the world and reappeared in front of Tempest. He charged on after the car, but I matched his pace, floating backwards as he moved.

"You look stressed," I said. "You know what you need? A massage. A Thai massage. Deep tissue stuff. I know a girl. Let me give you the phone number."

Tempest's form snapped his jaws at me. But they passed straight through me, doing nothing.

"Nice try," I said. "But to get rid of me, you'll have to talk."

"Talk?" Tempest roared. His voice screeched in my mind, dragging nails across the inside of my skull. "You want me to talk, human? I do not talk. I do not bow. I am the destroyer. I am the one who will wipe this planet clean of your filthy presence. I am your death."

"Jesus, where do you get these lines?" I glanced around. He was nearly at the car. I needed to distract him. "I don't know where you get off with all this grandiose shit anyway. It's not like you got where you are now through some great cunning. You're just lucky I came along and helped you break impulse control. Otherwise you would've stayed stuck as our little slave forever and ever, wouldn't you? Especially after Yllia decided to screw you over by killing herself."

It was a wild shot. But when Tempest stumbled in his chase, I knew it had hit home. Below me, the car screeched ahead, using the few seconds I'd bought to cut around the side of the island's central hill. Tempest bellowed and gave chase again. But in his wake, echoes of words leaked into the air around me, carried in Tempest's voice but somehow fainter, unconscious.

—Yllia. Betrayal.

I smiled to myself. *You're angry, big guy. You're having trouble keeping your thoughts in check.*

I blinked in closer, grinning into the black form's face. He swiped his claws at me like I was a mosquito.

"What a bitch, huh?" I said. "Screwing you over like that? But let's start at the beginning. I want you to know something. You listening? I'm in your head. I know you. I've dealt with people like you before. Smaller ones, I'll grant you. But just as full of themselves. So sure of their own strength, their own cunning, their own infallibility. You've got it worse than most. Big invincible monster. You never feared anything in your life. Nothing except those parasites. You certainly never feared us humans. After all, we're so small, so squishy. But let me tell you something."

"Be silent!" he growled.

I flicked in to his side, rested on his body's bulging shoulders. "We won. We beat you. The pond scum kicked your arse. And that galls you, doesn't it? Doesn't that just make you so mad? You want to cry about it? I'm here, big guy. Just let it out."

The form turned and snapped its jaws at me. I blinked out and reappeared on his other shoulder.

"It started with Garcia, didn't it? Your plans to get your revenge started when you drove away your last handler and Garcia inherited you. You searched his mind. And you found a weakness. Something Psi Division had missed. Some little thing to get your claws in and twist him to your use. What was it? You scared him, didn't you? I saw that in his eyes. But there was more than that. He was weak, he was afraid, so he wanted what the weak always want. Power."

Tempest didn't answer. But I knew I was right.

"That's right," I said. "Rule the galaxy together, as father and son. That's what you promised. He was just dying to suck your metaphorical cock, wasn't he?"

—*Weak fool*, a mind whispered.

I glanced behind Tempest. Another Mayday lumbered through the rain and mist. Nasir was up again. But he was still too far behind. I needed to keep Tempest distracted.

"I figure once you'd broken Garcia he was more than happy to do some digging for you. He couldn't do it alone, of course. So he conned some poor MPF members into breaking off from the group and helping him out. I bet they never even knew they were working for a Mayday all along. But I'm curious about how he got in contact with the MPF in the first place. They're not easy to get to. Even harder to talk to."

An image of Cunningham flashed into my mind, the reporter's body pierced by a huge claw. I was looking down at the watchtower through Tempest's eyes, feeling the thrill of freedom rush through me. I tasted blood in my mouth.

I clicked my metaphysical fingers. "Cunningham. That's it, isn't it? That's why he was hanging around, trying to keep us off the scent. Cunningham had been to the island before, Garcia had probably met him. Garcia enlisted Cunningham's help to get to the MPF, and used the MPF splinter group to do his dirty work." I shook my head. "Poor Cunningham. I bet he didn't know what he was in for either. Not until you opened up his insides.

"But if you were going to get free, you needed to get to Volkov. He was the key to your imprisonment. So Garcia and his new MPF buddies went looking into Volkov, and that's how they found Catherine Russell. And she told the two of you everything."

A sense of alien rage bubbled in the air around me. I grinned at Tempest.

"Oh my. You didn't even know, did you? You didn't know what Yllia had done until Dr Russell told you." I moved in front of Tempest, stared him in the eye. "You poor sap. Betrayed by one of your own. That stung, didn't it?"

"You know nothing!" Tempest screeched. He stopped in his tracks, flailing at me. But every time his claws were about to make contact, I blinked out and reappeared somewhere else. I slid in closer.

"She gave you up. She sold you out. To us. To a bunch of insects." I laughed. "What a poor fucking sap you are. You know what us humans call people like you? Fool. Sucker. Slave."

"I am no slave!"

"Maybe not." I pointed behind him. "But he is."

Tempest turned as Nasir slammed his fists together on either side of Tempest's head. The world shuddered for a moment, the picture breaking up like bad TV reception. A burst of voices came through the static. Somewhere far away I could hear Priya in pain. My own agony flared as Nasir landed another punch in Tempest's midsection. I forced it back down. Pain wouldn't win this.

Tempest grabbed Nasir and the two of them tumbled to the ground, wrestling as they crushed the forest beneath them. As they rolled, words and images tumbled from Tempest.

—*Betrayed me. Enslaved me. Betrayed me again. Took everything.*

I followed the wrestling giants down, flickering in front of Tempest's face as he stabbed at Nasir with his claws.

"You must've been so mad," I taunted. "And you couldn't do a thing about it. We've got a word for that as

well. Impotent. I think that fits you, doesn't it? But at least
you knew the truth now. You knew you'd been fucked over.
And you knew about the infant. You knew Volkov had his
grubby little hands all over it. And you knew there was
a weapon inside. The parasites. Not only did Volkov have
you enslaved. He could kill you on a whim. All because
Yllia hid the infected infant all those billions of years ago.
And now it was ours."

—*Mine,* Tempest's voice whispered. *Mine, mine, mine.*

"Mine." I rolled the word around inside my head. What
did he mean? Volkov was his? The world? No. It clicked.
My smile grew.

"Well, well, isn't that interesting?" I said. "I know I was
giving you a hard time before about not having a dick, but
I guess you can't have been as hard up as I thought. The
infant's not just Yllia's, is it? It's yours as well. Tempest's a
daddy. Congratulations! Got any cigars?"

I knew I was right by the roar of frustration that
came floating through the ether. Nasir rained blows on
Tempest's real body, each one driving the twelve-legged
Mayday deeper into the mud. Tempest screeched and
breathed flame in a wide gout, but it did nothing to divert
the attacks.

"You can feel it now, can't you?" I said. "We have your
baby. We're using it against you. My, my, I don't know how
you're staying so calm and in control. If it was me in your
shoes, I'd be furious."

—*Hate, hate, hate, hate.*

Tempest kicked, swiping with his claws. But his blows
were wild, disjointed. He couldn't get free of Nasir's grasp.

"Sorry," I said. "I just enjoy pushing your buttons. After all, you did it to me. You did it to everyone. That's how you got Dr Russell's cooperation. Find a weak point, press it. That's how you got her here. That's how you had her extract the parasites from the infant. But here's a funny thing. You didn't make her destroy them. Not right away. No, you had Garcia hold onto them for a while. Why would that be?"

Tempest rolled, dodging a blow from Nasir. With a swipe of his claws, he knocked Nasir aside and he was up and free again. But Lindsey had been tearing away for the minute Tempest was down. We had a few more seconds. If I concentrated, I could feel my own body in the car, thrown about by the turns, my palm still pressed against the infant's flesh. People were talking, yelling, but it was just noise. I brought myself back to the dream world. This was what mattered. Each second I kept Tempest distracted was a second more we lived.

"I figure you kept the parasites for one of the same three reasons someone buys a gun. To kill someone. To threaten someone. Or to protect yourself from someone. So which is it? They're no good for killing humans, so it could only be a Mayday on the receiving end. If you wanted one of them dead, you would've done it. You wouldn't be so grumpy about Yllia killing herself. So that's out. And I don't think you had anything to fear from your fellow Maydays. They can't kill you any more than we can. So that leaves one option. You were going to threaten a Mayday. Or more than one. To keep them in line once you broke free? Or maybe it was to break free in the first place? You knew Yllia held the key to your imprisonment. Did you threaten her? Did you tell her that if she didn't release you she'd be sleeping with the fishes?"

Tempest didn't answer, but I felt the tension in him. Something was wrong with my theory, but I couldn't put my finger on it.

"There's something I'm missing. You're desperate. You're afraid I'm going to work something out. I can feel it. It radiates off you. So what is it? Tell me. Get it off your chest."

Tempest ignored me as he roared across the island. The car was heading back down the north-eastern side, making for the coast. We were rapidly running out of road. I could feel my heart pounding in a body far away. Somewhere else I could feel Priya's pain as she whimpered. Tempest was doing it on purpose, he had to be. He was trying to distract her like I was trying to distract him. Make her break the connection.

Hold on, I tried to broadcast my thoughts to her. *Just a little longer.*

I chased Tempest across the landscape. "You're afraid of her, aren't you? Afraid of Priya. There's something about her. What was the first thing you did when Yllia killed herself? You didn't go after the infant first. You tried to flush Priya out. You had Garcia send your thugs to go after her family. But I got to her first. You're big, but you were still under impulse control. Garcia only had a handful of thugs under his command. He couldn't get to her while I had her in custody." I turned the thoughts over in my mind. "And that's why you didn't kill me when I gave you the impetus to break impulse control. I was nobody, you could kill me anytime. But if you didn't manage to get to her, you knew I'd go looking for her. You knew I'd bring her into the open so Garcia could get to her. That's why you chased down Healy's car. That's why you killed him."

Healy had been right. I wasn't cut out for this case. And he'd died for it. *I'm sorry, kid.*

But I couldn't let that guilt drive me now. I had to be calm in the face of Tempest's fury. I had to keep thinking.

"You killed Healy. But you missed Priya. And that terrified you. You could've immediately gone and broken the other Maydays out of impulse control, left the island while Garcia went to retrieve the infant. But you didn't. You went on a rampage through the city. Cause chaos, take out your fear and anger on Volkov. Maybe take out Priya in the madness. But why? What's so important about her?"

I wracked my brain, tried to fit the pieces together. She was Yllia's handler. And her killer. She'd already been unconsciously controlled by Yllia. Was that it? She was part of some plot by Yllia? To do what?

What had this always been about? Control, freedom, imprisonment, slavery. Tempest had discovered Yllia's treachery in selling out the Maydays to Volkov. In retaliation, he got his hands on the infant and the parasites. He threatened her. Maybe he sent Garcia to show her the parasites, tell her that if she didn't have them released, he'd kill her or the infant.

But that couldn't be all. I searched Tempest's mind as he closed on the car again. He was afraid, all right. But he was guarding himself, pushing me out.

That didn't matter. Work it out. What did I know about

Tempest? Vengeful, strong, held a bit of a grudge. He considered himself a saviour of his people, and one of them had betrayed him. So what else would he want from Yllia? Revenge? Maybe. But not if he could get something else from her.

Control.

"You cheeky bastard," I said. "You wanted to steal Volkov's idea. You were the Maydays' leader, but you couldn't trust them. So you wanted to control them. You thought you could threaten Yllia into giving the secrets of impulse control to you. The Maydays would've been giving up one slavemaster for another." I tsked. "That's not very cricket, is it?"

—*Necessary*, Tempest's mind whispered.

I glanced ahead. Our car was nearly at the coast. We could loop back, but we'd be in clear view of Tempest and the road would no longer be taking us away from him. I didn't think we could keep him off us much longer.

Come on, think. There was something else. Maybe he wanted to control the other Maydays, but that didn't explain why he was so afraid. Control would be nice for him, but it wasn't a matter of life and death. So what was it? What was he afraid we'd do to him? What had he worked out that I couldn't see?

I flickered back in front of Tempest. "Come on!" I yelled in his face. "You big goddamn hypocrite. Yllia betrayed you, so you do the same to the other Maydays. Fine with me. But Yllia must've been pissed off when she found out what you really wanted. Being controlled by humans was all right, as long as her infant was safe. But being controlled by the likes of you? Who could stand it? She said, 'Fuck you' and offed herself. She made it so you'd never be able to use her to control the Maydays. If I hadn't come along, maybe you'd have spent the rest of your pitiful life in human control. But she did something else before she ended up as a big corpse, didn't she? Something with Priya and the infant. Something that terrifies you. What? Tell me!"

A hissing sound swept across the island. Not from Tempest. From out to sea. I turned towards the coast as a set of spines rose out of the water. Grotesque leaped out of the sea, onto the coastline, and headed straight for the car as it tore down the road.

If I still had a heart, it would've stopped. In the sea beyond Grotesque I could see Serraton slither after the other Mayday. But there was no chance of an intercept. Grotesque hissed in triumph and charged towards the car on all fours.

Something slammed into my physical body. The dream world faded around me. I groped at its ethereal edges. I had to hold on. I had to stay!

But with a snap and a spike in my brain, I was back in the car, being thrown to the side as Grotesque's massive paw slapped us off the road.

We rolled. I don't know how many times. The car bent and shattered and screamed all around me. Grotesque's foul smell filled my nostrils. My head was thrown about, smashing again and again into the window. The others cried out, shouted. I probably joined them. The infant was squealing.

And then we were still. The car was balanced on its side, my side closest to the ground. Blood dripped into my eyes. My broken arm burned. The engine ticked and wound down. Someone was moaning. Lindsey. Her face was pale, her body trembling. Dazed, I looked into the back seat. Dr Russell's arm was twisted at an impossible angle. Su-jin was unconscious. And Priya whimpered, her eyes closed, still clutching the squirming infant in both hands.

I opened my mouth, but nothing came out. I was so tired. I tried again, and this time I worked out how to make words.

"Hey," I said. I reached back with my good arm. The car groaned as I shifted my weight. I grabbed Priya's knee, shook it. She whimpered something. Maybe it was in Hindi, or maybe I was just brain damaged and couldn't understand her. Everything was echoing in my head. A footstep stomped outside. I glanced through the shattered back window and saw Grotesque's tail slither past.

I grabbed Priya's knee again and shook it harder, digging my fingers in. "Hey. Wake up. Come on. Don't do this now."

The whimpering faded, but her eyes remained closed. She was still there, I realised. Still in the dream world with Tempest.

"He's coming," she whispered.

"Yeah," I said. "Yeah, he is. We don't have much time."

"He'll kill us."

"Me and the others, yeah," I said. "Not you. He wants to use you. You can use that against him. There's something, something in you he's afraid of." I coughed and had to wipe the blood out of my mouth. My mind was still spinning along with the car. "I couldn't find out what. I'm sorry. But maybe you can figure it out. Maybe you can use it."

Tempest roared outside. He was close now. Grotesque circled the car. I could barely think with his stench overwhelming me. But I had to keep talking. It was the only thing I could do.

"I think Yllia did something to you. She wanted to use you as a pawn against Tempest. A weapon. It's the only thing that makes sense. But you're not a pawn anymore. You're free. For a few seconds, at least. So you have to think. I can help you. But you have to think. Can you do that?"

"I...I don't know what I'm trying to think of."

"Neither do it." My eyes drifted closed and my head dipped to the side. No! My eyes snapped open. *Stay awake. Think.* "What does he fear? You're there with him. He fears what you can do to him. Death. He must fear death, right?"

She shook her head, eyes still closed. "He doesn't understand death. Not truly."

"Then what? Dig into his mind. You can do it."

She was quiet a few seconds. The car vibrated with every footstep that carried Tempest closer. It was getting harder and harder to keep my mind clear. I felt cold. My body was shutting down. At least it'd save me experiencing the joy of Tempest's digestive tract.

"A prison," Priya said finally. "He fears being trapped again."

I slumped. "But you said you can't bring him under impulse control. Not without a LIM designed for him."

"Yes," she said. "I'm trying. But the infant can't do it. Not by itself."

I sighed. All right. Fine. It looked like that was that. I felt like I needed to throw up. Being perched on my side probably didn't help. With fumbling fingers, I unbuckled my seatbelt. Gravity took me and I thudded against the passenger door. There was no way out of the car. I fished my cigarettes out of my pocket. The whole packet was bent and crumpled. I opened it. Not a good cigarette in the bunch. It figured. I tossed them away and sat there, waiting for my death.

The first rays of dawn were creeping through the shattered car windows. Twenty-four hours since Healy called, telling me about Yllia's death. Christ, how excited I'd been. Giddy as a goddamn schoolgirl. Career case. I snorted. Yeah, some career. Some legacy I was leaving behind.

Tempest's footsteps stopped outside. I couldn't see him from here, but I thought I could feel his shadow fall across the car. I could hear him breathing. The rain seemed to be fading, if you could believe it. I suppose that was something.

Claws closed around the car. I shivered at the squealing of the metal.

Prison. Something about that word kept bouncing around my head, even now, at the end. Not enslavement. But prison. Being trapped, Priya had said. I suppose impulse control was a kind of being trapped. But it just didn't quite seem to fit.

I thought back. Priya had said that before she'd given Yllia the parasites, the Mayday had tried to tell her something. No, that wasn't what she said. I tried to remember the exact words she'd used. Something about a chemical message, and a pressure in her mind. Some key to impulse control?

No, to hell with impulse control. That wasn't it. There was something else.

The car shuddered and began to rise off the ground. I didn't know if Tempest was drawing this out or just being careful. He didn't want to kill Priya and the infant. Not if he still wanted control of the other Maydays. I looked up and saw his black eyes staring down at me. His mouth spread in a grin. His teeth glistened.

"Ah, go fuck yourself," I said.

This wasn't right. He was a monster that shouldn't exist. We should've been separated from each other by four billion years, not by the thin, crumpled metal of the car's body. But no. He had to live. Most of his species died, but this son of a bitch lived. He got to hide in a hole and go to sleep and wait for the world to—

The ideas crashed together in my mind. Something Dr Russell had said at Yllia's pit, about the infant, how they found it in stasis. And something Priya had said as well. That vision she'd had at the pit. She'd watched the Maydays go into stasis, seal themselves away from the epidemic that threatened to wipe them out. That was their final survival mechanism. They put themselves into stasis in response to an outside signal.

That was the pressure she'd felt, the ache she'd carried since Yllia died. It wasn't a message that Yllia had given her. It was a signal.

And Tempest. Big, powerful, invincible Tempest. Maybe he didn't understand death. But he understood the next best thing. He was afraid we would trap him. That we'd put him to sleep again. And this time he'd never wake up. That all his strength, all his power, would be undone by a single involuntary reflex.

I jerked around and shook Priya again. "Priya. Priya! Tell me you're still there. Talk to me."

She mumbled something incoherent.

"Dr Russell said that the infant secreted that gel stuff to put itself in stasis, right? The other Maydays had to do that as well. Something triggered that reflex to put them all into stasis. It had to be Yllia. She was the only one with the psychic ability to do it."

I couldn't tell if Priya understood me. The car continued to rise.

I kept talking, faster now. "What if Yllia gave you the same signal? So that if Tempest made a move on the infant, tried to use it to control the other Maydays, you'd be able to trigger them all to go into stasis. One last 'fuck you' to Tempest after he tried to manipulate her. She probably thought the infant would take up the signal from you and broadcast it as soon as it was out of stasis. She didn't anticipate that it'd be too brain damaged for that. But maybe you can still do it. You boosted the infant's psychic activity. So just plug in the signal and broadcast that. If I'm right, you've got the signal inside you. Yllia gave it to you before she killed herself. Priya? Can you hear me? Do you understand?"

Priya's lips moved, but no sounds came out. Her face

was grey, the muscles of her jaw tense. The infant pulsed in her arms. I glanced up through the window as Tempest brought his other claws overhead, ready to pluck us out one by one.

I lurched forward and grabbed Priya with my good arm. My battered body groaned at me. It could groan all it liked. I wanted to live, goddamn it.

"Priya, do it! Just try. Do it now!"

Her eyes tightened. I couldn't feel anything. I didn't know if she'd heard me. I didn't even know if she was still conscious.

Until Tempest screamed.

I'd heard him roar before. I'd heard him frustrated, triumphant, furious. But this, this piercing, pitiful sound, it was a scream. It was fear. I delighted in it.

Tempest's claws snapped open. We dropped.

My stomach lurched into my throat for the second before we crashed into the muddy ditch and rolled again. My foot caught somewhere and I felt the crack of bones breaking. Nausea churned in the pit of my stomach and my vision blackened.

When I could concentrate past the pain, we'd stopped. The car had only rolled once or twice this time, but my head spun and every inch of me ached. I groaned involuntarily as I pushed myself up and looked around.

Lindsey was slumped against the wheel, moaning softly. The others were all unconscious. The infant sat shrivelled up in Priya's arms, no longer moving. Something grey oozed from its pores, coating its flesh.

It took my dazed mind a few seconds to understand

what was happening. Tempest's screams still filled my ears. I had to get outside. I had to see.

The car had landed on its tyres this time. The doors were crumpled, no hope of opening them. I pushed what remained of the shattered windscreen out of the way and crawled out onto the hood of the car, dragging my broken foot behind me. The dying rain peppered my skin, as refreshing as a shower after a long day's work. I rolled onto my back and looked up at the sky.

Tempest, Nasir, Serraton, and Grotesque all stood above me. Each of them moved in super slow-mo. Their muscles bulged, straining against nothing. Grey fluid leaked out from between scales and out of pores and from tiny slits in folds of skin. Nasir was already coated head to foot in the fluid as it solidified around him. At the outer edges, where the fluid met the air, a darkened, translucent skin was forming, trapping the Mayday in a massive pouch. His last movements slowed, and then he was still.

"Yes," I whispered. "Yes."

The Maydays struggled, screeching and roaring. But it was useless. They couldn't fight their own physiology. They were perfect, invincible. This last defence mechanism was supposed to protect their species against the one thing that could kill them. And now it had been turned against them.

Serraton's movements stopped next, then Grotesque's. The fluid grew solid. Both of them froze in mid-scream. I hoped they enjoyed their nap for an awful long time. Another four billion years would suit me just fine.

Tempest was the last. Even now he fought, muscles trembling with the exertion. I looked into his eyes. No glee now, no sadism, no power. Just terror. Pure, human terror. I guess that was another thing he'd learned from us.

As the fluid engulfed Tempest's head, he stared down at me and roared. Fire glowed in the back of his throat.

I grinned back and showed him my middle finger.

The fluid swallowed his mouth, his nostrils, his eyes. He was completely enveloped now. His eyes held on to life for another second. The pouch solidified around him. With a final growl, the fire died in his throat.

And the bastard was gone.

I laid back and closed my eyes. "Sweet dreams, pal."

28

We sat against the broken car in the shadow of the Maydays and watched the Alliance fleet grow on the horizon as the sun slowly climbed into the sky. They'd arrived just in time to do absolutely nothing. Typical.

It was going to be a long wait before they got to us, but we weren't going anywhere. We were near the coast beneath four frozen Maydays. We weren't hard to spot. A little first aid had made sure none of us had died in the couple of hours since the Maydays went still, and careful rationing of the Panadol kept us from passing out. All five of us would be seeing the inside of a hospital once we got back to the mainland. Lindsey looked like she'd just come out on the wrong side of a heavyweight prize fight. Between me, Su-jin, and Dr Russell, we had enough broken bones to keep an orthopaedic surgeon in caviar and fast cars for the next year.

Priya had come out the best of us, nursing some nasty whiplash but with all her limbs intact. For some reason I didn't understand, she still held the infant. It was in stasis now like the rest of the Maydays, contained within a translucent pouch of greenish-grey fluid. It was still an ugly little bastard.

The morning wore on. I watched Priya for a while, mostly to keep my mind off the pain. After a few minutes, she glanced at me and met my eyes. I nodded at her. A half smile flashed across her face, and then it was gone. It hadn't been a smile of happiness or relief. Not yet. It was an acknowledgment. She was right. It had been up to us to stop them. Not because we were the only ones who could. But because it was our responsibility. Our penance. I could see the pain on her face. Her body had survived the ordeal, but I figured her mind had a lot of healing to do.

After another hour or so, Dr Russell started crying silently. We let her. After a while, she stopped.

When the throbbing in my foot and arm became almost too much to bear, I leaned back on the car and looked up at the Maydays above us. It was unnerving, seeing them frozen like giant statues. "How long do you reckon they'll stay like that?"

"It's hard to say," Dr Russell said. "We don't know exactly what triggered them to leave stasis in the first place. Maybe they were on a timer. Maybe there was something else, some change in the environment that they detected."

"What will the Alliance do with them?" Lindsey asked. "Because my vote is to load them on a bunch of rockets and send them into the heart of the sun."

"Seconded," I said.

We hadn't seen or heard from anyone else since Tempest had stopped screaming. The rain had finally stopped, at least for a little while. I didn't know where the other handlers were. Probably alive. I'd have to ask after them later.

Except I still didn't know their names. Oh well. Nuts to it.

None of the others had any way to contact their family and loved ones. I knew Lindsey was itching to head back to the port, make sure her girlfriend was alive. And I'm sure Priya must've been thinking the same about her own family. But it was hard to tell with the blank mask she was wearing.

Me, I was just ready for a break and a nap. And some morphine. And maybe a smoke. I hadn't yet decided whether or not to quit again. I hadn't decided much of anything. There'd be time for that later. Once I worked out who I was now. And who I wanted to be.

"Say," I said as a thought occurred to me. "How sure are we that these five Maydays and the infant are the only ones who survived the parasite infection all those years ago? What if there's others in stasis somewhere, at the bottom of the ocean or buried underground?"

Everyone was quiet for a few seconds. I felt their eyes on me.

"Escobar," Dr Russell said. "Shut the fuck up."

I nodded. "Okay." I glanced up at the frozen Maydays, then out to sea. "I guess we're all out of work now."

"I guess we are," Lindsey said.

"Anyone know someone who runs a trucking company?"

"What?" Dr Russell said.

"I used to have this fantasy about becoming a truck driver. I know, I know, what the hell do I know about driving trucks, right? But there's this little town I know of, and they've got this cafe where they make the best damn custard tart in the world. And in this cafe there's a shelf of paperback novels."

"Boss," Lindsey said. "What the hell are you talking about?"

I grinned and closed my eyes.

"Never mind. Never mind."

ABOUT THE AUTHOR

Chris Strange discovered at an early age that he was completely unsuited to life among normal human beings. After experimenting with several different career paths, he said to hell with it and went back to writing, his first love.

Chris is the author of *Don't Be a Hero* and the Miles Franco series of hard-boiled urban fantasy novels, beginning with *The Man Who Crossed Worlds*. He writes for the daydreamers, the losers, the cynics and the temporarily insane. His stories are full of restless energy and driven by a passion for the unorthodox. He loves writing characters on the fringe of society: the drifters, the knights errant, the down-and-out.

In his spare time, Chris is an unapologetic geek, spending far too long wrapped up in sci-fi books, watching old kaiju movies and playing video games. He lives in the far away land of New Zealand, and is currently working towards a Master's degree in Forensic Science.

He doesn't plan on growing up any time soon.

Want to be the first to hear about Chris's new releases? Sign up for the email list at: **http://bit.ly/StrangeList**

Contact Chris at: **chrisstrangeauthor@gmail.com**

www.chris-strange.com